* * * * * * *

"What are you going to be arrested for, Mr. Carlson?" I asked.

I spoke to him as calmly as I could. My hope was to keep him from becoming hysterical to a point where he made no sense at all.

"For murder," he said sharply.

"I would think you would be better off calling a good attorney," I said as I straightened up and started paying closer attention. "I can certainly recommend one if you don't have one."

"I've already called one. What I really need is someone to prove I didn't do it."

The sound of his voice was beginning to show that panic was beginning to set in. I wasn't sure how long he would be able to keep it together. This guy needed help, all right, but I wasn't sure what kind of help, or what I could do for him.

"Who did you kill?"

"I didn't kill anyone," he screamed into the phone.

"Okay. Okay," I said in an effort to get him to settle down a little. "Who are you supposed to have killed?"

"My wife. Oh, God, my wife, but I didn't do it," he cried.

* * * * * * *

Other titles by J.E. Terrall

Western Short Stories	Western Novels
The Old West	Conflict In Elkhorn Valley
The Frontier	Lazy A Ranch (a modern
Untamed Land	western)
Tales From The Territory	The Story of Joshua Higgins

Romance Novels	Mystery/Suspense/Thriller
Balboa Rendezvous	I Can See Clearly
Sing for Me	The Return Home
Return to Me	The Inheritance
Forever Yours	

Nick McCord Mysteries
    Vol – 1 Murder at Gill's Point
    Vol – 2 Death of a Flower
    Vol – 3 A Dead Man's Treasure
    Vol – 4 Blackjack, A Game to Die For
    Vol – 5 Death on the Lakes
    Vol – 6 Secrets Can Get You Killed

Peter Blackstone Mysteries
    Murder in the Foothills
    Murder on the Crystal Blue
    Murder of My Love

DEATH BY DESIGN

A Frank Tidsdale Mystery

J.E. Terrall

ISBN: 978-0-9916232-9-7

This is a work of fiction. Names, characters, and incidents are either a product of the author's imagination or are used fictitiously, and any resemblance to actual persons, living or dead, is purely coincidental.

Printed in the United States of America
First Printing / 2010 – www.lulu.com
Second Printing / 2014 – creatspace.com

Cover: Design concept for cover by Phyllis J. Terrall with blue print and drafting tools provided by Rex Harris. Cover photos taken by author, J. E. Terrall

Book Layout/
Formatting: J.E. Terrall
                     Custer, South Dakota

DEATH BY DESIGN

A Frank Tidsdale Mystery

To Craig Luze

CHAPTER ONE

It was getting late in the day when my phone began to ring. It had been a long day. I was more interested in going home than in answering the phone that rang annoyingly on the corner of the desk. Since it was not my nature to let a phone ring without answering it, I half-heartedly reached out and picked up the phone.

"Tidsdale Investigative Agency"

"Is this Frank Tidsdale?" a male voice asked.

I noted a hint of urgency in his voice.

"It is. Who is this?"

"My name's Jim Carlson and I'm going to be arrested at almost anytime now. I need your help."

It suddenly became clear why he seemed in such a hurry, and why the man's voice carried a trace of nervousness. He spoke very rapidly. He sounded as if it would not take too much for him to become hysterical and start yelling uncontrollably, or completely break down and cry. I wasn't sure which, but I could certainly understand the reason for his urgency. Getting arrested can be a very frightening experience.

"What are you going to be arrested for, Mr. Carlson?" I asked.

I spoke to him as calmly as I could. My hope was to keep him from becoming hysterical to a point where he made no sense at all.

"For murder," he said sharply.

"I would think you would be better off calling a good attorney," I said as I straightened up and started paying closer attention. "I can certainly recommend one if you don't have one."

"I've already called one. What I really need is someone to prove I didn't do it."

The sound of his voice was beginning to show that panic was beginning to set in. I wasn't sure how long he would be able to keep it together. This guy needed help, all right, but I wasn't sure what kind of help, or what I could do for him.

"Who did you kill?"

"I didn't kill anyone," he screamed into the phone.

"Okay. Okay," I said in an effort to get him to settle down a little. "Who are you supposed to have killed?"

"My wife. Oh, God, my wife, but I didn't do it. Honest, I didn't do it," he cried.

He had no more than said that when I began to hear the sounds of sirens in the background. They were getting louder by the second, and he was getting more agitated. I was afraid that he was going to loose it at any moment.

"They're almost here," he yelled, the fear in his voice growing rapidly.

"Mr. Carlson, listen to me. You've got to listen to me. When they get there do not, I repeat, do not say anything until you talk to your attorney. Do you understand?"

"Yes, but they're here. Oh God. They're here," he shouted, his voice breaking up.

"Do you know where they will take you?"

"No. Oh, God. They're right out front. You've got to help me."

"Whatever you do, don't resist them. Go to the door, open it and let them in. Don't worry. I'll find you. Just don't talk to the police without your attorney."

"Oh, God, they're here," he cried.

"Keep cool and raise your hands. Don't resist."

I could hear the sound of a door opening with a crash. It was followed by the yelling of police officers as they told Carlson to drop the gun, to get down on the floor and put his hands behind his head. I heard the phone as it fell crashing to the floor. I could hear the scuffling of feet and a hard thud like someone falling to the floor. Actually more like someone being taken down hard. The last thing I heard was the click of the phone as it went dead.

I hung up the phone and looked at it as if it would help me figure out what had been going on, but I already knew. What I didn't know was why this guy called me. I had to wonder if he really did kill his wife. The other question that came to mind was who was Jim Carlson? I could not remember ever having heard that name before. I was sure that it was no one I knew.

The police cars squealed to a halt in front of the Carlson home. Four officers, with guns in hand, rushed to the front door. They immediately kicked in the door and charged through it as if they where there to rescue someone. Carlson was standing in the hall with the phone in one hand and a small caliber gun in the other. He had a frightened look on his face. There was blood on his hands, on the front of his shirt and on his pants. There was even blood on his face. He was shaking all over.

"Drop the gun. Drop - the - gun," the lead officer yelled while pointing his gun at Carlson.

Scared that he was going to be shot if he didn't comply, he dropped the gun. He threw his hands in the air, dropping the phone on the floor.

"Down on the floor. Get down on the floor, face down."

Sweat was running down Carlson's face. Every nerve in his body was trembling with fear. He knew he was going to be killed. He started to do as he was told, but apparently not fast enough for the police officers. He was pushed to the floor, hard. He had never been so scared in all his life. His breath came in short gasps and his heart pounded in his chest.

"Put your hands on the back of your head," the officer ordered.

He put his hands on the back of his head. Although he knew what was happening, he couldn't believe that it was really happening to him. Almost immediately he felt a knee press down in the middle of his back. The officer took hold of one of his wrists and twisted his arm around behind his back. He could feel the cold hard steel of the handcuffs as the officer locked it firmly around his wrist. The officer then did the same thing with his other wrist.

As soon as he was handcuffed securely, two officers grabbed Carlson under the arms, lifted him up off the floor and stood him up on his feet. One of the officers reached over and hung up the phone while Carlson was taken out the door. As they took him to a patrol car he was given his rights. When they reached the patrol car, he was unceremoniously pushed into the back seat. Carlson looked out the window at the front of his house as all but one of the police officers returned to the house.

Suddenly there was a photographer's camera in his face. He had no idea where the photographer had come from, he had just suddenly appeared. He quickly shut his eyes and tried to turn away as the camera flashed in his face, but it was too late. He just knew his picture would be splashed all over the morning newspapers and on the television.

His heart was pounding in his chest so hard that he could feel it. All he could think about was his wife lying on the floor of their bedroom with blood all around her. His wife was lying dead on their bedroom floor next to the bed, the same bed they had shared for the past eight years. He knew that he was going to be hauled off to jail where he would be charged with her murder.

Tears began to fill his eyes as an officer approached the car. He could hear him talking to the policeman who had remained in the car with him.

"The call was right. The guy's wife is in the upstairs bedroom. She was apparently shot," the officer said, then glanced back at Carlson sitting in the back seat of the police car.

"You think he did it?" the second officer asked.

"I don't know, but it sure looks like it. I'll call in for a homicide detective."

Carlson could hear the officer make the call. He could only hear one side of the conversation, but it was enough for him to know that he was in very deep trouble.

After the call was made, the officers got in the car and started to drive away. Carlson could see the officers from the second car as they started wrapping bright yellow crime scene tape across the front porch of his home. The yellow tape was telling the whole world that something terrible had happened in that house.

As the patrol car headed down the street, there was no doubt in Carlson's mind that he would never see his house again.

CHAPTER TWO

I didn't remember ever having heard of Jim Carlson before, but it was time to find out as much about him as I could before I decided if I would get involved. The first thing I needed to do was to find out where he lived. I swung around in my chair and reached for the telephone directory. There were nine Carlson's in the Denver telephone book with the first name of James, or Jim, or with the first initial of J. That didn't include the surrounding suburbs. I began calling each of the numbers. It wasn't until I got to the sixth number that I didn't get someone to answer the phone. I tried the remaining three just to be sure, and got answers to my calls. Simple deduction told me it was probably number six.

The James Carlson that didn't answer the phone lived on Spruce Street across the street from Washington Park. It was a rather affluent area of town, an area where doctors, lawyers and successful business people tended to live. Since there was nothing in the white pages to indicate what Mr. Carlson did for a living, and the library was closed, there was only one thing for me to do. I would have to drive over there and see if anything was going on. If this particular Jim Carlson had just been arrested for killing his wife, the place would be crawling with police.

It took me only about fifteen minutes to get to Spruce Street. When I got to the corner of Wilson and Spruce, I looked down Spruce Street. I could see a lot of flashing lights near the middle of the block. There was an ambulance and several police cars in front of a large two-story stucco home. It was not a new home, but it had been well maintained, possibly remodeled.

I turned onto Spruce Street and pulled over to the curb near the corner to watch. I wanted to see what was going on, before I decided what I should do, if anything. Sitting behind the wheel of my car, I watched the police milling around as if they were waiting for someone. I had to wonder if the lead detective had not shown up, yet. I took my binoculars out of the glove box and watched as a stretcher was brought out of the house. There was a black body bag on it. That was a good indication that I had the right house, assuming that the person in the body bag was that of Mrs. Carlson.

The body bag was placed in the waiting ambulance, then taken away. There were no sirens, as there was no need for them.

More important to me than the body at this time, was who was in charge of the investigation. I knew a few of the detectives on the Denver police force, but not all of them were very friendly toward private investigators, especially me. To some of them, I was a maverick and more trouble than I was worth. Some of them thought I simply got in their way.

However, I had made a few friends over the years by helping them solve a case or two. I could get away with things that a policeman would get in trouble for, and some of them understood that. They also understood that we could work together if given the chance.

Since the body had been removed from the house, I assumed that the lead detective was already in the house. Just as I was about to get out of my car, I saw the lights of a car turning onto Spruce Street flash across the rear window of my car. I quickly slide down in the seat and looked out at my side rearview mirror. There was a flashing red light on the dash of the car.

I waited for it to go by before I sat up again. If I had to guess, the man in the car would be one of the detectives assigned to finding the murderer.

The car pulled up in front of the house and stopped at the curb. A tall, well-built man got out of the car. He looked both ways then walked across the street toward the house. Just as he stepped up on the curb, another man in a suit came out of the house and stepped down off the porch. I noticed he was wearing rubber gloves. The two men met on the lawn and talked for several minutes before they went into the house together.

I didn't recognize the detective who came out of the house, but I did recognize the one who had just arrived on the scene. His name was Donald Wright. He had been a detective for a long time and was considered to be one of the best. The good thing was that I had a fairly good working relationship with him. I decided to wait and watch for a few more minutes to see what was going on.

"What do you have, Latimer?" Wright asked as he walked toward the house.

Robert Latimer was a young detective who had just been promoted to the rank of Detective and assigned to Homicide. It was his first murder case.

"We got a woman that was shot twice, one to the chest and one to the head. Her husband has identified her as Jennifer Carlson, his wife. Her husband was found with the gun in his hand," Latimer said as he held up the weapon.

"Are you sure it's the murder weapon?"

"Yeah. It's the murder weapon, all right. There's no doubt."

"Bag it and get it to the lab. I want to know everything there is to know about it, fingerprints, ballistics, the works. I also want Mr. Carlson's hands checked to see if he actually fired the gun, and I want it done before he's cleaned up."

"Yes, sir."

"Have the forensic people been notified?"

"Yeah. They're on their way now."

"Let's take a look and see what we have."

Wright and Latimer turned and went inside the house. Just as they were about to go up the stairs, Wright stopped, put out his hand to stop Latimer.

"The murder took place upstairs, right?"

"Yeah. In the master bedroom."

"Then where did all the blood come from on the steps?" Wright asked as he pointed to several droplets of blood on the steps and several spots where the blood looked like it had been stepped in.

"I didn't notice that."

"That's clear by the fact that someone has stepped in it. Do we know who stepped in it?

"Not really, I guess," Latimer replied after thinking about it for a minute.

"You have to watch where you put your feet. Now step around them," he said with a note of anger as he started up the stairs watching their every step. "There's no need to ruin any more of the evidence."

Once they reached the top of the stairs, Wright followed the blood trail down the hall toward the master bedroom. He looked in each room that was unlocked as he worked his way toward the master bedroom. Sticking his head inside the door, he looked around. The bed was a mess. It looked as if there had been a wrestling match held on it. Even the mattress was not straight on the bed indicating someone had resisted being dragged off the bed. The sheets and blankets were twisted and wadded up, one pillow was on the floor and the other was up against the headboard. There was a lot of blood on the bed.

On the floor next to the bed was a small rug. It was covered in so much blood that it was hard to tell that it had been white at one time. The lamp next to the nightstand was on the floor and the light bulb was broken indicating it had been knocked off the table. There was no question that there had been a violent struggle in the room. It was hard to determine who had fought with whom. It had all the earmarks of a case of a domestic argument turned violent, but that was yet to be proven. Wright looked around the room before he spoke.

"Where's the body?" Wright asked, looking at Latimer.

"I had the ambulance crew take her to the ME."

Wright just looked at Latimer. He couldn't believe that Latimer could be so careless as to remove the body before the lead detective had seen the crime scene.

"Anytime there is a dead body, you do not move or remove the body from the scene until the lead detective gives you permission, do you understand that?"

"Yes, sir. I didn't think it mattered. Carlson killed his wife. He had the weapon in his hand when he was arrested."

"I sure hope you are right. Did you have pictures of the scene taken before the body was moved?"

"No, sir," Latimer replied sort of sheepishly.

"Great," he said with a note of disgust. "Understand this. The position of the body often goes a long way in determining just what happened here. Without pictures, our case may be seriously weakened in court. We could lose the case without pictures."

"Yes, sir. He had the gun in his hand when the police came in the door," Latimer said.

"That does not make him guilty," Wright replied as he shook his head.

Wright looked around the room for a minute. He was hoping that the forensic team could find something solid that would prove what happened and who might have killed Mrs. Carlson.

There was nothing that could be done about Latimer's screw up now. He let out a long sigh as he looked at Latimer. He wondered how Latimer had passed the exam for detective. It was looking like half the evidence had been compromised just by his carelessness and his failure to follow departmental procedures.

"We need to know if any of the neighbors heard anything and if the Carlsons were prone to arguments or fighting. Do you think you can handle that without screwing it up? I'll wait for the forensic team to get here then I'll join you."

"Yes, sir," Latimer said, the tone of his voice showed that he was not very happy that he was being dismissed.

Latimer left the house being very careful not to step on any more of the blood on the stairs. Wright remained behind and continued to look around the room from the door before entering the room. He then stepped into the room to get a *better look at the crime scene. He noticed that the drawers of the dresser had been pulled out, something he couldn't see from the doorway. The more he looked around the room, the more he wondered what had really happened here. It almost looked like the room had been searched, or at the very least ransacked.*

Wright stepped back out of the room and went downstairs. He couldn't help but think that there was something about the crime scene that didn't quite add up. It suddenly crossed his mind about what Latimer had said with regard to the murder weapon. He had indicated that Carlson had a small caliber pistol in his hand when he was arrested. Yet the blood splatter on the walls of the bedroom indicated that she had been shot with a much larger caliber gun. There were also blood patterns indicating that a knife may have been used, but with so much blood and no body, it was hard for him to tell what had been used to kill the woman.

Wright knew that he would have to wait for the autopsy to find out what weapon or weapons were used in the crime and what the actual cause of death was. Hopefully the forensic team could shed some light on what really happened in the house.

CHAPTER THREE

After sitting in my car for about twenty minutes and watching four uniformed officers standing around in front of the house, I saw the young detective come out and talk to the uniformed sergeant. Within a couple of minutes, the uniformed officers spread out and began going from house to house knocking on doors.

I continued to watch and wondered what they might find out about the Carlsons by questioning the neighbors. I had a pretty good idea of what they were interested in finding out. Was the murder of Mrs. Carlson the result of a family argument that became violent and ended in her death? Could it have been an accidental shooting, or was it something else like a robbery that went sour? There was still the possibility that it was something entirely different. There were just too many unanswered questions at the early stage of the investigation to look in any one direction. At this point in time, looking in one direction could prove to be a very big mistake.

I was still sitting in my car about a half a block away from Carlson's house when the forensic team arrived in a van. Three forensic specialists got out of the van and went into the house. There was no doubt in my mind that they would be spending a lot of time looking over the house while the M.E. examined the body at the morgue. The forensic team would gather blood samples, dust for prints and gather anything that might be even remotely relevant to the crime. One thing I knew was that they were good at their job. It was very unlikely that anything would go unnoticed. Every piece of evidence would be scrutinized for its value in figuring out how the victim had been killed, who had killed her, and what had happened in the house.

With those thoughts firmly planted in my mind, I still had to wonder if that would actually be the case. From what I had heard over the phone, it might not. After all, they had found Carlson in the house with a gun in his hand. That much I knew from his phone call to me.

The first thing that came to my mind was the gun Carlson had in his hand when he was arrested. I had to wonder if it was actually the murder weapon. Since I had nothing to make me think otherwise, I could only assume that the police would think it was the murder weapon until testing proved it wasn't, or proved that it was the murder weapon. At the moment, it almost looked like a case where the perpetrator of the crime had been caught with the smoking gun in his hand. So to speak.

However, I had seen too many cases where it wasn't as clear-cut as it first appeared to be. It often would prove to be something entirely different. I would have to wait to see what could be proven.

Whatever had happened in that house, it was time for me to have a talk with Don and see if he could give me something to go on. Being so early in the case, I doubted that he had anything solid to go on but his gut feeling. Even that could prove helpful in deciding if I wanted to take on the job of doing my own investigation, or not.

I got out of my car and walked down the block toward the house. I was just about to turn up the sidewalk when Don came out. He stopped on the front porch and looked around while he reached for a cigarette. He was about to light it when he spotted me.

"Those damn things can kill you, Don," I said as I stepped up on the first step, stopped and looked up at him.

"Yeah, I know. What are you doing here, Tidsdale?"

"I got a call from Jim Carlson just minutes before the police broke down his door and arrested him."

"You're kidding?"

"No. He was on the phone with me when the police arrested him."

"What did he want with you?"

"He said he was going to be arrested for killing his wife and asked me to look for who really murdered her."

"He called you before we got here?" Don asked, looking a little confused.

"Yeah."

"How would he know we were going to arrest him for it?"

"Don't know. He didn't say. Maybe he's had run-ins with the police before. Maybe he knows that the husband is usually the primary suspect in cases like this. Then again, maybe he's just watched too many cop shows on television."

"I'll look into any run-ins he might have had with the police, but he doesn't strike me as the kind to have problems with the police. You know as well as I do that we are going to look at him. I'm not limiting my investigation to any one person until I have a lot more to go on than what I have right now."

"I know you're not, but how's it looking?" I asked in the hope of getting some idea of the direction Don planned to take.

"Not good. It's a real messy job, this one. I get the feeling it's an amateur."

"Or maybe it was meant to look like an amateur job?"

"Possible, but I've got nothing to point that way, yet."

"Any idea why she was murdered?" I asked.

"Not yet. We're canvassing the area to see if anyone heard anything that might help."

"I think I'll go have a talk with Carlson and see if this is anything I want to get involved in."

"Okay. Let me know what you decide," Don said.

"Sure."

"I'll talk to you later."

Just as I was about to leave, the young detective returned. He looked at me as if he was wondering who I was and what I was doing there.

"Frank, this is Detective Robert Latimer. He's new to Homicide. This is his first case," Don said.

Latimer smiled and stuck out his hand, but quickly pulled it back when Don added, "This is Frank Tidsdale, a local private investigator."

It was obvious that Latimer had some preconceived ideas about private investigators. From his reaction, I got the feeling they weren't good. The smile disappeared, his eyes narrowed slightly and he looked like he was about to say something. Instead, he glanced over at Don and decided to keep his mouth shut, which was probably a good idea.

"It's all right. You're not the first detective to dislike private investigators," I said.

"Yeah. Well, you guys usually get in the way of an investigation and make it harder for us."

"I take it you're speaking from long years of experience?" I asked sarcastically, knowing full well he hadn't been a detective long enough to have had any experience.

"Just don't get in my way," he said sharply.

I looked at Don and said, "I think I'll go visit with Carlson. See if there's any reason for me to take him on as a client."

"He did it and that's all there is to it," Latimer said sharply.

I looked at the rookie and smiled.

"You might just want to look at the evidence before you go jumping off the deep end with a statement like that. It could come back to bite you in the ass," I said with a grin.

I turned and looked at Don.

"See you later, Don."

Don nodded, then I turned and walked toward my car. There was no need to look back to see what Latimer was doing. I could feel the heat from his eyes as they pierced my back. Latimer was not very happy with me, which made no sense to me. Hell, he didn't even know me.

I got in my car and drove on past the house. Latimer never took his eyes off me as I drove by. I couldn't resist the temptation to smile and wave at him.

Wright looked at Latimer and shook his head. He took a minute to light his cigarette and took a long draw on it before saying anything.

"You might think twice about what you say to Tidsdale. He can sometimes be of help if you don't piss him off."

"I've had run-ins with private investigators before. They usually just get in the way."

"Tidsdale is good at what he does. You piss him off and he'll tell you nothing. You treat him with a little respect, he might just help you."

"I don't want and I don't need his help. And I don't care if I do piss him off."

"Suit yourself, but I'd rather have him on my side than have him keep what he knows to himself."

"He doesn't know anything."

"He may or may not know anything, yet, but I wouldn't be so sure it'll stay that way very long. Like I said, 'he's good at what he does'."

"If he keeps information from us, I'll have him arrested for interfering in an investigation."

"You do that and find out what it gets you."

With that said Wright took another draw on his cigarette, crushed it out and went back in the house. Latimer looked at Wright, but didn't say anything more. He simply turned and followed Wright into the house.

Wright stood in the hall and waited while the forensic team worked upstairs. There wasn't much he could do until they were finished with their job of collecting evidence.

CHAPTER FOUR

When I arrived at the precinct where Carlson had been taken, I was greeted by the Desk Sergeant. He was a large man in his mid-fifties. At well over six feet tall and weighing in at over two hundred and fifty pounds, he was an impressive man. His hair was gray and his brown eyes looked tired. He looked like a man that had seen about everything there was to see and was no longer impressed by anything or anybody. I had known Sergeant Charles Monahan for close to fifteen years and knew he was getting close to retirement.

"What's up, Tidsdale."

"Not much. How's it going, Charley?"

"You know, about the same. Nothing changes much around here. Who ya here to see?"

"A guy by the name of Carlson, James Carlson. He was brought in tonight. I'd like to have a talk with him."

"Can't do it right now."

"Why's that?"

"Forensic guys are processing him for trace evidence, gunshot residue and anything else they can find on him or his clothes. After that he will be talking with his lawyer. Then you'll have to wait until the detectives have their talk with him. You working for him?" he asked.

"Not sure. He called me, but I haven't decided."

"Have a seat and I'll let you know when you can see him, but it might be a while."

"Okay. By the way, what's the name of his attorney?"

"Albert Moore."

"Pretty expensive attorney," I said.

"I'll say."

I had heard of Albert Moore. If what I had heard about him was true, he was the best criminal attorney in the city. He had defended several people accused of murder in recent years. If my memory served me right he got most, if not all, of his clients off.

"Say, Charley, have you got a City Directory?"

"Yeah, sure. I'll get it."

I watched as Charley got up from behind the desk. He went over to a bookshelf in the corner and pulled out a book. He handed me the book. I thanked him, then moved over to a bench, sat down and began thumbing through it looking for James Carlson.

It didn't take long for me to find him in the directory. It listed Carlson as a Certified Public Accountant with an office in one of the downtown high-rise buildings, the one called the Hammond building. The Hammond building had a number of investment firms in it and a few other businesses that I couldn't remember.

I also discovered that Mrs. Carlson's first name was Jennifer and that she worked for an architectural firm that was located on the top couple of floors of the same high-rise Carlson's office was located in. My first thought was that it was convenient for the Carlsons. I also had to wonder if the architectural firm had a contract with Carlson to help keep their books. Even if they did, I had no idea if it meant anything.

The architectural firm was Mile High Design. The only thing I knew about the architectural firm was what I had read in the newspapers. It seems they had recently obtained a contract with the city to build a rather large office complex to replace two of the aging city buildings located downtown that had become overcrowded. Being the suspicious person that I am, I had to wonder if there was something going on that might have put the Carlsons at risk.

Since I had not talked to Carlson, I had no idea what was going on. Looking at it from what little I knew, I had to look at something other than a family dispute turning ugly. If he didn't kill his wife as he claimed, then who did and why?

Jim Carlson had been taken to the precinct where he was placed in a holding cell under close guard. Two investigators from the forensic team came into the cell and took all his clothes. They processed him for any trace evidence that might be on his person. They took a DNA sample, checked his hands for gunpowder residue, took scrapings from under his fingernails and scanned his entire body for any indication that he had been in an altercation with anyone recently. They looked for recent things such as cuts or bruises. They also took samples of the blood on his hands, face and other parts of his body.

After they had finished gathering what evidence they could, they gave him the typical orange coveralls to wear with the word "Inmate" printed in large black letters across the back and down the outside edge of the right leg. He was then handcuffed again and taken to an interrogation room where he was set down on a chair and left there to wait for his lawyer and the detectives.

As soon as he was left alone, Carlson began to look around the room. The room was only about ten by ten. It was painted a dull ugly green making it look as depressing as he was feeling, if that was possible. There was only one light hanging from the ceiling. The metal shield over the light was a dark green as was the wire guard over the bulb. The light did little to brighten up the place.

There were no pictures, calendars or clocks on the walls, nor was there anything to give the room some color. The only furniture was three steel chairs with green vinyl seats and backs, and a heavy steel table with a black rubberized top. The table was securely bolted to the floor and had a large steel ring attached to the top near one end of it. There was a large one-way mirror on one wall. On *another wall was a door with a small mirrored window in it that was covered with steel bars.*

Carlson sat in one of the chairs shaking, but not because he was cold. It was because he was scared. He had never been in an interrogation room before. He had no idea what was going to happen to him. Was he going to be yelled at and bullied by the police like he had seen so many times in the movies and on television? Was he going to be intimidated with threats of getting the dreaded needle in his arm if he didn't confess?

The room gave him a feeling of being shut out of the world as he knew it. At that moment, he was feeling very much alone and trapped like an animal in a small cage. Although he had been there only about twenty minutes, he felt like it was forever before his lawyer showed up.

Carlson turned when the door suddenly opened. His eyes were big with fear of who might be coming into the room.

The man who entered the room was a tall man with slightly graying hair. He was wearing an expensive suit and tie, and carrying a briefcase. The man's name was Albert Moore.

"Oh, God, am I glad to see you," Carlson said with a big sigh of relief.

"It's going to be all right. Have you talked to anyone?" Albert asked as he sat down across the table from Carlson.

"No."

"No one?" he asked again.

Carlson looked at his lawyer as if he was a stranger to him. The fact was he had known Albert for a good many years.

"I - - - I called Frank Tidsdale right after I called you."

"What did you tell him?" Albert asked with a concerned look on his face.

"All I told him was that I was going to be arrested for murder and I needed his help."

"That's all?"

"Yes. I didn't have time to say much more. The police were breaking down my front door," he said.

"Did anyone hear your conversation with him?"

"No, I don't think so."

"Are you sure?"

"Yes! There was so much yelling when the police broke in I don't think they could have heard anything," he said as he relived the incident in his mind.

"Okay. That's good."

"Albert, you've got to get me out of here."

"I don't know if I can. They haven't charged you with anything, yet. They can hold you for questioning for awhile as a material witness, if nothing else. I'll be here with you when they question you. Everything is going to be okay."

Carlson looked at his attorney, then looked at the mirror. He was sure there would be someone behind the mirror listening to everything he said. He knew that from all the TV shows he had watched. He leaned closer to his attorney.

"What happens if they charge me with murdering Jenny?" he whispered.

"That depends," Albert replied.

"What do you mean, it depends?" he asked angrily. "You've got to have a better answer for me than that."

"Take it easy, Jim. It depends on what they charge you with. If they have what they think is enough evidence, you will most likely be arraigned sometime tomorrow, otherwise, within a day or two."

"A day or two?" Carlson yelled angrily.

"Yes. They have a day or two to charge you, or let you go."

"Okay," Carlson replied after taking a deep breath and trying to understand. "If they charge me, then they'll set bail, right?"

"Well, that will depend on the charge. There will be no bail if they charge you with first degree murder. If they charge you with a lesser crime, we might be able to get you out on bail."

Carlson sat and looked at his attorney in disbelief. What little hope he felt when Albert arrived quickly vanished into thin air. He could feel his whole world falling apart and there was nothing he could do about it. A cold chill ran through his entire body. It seemed that even his life was in someone else's hands. It was a strange feeling that came over him with the thought that he no longer had any control over his life

CHAPTER FIVE

I had just finished making a couple of notes for my daily record of things I didn't want to forget when Don and Latimer came into the precinct. Latimer was busy thinking about something and didn't notice me right away, but Don saw me and turned toward me.

"You still here?"

"Yeah. I haven't been able to talk to Carlson, yet. Charley told me that I couldn't talk to him until after you guys do."

"We're going to talk to him right now," Don said.

"You might want to know he's with his lawyer."

"His lawyer is here already?" Don asked, the tone of his voice showing his surprise.

"Yeah."

"That was pretty quick."

"Yeah. Real quick. He was here when I got here," I said as Latimer walked up next to Don.

"I'll bet you had something to do with that, too," Latimer said sharply.

"Sorry to disappoint you, hot-shot, but he had already called his attorney before he called me."

"I'll bet," he said as if he didn't believe me.

I didn't really care one way or the other what Latimer thought. He had a hell of a lot to learn before he would become anything close to a good detective. I sure wasn't in the mood to be the one to teach him.

"If you want to talk to me," I said to Don, "leave this rookie behind."

"Who you calling a rookie?"

I looked at Don, smiled and said, "I rest my case."

Don smiled at me then quickly wiped the smile off his face when Latimer started to turn to look at him.

"Come on, Latimer, we've got work to do before we can go home. See you later, Frank."

"Yeah."

I watched as Don turned and started down the hall. Latimer waited until Don was out of hearing range.

"We've got this guy dead to rights. He murdered his wife and that's that. You're not going to screw things up and get him off."

I couldn't help but smile before I said, "I don't suppose a little thing like evidence plays any part in your decision in finding him guilty so quickly?"

"Listen, smart ass, he did it. Nothing's going to change that."

"Right," I said with a strong note of sarcasm.

"You get in my way and you'll wish to hell you had never heard of me," Latimer threatened.

I didn't say a word. I simply smiled at him. Hell, I already wished I'd never heard of him.

Latimer didn't like my smile very much, but then I didn't like him; so I figured we were about even. I got the feeling he wanted to take a swing at me, but with Charley as a witness it was not a good idea if he wanted to keep his shield. Latimer turned and walked on down the hall.

As soon as he was gone, I turned and looked at Charley. I shook my head and Charley just grinned.

There was little doubt that it was going to be a long time before I would be able to see Carlson, so there was no need for me to hang around. I returned the City Directory to Charley, thanked him, then told him I would be back in the morning and left the precinct building. I walked out to my car and got in. I sat behind the wheel and thought about what had just happened.

Latimer might know something I didn't. Whatever it was, it didn't look like Don was buying into it. Don was the kind of a detective that knew nothing was for sure until everything had been checked, re-checked and re-checked again. That was one reason that Don rarely lost a case.

The one thing I seriously doubted was that they had found a motive. It was a small, but usually a very necessary item in most murder cases. As far as solid evidence, I doubted they had any at this point. It would be a while before the tests by the forensic team and the M.E. would be completed. Until then, everything was just speculation.

There was nothing more I could do tonight. I had not been hired yet, but it wouldn't hurt to look into it if for no other reason than to find out if I wanted Carlson for a client. It was time to drive home and get some sleep. Tomorrow I would talk to Carlson and his attorney. Maybe then I could get a feel for this case and make a decision on whether to take it on, or not.

Detective Wright entered the interrogation room and found Carlson and his attorney sitting at the table. Latimer followed Wright into the room just as introductions were completed. Wright sat down across the table from Carlson while Latimer stepped sideways and leaned up against the wall next to the door. He crossed his arms across his chest as he looked with squinted eyes at Carlson. He looked as if he was looking at someone he hated.

"You want to tell me what happened?" Wright asked Carlson.

"Are you arresting my client for anything?" Albert Moore asked.

"Not at the moment."

"You will be arresting him, though?"

"You can bet on it," Latimer said with a sharp, angry tone in his voice.

Wright turned and looked at Latimer. His eyes narrowed and the look on his face told Latimer that he didn't appreciate his remark; and he should keep his mouth shut.

"Well, in that case, I will instruct my client not to say anything until he is formally charged and given his rights," Moore said as he glanced over Wright's shoulder to Latimer.

"Excuse me for a moment, please," Wright said to Moore, then stood up without waiting for an answer.

As he walked to the door, he grabbed Latimer by the arm and jerked him out of the room. As soon as the door shut, he turned Latimer around and stood in front of him. The look on Wright's face showed that he was mad as hell.

"When I'm questioning someone, you keep your damn mouth shut. Do you understand that?"

"Yeah, I understand. That guy's as guilty as hell."

"Maybe, maybe not. I don't really care right now. I want to know what happened in that house. Since you screwed up by not following procedures, I have no idea what happened in that room. The only way I'm going to find out what happened is to talk to Carlson. And the only way I'm going to get anything out of Carlson is if he is willing to talk to me. Your smart ass comment may very well have caused him to clam up."

"You're not going to get anything out of him anyway," Latimer retorted. "That lawyer of his won't let him talk."

"Maybe not, but if he buttons up because his attorney tells him to, I'm certainly not going to get anything, am I? I want to know what his frame of mind was and what he's thinking. I can't get that unless he talks to me, can I?"

Latimer looked at Wright for a moment, than looked down at the floor. He knew he was not making any points with Wright. He also knew that since he was a probationary detective, Wright could prevent him from becoming a full-fledged detective with just one word to the right people.

"You stay out here and watch through the window. Don't knock on the window, don't open the door, and don't make any sound what-so-ever. Do you understand that?" Wright asked sharply.

"But," Latimer said.

"But nothing. You've made it so that just being in the same room as Carlson would cause him to clam up. Now stay here or go home, and I frankly don't give a damn which."

"You can't send me home," Latimer said in defiance.

Wright stepped up a little closer to him and said, "Like hell I can't. If you say one more word, I'll prove it. If you step out of line one more time, I'll have you back in uniform and pounding the pavement in the worst neighborhood I can find. Is that clear?"

Wright looked him in the eye for a moment. When he didn't reply, Wright turned around, took a deep breathe and went back inside the room. Latimer did not try to follow him.

Once in the room, he slipped off his coat and hung it on the back of the chair. He then pulled the chair out and sat down across the table from Carlson.

"Sorry about that. Just to make things clear, I'm not sure what's going to happen, yet. I would like to hear from your client, in his own words, what happened at his house tonight?" Wright said to Moore.

"Okay. I'll let him talk to you," Moore said, "But only if you keep that hothead out of here and keep him away from my client."

"Agreed," Wright said as he nodded his head.

Carlson looked at his attorney, then back at Wright. He looked down at the table for a second, but didn't say anything.

CHAPTER SIX

I drove across town to my apartment. There were a lot of things running through my mind. One of the more nagging questions was why had Carlson called me? He had to know something about me, but at this point I knew virtually nothing about him. I couldn't help but think that it would be in my best interest to find out a little about him before I stuck my neck out too far.

By the time I got to my apartment, I was as frustrated as ever. The only thing I knew for sure was there was nothing I could do until I had a chance to talk to Carlson. I wouldn't be able to do that until morning.

As I walked up to the door to my apartment, I noticed a light on inside. That could only mean one thing. Jackie was waiting for me, and that thought caused me to smile.

Jackie was my best friend and a very sexy lady. We had grown up as friends from junior high school. She had been my first love, and I hers. We had dated a few times in high school and in college. She had been there for me when my marriage ended. I had been there for her when her boyfriends would dump her. In short, we had a long history together. I had to wonder what brought her to my apartment so late in the evening.

I opened the door and stepped inside. The small dining room table had been set with my best table settings and two tall white candles were glowing brightly. It didn't take me long to figure out what was going on. Apparently, Jackie was trying to impress me, or she wanted something. Maybe she just wanted to show me that she could be very domestic. I could hear her in the kitchen and walked to the door.

"What's going on?" I asked as I leaned against the doorjamb.

"Oh, hi," she said after looking over her shoulder.

"Whatever you're cooking smells great."

"I hope you're hungry," she said as she walked over to the door and gave me a kiss on the cheek. "You have about fifteen minutes before its ready."

"Isn't it kind of late to be fixing a meal?"

"I happen to know you have been working late. I thought you might like something before we go to bed."

"Oh. How is it that you know I was working late?"

"My powers of perception. Actually, I called your office and here with no answer at either place."

"Oh," I said, not missing the fact she had said "we" when it came to going to bed.

"Get washed up," she said, then returned to cooking.

I went to my bedroom and hung up my sport coat and put my gun in the closet. After washing up, I went back to the kitchen and stood in the doorway watching her. With Jackie there was no telling what I might get when she had the entire kitchen to herself. She could come up with some of the strangest combination of foods. The strangest part of it all was they often didn't taste all that bad. The only good thing was it was my kitchen. Unless she had stopped off at the store first, I had a pretty good idea of what there was available to eat.

"What are we having for this late night dinner?"

"It's a surprise," she said with a smile.

"With you, it's always a surprise."

"Good. Sit down. I'll bring it in, in a minute."

I sat down and waited for her surprise. Before long she came in carrying a casserole. She set it down on the table, pulled out a chair and sat down across the table from me.

I leaned over and looked at the dish she had prepared. I had to admit it smelled good, but it looked a little green. I had no idea if it was supposed to look green or not, but I was secure in the fact that I didn't think she would intentionally poison me.

"Okay. Before I'm going to eat this, I want to know what it is."

"It's my own creation. It's a crab meat and asparagus casserole with egg noodles in an Alfredo sauce," she said proudly.

Naming it didn't seem to help very much, but there was nothing in it I couldn't eat; so I decided I would give it a try. I dished some on her plate then put some on my plate. I took a little on my fork and looked at her as I put it in my mouth. It was creamy, rich, and surprisingly good in spite of how it looked.

"This isn't bad," I said then took another bit.

For the next few minutes we did very little talking. I had to admit the dinner was good and I was hungrier than I thought. After dinner I helped her clean up the kitchen. She asked me what I was working on and I explained.

After watching the nightly news, she suggested we go to bed because she had to be at work early. I didn't need a great deal of encouragement.

Once we were in bed, we did a lot of petting and then we proceeded on to more important things. I had to admit that what she thought was important I found to be very pleasant. Before long we were off in a dream world of our own.

It took Jim Carlson a little while before he began explaining what had happened at his house. He told Wright that he had been working in his workshop in the basement. He had been there for several hours working on a wooden bench for the porch.

"Since I was using a couple of my power tools on the project, I didn't hear anything until I shut my sander off. That was when I heard a noise upstairs that sounded like something falling. I called for Jenny, but didn't get an answer. I waited a couple of minutes, but didn't hear anything else. I became concerned and decided to go upstairs to see what was going on.

"When I got upstairs, I called for Jenny again, but I still didn't get a response. I began looking for her. That was when I discovered the blood on the floor at the bottom of the stairs and became very concerned. I followed the blood trail up the stairs to our bedroom," he said, then choked up and had to take a breather before he could continue.

"I - - - I found Jenny on the floor in our bedroom. She was next to the bed - - in a pool of blood."

Carlson broke down and began to cry. No one said anything. They just gave him a moment or two to gather himself together. As soon as he was ready to talk, he began again.

"I knelt down beside her - - to see if she was still - - alive. That must have been when I put my hand on the gun. I don't even remember doing it, but I picked up the gun without thinking. I called 911 and told them my wife had been shot."

"It looks like you called 911 from the phone downstairs in the entry. Why didn't you use the phone in the bedroom?" Wright asked, keeping his voice calm and soft.

"I don't know. I'm not sure what I did."

"You remembered enough to hang up the phone and call your attorney. You also were thinking clearly enough to call Tidsdale and ask him for help."

"I don't remember calling Albert or hanging up. I'm not even sure in what order I made the calls to 911 and to Mr. Moore. But at some point, I realized that I still had the gun in my hand and I was going to need help. Somewhere in the back of my mind, I knew that the police would think I shot my wife and would arrest me. That was when I called Mr. Tidsdale."

Carlson seemed to have his story down pat. Wright had to wonder if he was telling the truth, or if he had rehearsed what he was going to say ahead of time. It sounded just a little to pat for Wright, but he didn't know Carlson well enough to know if he should believe him or not.

Wright still had a lot of questions to ask Carlson, but it was getting late. Mr. Moore suggested that Wright stop questioning his client for the night; so they all could get some much needed rest. It had been a long day for all of them.

Once Moore had suggested that they stop the interview, Wright knew he didn't have a choice. Carlson's attorney could stop the questioning anytime he wanted by simply telling his client not to speak to the police. Wright agreed immediately. In a way he hoped to build a little willingness for them to work with him.

After some minor negotiating with Mr. Moore, Wright agreed to keep Carlson in jail for the night as a material witness instead of booking him for murder. Moore didn't want it on record that Carlson had been charged with murder until there was more information from the crime scene.

Much to Carlson's displeasure, he was escorted to a holding cell. He was guided into the cell and the guard closed the cell door behind him. The sound of the cell door closing and locking startled Carlson. It was a sound that he was sure he would never forget.

Carlson was soon left alone. He looked around the cell. He found the cell to be dark and dingy. The walls had at one time been painted an off-white, but now had places were the paint was chipped. There were also places where those held in the cell before him had scratched messages and foul words on the walls.

In one corner of the cell there was a combination stainless steel sink and toilet that was bolted to the wall and floor. The bed was made of steel band springs stretched over a steel frame and it was also bolted to the wall. It had a three inch thick mattress that was very hard. The only cover he had was a single wool blanket in a dingy gray. He had been given only a small towel, a wash cloth and a small bar of soap similar to those found in the less expensive hotels to clean up with. There was a dim light in the passageway, but no lights in the cell.

Carlson stood looking around the cell hoping that what he was seeing was not true. He could not believe that he was locked up in such a place. After a while, he climbed onto the bed and laid down. He put his hands behind his head and looked up at the ceiling. Tears came to his eyes and slowly ran down the side of his face. In all his wildest dreams he had never expected to end up in a jail cell. It began to occur to him that he might spend the rest of his life in a place just like it.

Carlson found it very difficult to fall asleep. There was the sound of a drunk in the holding cell next to his and the loud sounds of someone snoring somewhere down the narrow hall. He guessed that the holding cell next to his was what was called the "drunk tank". These were sounds he was not used to hearing. They were certainly not the sounds he was used to in the nice home he had across the street from Washington Park. That along with everything that had happened made it almost impossible for him to fall asleep.

He finally did fall asleep, but more from exhaustion than from a desire to sleep.

CHAPTER SEVEN

Morning came with a flash of lightening and the crash of thunder. The suddenness of the loud sound made me sit straight up in bed. It took me a couple of minutes to clear my head and understand what was happening. After taking a deep breath, I laid back down. I took a moment to see what time it was. It was still early. I tried to close my eyes in the hope of getting a little more sleep, but it was not to be. I had too much going through my head to allow myself to get any more sleep.

Instead of getting up, I looked over at Jackie. She was looking at me. From the look on her face, I could see that she knew I would not be able to go back to sleep.

"Good morning," she said with a sexy smile.

I had never known any woman to look so good so early in the morning.

"Good morning," I replied. "You ready to get up?"

"Not really, but I should. I have to go to work."

"Okay."

I rolled over to her and kissed her. I then sat up and swung my legs over the side of the bed. After taking a couple of seconds to look at her lying on my bed, I went into the bathroom. It didn't take long for me to get ready to face the day. A quick shower and shave, and I was ready. I dressed in a pair of slacks and a polo shirt. I would put on a sport jacket before I left the house to cover my gun.

It didn't take Jackie very long to dress and be ready to leave, either. Neither of us worried about breakfast. We could grab something to eat somewhere along the way.

As soon as we were ready, we left my apartment hand in hand. I walked her to her car, gave her a kiss and held the door for her while she got in.

"Will I see you tonight," she asked.

"I'm not sure. At the moment I don't know if I have a case or not. Maybe I better give you a call later."

"Okay. Be careful."

"You, too."

After giving her another kiss, I stepped back and watched her as she drove away. As soon as she was gone, I went to my car and headed for my office.

The rain seemed to have slowed traffic a little, but there were still those who would drive fast no matter what the weather. The drive to the office gave me time to think about Carlson and sort of put together what I knew, which was very little. I still hadn't decided if I was going to take him on as a client. I didn't have enough information to make that kind of a decision.

I made a stop at a local bakery about a half block from my office to grab a roll and a cup of coffee. While I was eating, I watched the news on the television above the counter. The reporter was telling the world about the "brutal murder" of Mrs. Jennifer Carlson and that the prime suspect was her husband, James Carlson. I couldn't help but think that he was probably the only suspect, at least for now.

I didn't wait for the rest of the news. My mind was too cluttered with thoughts of Carlson and who else might have had a reason to kill his wife to show much interest in anything else at the moment. Instead, I went directly to my office and checked the answering machine. There was a message from Carlson's lawyer, Albert Moore, to call him as soon as I could. He had left me a number which I jotted down then placed the call.

"Hello."

"Is this Albert Moore?"

"Yes."

"This is Frank Tidsdale. I'm returning your call."

"Ah, yes. I was wondering if I could meet with you."

"Certainly. I take it this would be about Jim Carlson and his present situation?"

"Yes, it would. He told me that he talked to you last night on the phone. I need to know what he told you."

"You mean he hasn't told you, yet?"

"As a matter of fact, he has. However, I would like to hear it from you."

"In other words, you would like to know what I might have told the police."

"Well, yes. That is really what I want to know."

"I can tell you that right now."

"I would rather talk to you in person."

"First of all, Jim Carlson did not hire me to work for him. We didn't get that far. Anything he told me is not privileged."

"I understand that, Mr. Tidsdale. I would still like to meet with you. It may prove to be important to me as well as beneficial to you. In fact, I may need your help and I'm more than willing to pay you for your services."

Now that was music to my ears. I always liked getting paid for what I do. It tends to keep groceries on the table and helps pay the bills.

"When would you like to meet and where?"

"Could you meet me at my office in, say, about an hour?"

"I'll be there," I said then hung up.

As soon as I put the phone down, I sat back in my chair and looked at it. I had a feeling that Albert Moore wanted more than to know what Jim had said to me. I had to wonder if he had some idea of what had gone on in the Carlson house. I also wondered if there was more to it than wanting to know what I might have told the police. Either way, I wasn't going to find out until I talked to him.

I left my office and drove to Mr. Moore's office. It was in a nice new three story building on the edge of the downtown district. I parked in the underground garage and took the elevator to the third floor where Moore's office was located.

Carlson was awake early, but not because of the thunderstorm. He woke wondering if what had happened to him had all been some terrible nightmare. He quickly discovered it was about as real as it gets. His world had fallen apart last night. His wife was dead and he was being blamed for it. It couldn't get much worse than that.

He still could not believe that he had been arrested and put in jail. It was so depressing that he wanted to sit there and cry, but what good would it do. Besides, he would have plenty of time for that later. Now he had to get help in proving that he didn't kill his wife.

He looked around the drab surroundings of the holding cell. Until last night he had never even seen the insides of a jail cell, let alone be locked up in one. He stood up and walked over to the cell door and gripped the bars with both hands as he looked out. There was no one in the aisle. He couldn't see in any of the other cells, but he knew there had been at least two other men locked up last night. He had heard them, but it was quiet now.

Just then he heard the steel door at the end of the aisle being unlocked and opened. The thought ran through his mind that someone was coming to get him out. He was sure that everything was going to be okay as he smiled to himself. The excitement of just the thought that he was going to get out sent a feeling of joy through him that was hard for him to contain. He could hear the solid footsteps of hard street shoes on the gray painted cement floor of someone coming toward him.

A man in a policeman's uniform walked up to his cell and looked at Carlson. He had a steel tray in his hands that was dented and looked as if it had been used as a shield in a fight.

"Step back," the officer said in a demanding tone.

Carlson looked at him for a second then glanced at the tray he was carrying. He suddenly realized that he was not getting out. Carlson slowly stepped back away from the cell door. The officer opened a small section of the bars of the cell and slid the tray into the cell onto a narrow shelf.

"Your breakfast. Eat up. I'll be back in fifteen minutes to get the tray," the officer said without any feeling or emotion.

Carlson just looked at the officer as he turned and walked away. Seeing him leave caused Carlson to feel panicky. He had been so sure that he was going to get out.

"Wait. Please wait," he called out, but the officer ignored him and left shutting the steel door at the end of the aisle.

The sound of the door shutting was like shutting out the entire world that Carlson had known. It was so quiet he could hear his own heart beat. He looked at the tray of cold scrambled eggs and toast, orange juice and black coffee. The food looked so unappetizing on the dull and dented metal tray that he thought about not eating it.

Carlson stared at the food not feeling very hungry. But the longer he looked at it, the more he wondered if he would ever see a meal on china plates with real silverware, or coffee served in a delicate china cup, or a crystal glass or goblet with a nice red wine in it again. It occurred to him that he had better eat if for no other reason than to keep up his strength. He would need it if he was going to beat the charges that he was rapidly becoming convinced would be filed against him.

He took the tray and sat down on the edge of the bunk. Carlson slowly began eating. He found the food to be as tasteless as it looked. It was almost as if he could taste the metal of the steel tray in the food

CHAPTER EIGHT

When I walked into Moore's reception area, I was greeted by a very nice looking woman who was sitting behind a large solid walnut desk. A quick look around the office assured me that Moore was probably a very expensive attorney. The office had all the appearances of someone with money. There wasn't anything there that wasn't expensive.

"May I help you?" the woman asked with a pleasant smile.

"Yes. I'm here to see Albert Moore. He's expecting me. I'm Frank Tidsdale."

I watched her as she picked up the phone, pressed a button and announced to Mr. Moore that I was waiting to see him. She nodded her head and said "Yes, sir," into the phone.

After hanging up the phone, she looked up at me, smiled and said, "Mr. Moore is expecting you. He will see you now."

"Thank you."

She stood up and walked over to a large door and opened it for me. I nodded a "thank you" as I stepped into Moore's office. His office was just as impressive as the outer office, maybe more so. The furniture was large and very expensive. One wall was covered with walnut book shelves and each shelf was full of law books. There were several paintings on the other wall that were more than likely originals.

"It is so nice of you to come on such short notice," Moore said as he stood up.

"No problem. What is it you think I can do for you?"

"I see you like to get right to the point. I like that," he said with a smile.

Mr. Moore sat down and motioned for me to sit down in front of his desk. I sat down then waited for him to speak first since he was the one who had asked for this meeting.

"First of all, I need to know what Carlson told you last night."

"He told me nothing more than I have already told you. Carlson called me and said that he was going to be arrested for murdering his wife. I told him to call an attorney and not to resist the officers. I also told him not to say a word without his attorney present."

"That's it?" he asked as if he expected more.

"He did say that he didn't do it."

"I take it you don't believe him."

"I wouldn't say that I don't believe him. But from what I know about it, it doesn't look good for him."

"I see," Moore said as he looked as if he was expecting more from me.

"That's it. There wasn't anything else to say. I heard the police enter the house and tell Carlson to drop the gun. I heard what sounded like a scuffle then the phone went dead."

"So you don't really know very much, do you?"

"No."

"What did you tell the police?"

His last question gave me the feeling that he knew that I had talked to the police. I didn't know how he might know that, but it seemed that he did. I also got the impression that he expected me to know more and to tell him everything I knew. I had to wonder what it was that he thought I might know. I decided that it would be a good idea on my part to be very careful about what I said to him. I decided not to tell him what Don had told me at the house. In fact, I decided not to tell him that I had even talked to Don.

"You have to remember, I was not retained by Mr. Carlson. We had agreed to nothing. I had no reason to ask anyone any questions, including the police, with regard to what happened at Mr. Carlson's home. Having said that, I went by Carlson's home, and I went to the police station to see if I could talk to him. All I wanted to find out was whether or not I wanted to take Carlson on as a Client."

There was something going on in Moore's mind, but I had no idea what it might be. I had no idea what he thought I might know, or what he expected me to know.

"So you didn't talk to the police?"

"I talked to Detective Wright at the precinct while I was waiting to talk to Carlson. That was only to say 'hi' as we have known each other for a good many years."

"I see. Did you ask him anything about the Carlson case?

"No. I had no reason to. As I've said before, Carlson was not my client at that point, and still isn't my client."

Moore looked at me as if he was trying to decide if I was telling him the whole truth. I had no idea what he had decided when he asked another question.

"Do you know what Mr. Carlson does for a living?"

"Sure. He's an accountant."

"How is it that you know that?"

"After he called me, I looked it up in the City Directory. His wife worked for an architectural firm in the Hammond building where Carlson has his office. Mile High Design, if I remember correctly. I'm not sure what her job was, though. That's about it."

"What do you suppose Mr. Carlson wanted you to do for him?"

"From what he said on the phone, he wanted me to find proof that he didn't kill his wife. At least that's what he said."

"Anything else?"

"I seriously doubt we had much time to discuss details. The police were about to break into his house. All he said was that he wanted me to find out who killed his wife. I believe what he said was "what I really need is someone to prove I didn't do it". That was all he had time to say about it. He was very nervous. We didn't have time to discuss a contract, even a verbal one."

"Do you think you can do that?"

"What? Prove he didn't do it?"

"Yes."

"I don't know if I can prove it or not because I don't know if he killed his wife."

"I don't think he did," Moore said, his voice sounding like he really believed what he said.

I wasn't sure if it was something he practiced, or if he really believed it. Moore was looking for something. I just didn't know what it was he was after.

"I want to hire you to find out who did kill Mrs. Carlson and why."

"Even if I find out that he did do it?"

"Yes, because I don't think he did it."

"So you want to hire me?"

"That is correct."

"Okay, but I don't come cheap," I said.

"I'm sure you don't," Moore said with a smile.

We spent the next twenty minutes or so agreeing on a fee and a retainer. I found it interesting that he didn't try to negotiate a lower fee. I had heard that Moore was a penny pincher when it came to spending money, but didn't hesitate to charge high fees for his services. Moore paid me the retainer and told me that he wanted me to start immediately. I agreed and explained to him that I was going to have to talk to Carlson, alone, and I would like him to arrange it. He agreed.

Since everything was settled, I left Mr. Moore's office and returned to my own office. I sat down at my desk and began planning out how I was going to start. The first thing I needed to do was to have a talk with Carlson. I wondered if I would be as confident of his innocence as Moore seemed to be once I visited with Carlson.

I hadn't been in my office very long when I received a call from Moore. He told me that he had arranged for me to interview Carlson at the police station. I immediately left to see Carlson.

The officer returned to Carlson's cell in fifteen minutes, just like he said. He picked up the tray and left. He returned again within a few minutes.

"You've got someone here to see you. Turn around."

Carlson did as he was told. He stood up, turned around and put his hands behind his back and waited for the officer to put handcuffs on him. As the officer cuffed him, Carlson wondered who was here to see him, but didn't think he should ask.

As he was led down the hall, Carlson was thinking that it was probably Mr. Moore. He was even hopeful that Moore was there to get him out of jail. When he entered the interrogation room, he saw Latimer and Wright waiting for him. He looked around but didn't see his attorney. He didn't like the idea that Latimer was there. He was all too well aware of the fact that Latimer thought he was guilty.

"I'm not supposed to talk to you without my attorney present," Carlson said, the look on his face showing that he was worried about why his attorney wasn't present.

"Mr. Moore is unable to be here right now, but assured me that he would be along later," Wright said. "There's a Mr. Tidsdale here to visit with you at the request of your attorney. Is that all right with you? I believe you called Mr. Tidsdale just before you were arrested."

"Yes, that's true. Will you be here when he talks to me?"

"No. Mr. Tidsdale is a representative of your attorney and is therefore representing you. He has the same privileges as your attorney," Wright explained.

"You don't have to talk to him," Latimer said flatly.

Wright looked at Latimer as if to say 'shut your damn mouth'. Latimer looked at Wright then turned away.

Turning back to look at Carlson, Wright said. "Your attorney said it was okay for you to speak with him. Do you want to talk to him?"

"Yes. If my attorney said it was okay, I'll talk to him."

"I'll get him for you."

"Thank you."

Wright started to leave, but stopped when Latimer didn't immediately follow him. He noticed the look on Latimer's face. Wright knew that Latimer thought that Carlson was guilty and that he didn't like the fact that Wright was going to let him talk to Tidsdale. But Wright didn't care what Latimer thought, or what he liked or didn't like. Under the circumstances, there was no way he could stop Tidsdale from interviewing Carlson without breaking the law. Tidsdale was now part of Carlson's defense team and had every right to talk to Carlson.

"Latimer," was all Wright had to say.

Latimer reluctantly left the interrogation room mumbling something as he left. Wright followed Latimer out into the hall, then he reached out and touched Latimer's arm. Latimer stopped, turned and looked at Wright.

"I know you don't like the way I investigate a crime, but I don't care what you like. It will be done my way or you'll find yourself beating the pavement again. I have been doing this for a long time. There are things that they don't teach you in that high class college you went to that you will need to learn on the job. If you last long enough, you might find out what they are. If you continue to keep that holier than thou attitude of yours, your time as a detective is going to be one of the shortest in the history of the department. You get what I'm telling you?"

"Yeah, I get it," he said, not liking it though."

"I know you don't like PI's, but in spite of what you think, sometimes they can be a lot of help."

"Maybe so, but they do more harm than good."

"*I doubt that. You have to sort out the ones that can help you from the ones that just get in the way.*"

Latimer looked at Wright for a minute, then just shook his head, turned and walked on down the hall. Wright knew that Latimer wasn't listening to him. Wright was thinking that the kid had a lot to learn and wondered if he was going to last long enough to learn it. He was beginning to wonder how he got promoted to Detective in the first place. He couldn't help but think that Latimer had to know someone because he didn't have what it took to get promoted without some help from someone higher up.

Wright shook his head again then went into the hall and got Tidsdale.

"*He's all yours,*" Wright said as he pointed toward the interrogation room.

CHAPTER NINE

I entered the interrogation room, then turned around and looked at Don. I had a dozen questions to ask him, but not while Latimer was nearby.

Latimer was down the hall a little way. He was watching us rather closely, I thought. He had a look of disgust on his face, but, frankly, I didn't give a damn. I had little respect for an officer of the law that was so stupid as to express his belief in a man's guilt without any evidence to back it up.

"Don, would you be so kind as to make sure that no one listens in on us?"

"Sure. I take it you're referring to Latimer?"

"Yeah. I trust you, but I don't trust him."

"I certainly understand that," Don said.

I waited for Don to leave and closed the door before I turned around. The man sitting at the table looked like he'd had a rough night. He hadn't shaved and his hair was a mess. I could see the fear in his eyes. It was obvious to me that he had never been in jail before and had no idea of what to expect, or what was expected of him.

"I'm Frank Tidsdale," I said softly. "You called me the night your wife was murdered. Do you remember that?"

"Yes. You told me not to resist the police and not to say anything until my attorney was present."

"That's right. Because of the circumstances of last night, I couldn't get in touch with you after you were arrested. I did, however, have a talk with your attorney, Mr. Moore, this morning. He has hired me to find out the truth. Is that okay with you?"

"Sure," he replied, but didn't sound too sure.

"Are you ready to answer a few questions?"

"I guess so. Do I need to have my attorney present?"

"No. Not in this case. First of all, I'm not a cop. Secondly, I'm working for your attorney. Client privilege applies with me the same as it would if you were talking to Mr. Moore. Anything you tell me is confidential. I can't tell anyone else, except for your attorney, without your permission. Do you understand?"

"Yes."

"Are you ready?"

"I guess so."

"I need to know where you got the gun that you had when the police arrested you?"

"Like I told Mr. Moore, it just sort of appeared beside my wife. I didn't see it until I knelt down beside her. The only thing I can think of was that it was there on the floor. I felt it when I leaned over my wife. I guess I just picked it up."

"Do you know whose gun it is? Was it your gun, or maybe your wife's gun?"

"Neither of us owns a gun."

"Any idea as to how the gun got in your house?"

"No. I have no idea as to how it got there. It must have been brought in by the person who killed her. That's the only way I can think of that it got into the house."

"Where were you when your wife was killed?"

"I was in the basement."

"What were you doing in the basement?"

"I was working on a wooden bench for the front porch. I do woodworking to relax."

"It appears that your wife had been shot. How is it you didn't hear anything?"

"I don't know. I must have been working with my sander when someone came into the house - and - and - killed her," he said as he started to cry.

I sat back in the chair and watched him while he tried to compose himself. His tears seemed real enough, but I have seen enough people who could turn on the tears and shut them off like a faucet. It was going to take more than that for him to convince me that he was innocent. That's not to say that I thought he killed her, either. It's just that in my line of work I get lied to more often than not.

From what Moore had told me about Carlson's interview with the police, things didn't add up the way I thought they should. There were a lot of unanswered questions about what actually took place in the Carlson house, and I was hired to find the answers.

"Are you going to help me?" he asked looking up at me.

"I'm going to try to find the truth. If that helps you, then, yes, I'm going to help you."

"I guess that's fair enough," he said, but the look on his face didn't seem to agree with what he said.

"I don't like surprises when I'm working on a case. I especially don't like to be lied to. After I've been lied to once, it tends to make me not believe what I'm told even if they tell the truth. I expect to be told the truth by those I'm working for. Do you understand?"

"Yes."

"Is there anything that you have told me so far that you would like to change?"

He hesitated for a moment before he said, "No."

I wasn't sure what the look in his eyes meant as he looked into mine. What I needed to do now was to see all the evidence that the police had on him. Until I had that, I had no idea where he stood. Since he had the gun that supposedly had killed his wife in his hand when he was arrested, it didn't look good. I needed to know if it really was the gun that had been used to commit the crime. I also needed to know what other evidence they had on him and what evidence the police had that might point to someone else as the killer.

"I'm going to be leaving now. I have a lot to do."

"That's it? That's all you're going to ask me?"

"It is for the time being. I need to find out what evidence they have before I have any more questions for you. If you think of anything that might help prove your innocence, I want to know about it before anyone else. Do you understand that?"

"Yes. What about telling Mr. Moore if I can't get in touch with you?"

"You can tell Mr. Moore, but no one else. And I mean no one else."

"Will you come back to see me again?"

The look on his face told me that he was afraid. Maybe he was afraid that I would never come back. From what I had seen and heard so far, he had good reason.

"Yes, but I'm not sure when. Try to relax. I believe that Mr. Moore will be by later."

He nodded that he understood even though I doubted that he really did. He was out of his normal surrounding and I'm sure he felt very apprehensive and insecure. He had no control over what might happen, and he struck me as the kind of a man who liked to be in control.

I left him in the interrogation room and headed down the hall to Don's office. He wasn't in. I stopped and talked to Charley for a moment. He told me that Don had gone back to Carlson's house to look around. I decided that it might be a good idea to go to Carlson's house and have a talk with him there.

Detective Donald Wright pulled up in front of Carlson's house. He sat in his car as he looked at the house. It was an upper middle-class house in an old Denver neighborhood. It was obvious that Carlson and his wife had spent a good deal of time and money to remodel and restore the old two story house.

Letting out a deep sigh, Wright opened the car door and got out. As he walked toward the house, he continued to look it over. It wasn't that he was looking for anything, he was just thinking about what had taken place in the house. To his way of thinking, there was something about the case that didn't seem right. There were a lot of things that just didn't seem to add up like they should.

The bedroom where Jennifer Carlson had been murdered was a mess with blood all over the room, yet there was a trail of blood that ran down the stairs to the front hall, more blood than one would expect to see if it had simply dripped off Carlson's hand and the clothes he had been wearing.

From the look of it there may have been a struggle in the front hall. The fact that Mrs. Jennifer Carlson had been shot didn't seem to play into it. It was possible that she had fought with her attacker in the front hall then was taken upstairs where she was beaten and then shot. There was also the possibility that she had been able to escape her attacker after she cut him with a knife, or some other sharp instrument, and run upstairs to the bedroom before she was shot.

There was also the possibility that the struggle had been between the police and Mr. Carlson when he was arrested, but that didn't seem right. The struggle between the police and Carlson would not have produced the same results, at least based on what he had been told by the arresting police officers and Carlson. And if it had been blood resulting from a struggle between the police and Carlson, how did the blood get all the way up the stairs. It just didn't add up.

Wright was wishing that he had the coroner's report and the lab reports on the blood. He knew that the lab was very busy and he had been told that the reports would not be ready until early that afternoon. The actual cause of death might prove interesting, he thought. He was still a little angry with Latimer for not taking pictures and for having the body removed before he got there.

Just as he was about to go inside and take another look around, Latimer drove up. Wright let out a sigh of disgust and disappointment with his new partner. Even though Latimer was his partner, like it or not, he was wishing that he had not shown up. At that point, he felt he would accomplish a lot more if he didn't have to deal with the likes of Latimer and his arrogant attitude.

"Taking another look at the murder scene?" Latimer asked with a smile.

"Yeah. There might be something we missed."

"I doubt it, but it never hurts to take a second look," Latimer said with a grin.

Wright looked at Latimer. He wasn't sure why he wasted his time with him. So far, Latimer hadn't shown any indication that he was ready to be a detective.

"A second look doesn't do any good if you don't have an open mind while you're looking." Wright reminded him rather sharply.

Latimer didn't say anything, he simply smiled that stupid smile of superiority he used when he didn't have anything intelligent to say, which seemed to be the case most of the time. He waited for Wright to unlock the front door and enter the house. He then followed him inside

Wright walked slowly into the foyer where Carlson had been arrested, then stopped. Latimer stepped in and stood beside him. Latimer watched Wright closely. Latimer didn't *figure that there was anything in the foyer that they had missed the first time. Suddenly, Wright knelt down and looked closely at the floor.*

"See anything interesting?" Latimer asked.

"Yes. The blood trail that we found on the stairs last night leads right out the front door."

"It does?" Latimer said with a hint of surprise in his voice.

"Yeah. Why would it lead outside?"

"Maybe Carlson went outside before he called 9-1-1."

"Maybe. But maybe there was someone else in the house and he left by the front door," Wright said as he turned his head and looked at Latimer.

Wright wasn't sure what the look on Latimer's face meant. The one thing he was sure of was that Latimer didn't like the idea of another person in the house at the time of the murder. If that proved to be the case, it would certainly make him look bad since he thought he had the case all wrapped up in a neat little package. He didn't like to look bad. Looking bad did nothing to help him get through his probation period.

Wright opened the door and looked outside. The one thing he didn't find was blood on the porch just outside the door. If the blood trail led out the front door, why wasn't there any blood on the porch? Wright decided to keep that to himself for now.

"Let's take a look in the basement. I want to know if Carlson was doing what he said he was doing."

Wright headed straight to the basement with Latimer following along behind. The basement was typical of most basements in the area. There was a laundry area in one corner with a washer, dryer, a place to store things, and a table to fold clothes on. The ceiling was open between the beams with wiring, heat ducts and plumbing exposed. The walls had been painted white. Nothing had been done to remodel that part of the house other than to paint the walls white, probably to make it a little brighter.

Along the center support beam, a wall had been constructed with an unusually large door in the center of it. Wright opened the door and found a large open area. There were several workbenches, shelves, cabinets and a lot of woodworking tools. It was obvious that it was Carlson's woodworking shop.

Wright stood at the door and looked around then looked at the floor. The floor told him that whoever had been working there had not sweep up the floor after the last time he had worked. There were small pieces of wood, wood chips and sawdust on the floor near the workbench. There was also an electric sander on the workbench along with a single piece of sanded wood that looked like they could be part of a bench. The sander was still plugged in.

"Looks like Carlson might have been working on a wooden bench for his front porch after all," Wright said. "The only question is was he working on it last evening like he said he was, or had he worked on it at some other time."

"This doesn't prove anything. He could have been working on it almost anytime. It could have been weeks since he worked on it," Latimer said.

"That's true enough, but it does open up the possibility that he was telling the truth. Now we have to prove he was telling the truth, or that he was lying to us."

Latimer looked around the workshop for a moment then left for upstairs while Wright remained behind. Wright brushed a little of the sawdust from near the sander into an evidence envelope and put it in his pocket. He then took time to look at some of the tools. Satisfied that there was nothing else of importance to him at that time, he went upstairs to look around the main level of the house. As he went down the hall toward the living room, he saw a car pull up in front.

CHAPTER TEN

I parked behind Don's police car in front of Carlson's house. I noticed another police car across the street. It had to be Latimer's car. He was the last person I wanted to run into right now. I had been hoping to get to talk to Don alone.

Since I was here, I figured there was no reason for me to leave just because Latimer was there. I got out of my car and started for the front of the house. When I looked up at the door, I saw Don open the door and step outside.

"Hi, Don."

"Hi. What are you doing here?"

"For one thing, I came by to talk to you. For another, I came to see the crime scene."

"I take it you've decided to look into the murder of Carlson's wife?"

"Yeah. I was hired by Carlson's attorney."

"Let me guess. You're here to help get him off," Latimer said as he stepped out onto the porch behind Don.

"What the hell would you know? You can't even wait to see what the evidence proves before you're ready to hang the guy out to dry. And you think PI's are dumb?"

"You son of a bitch. I ought to toss your ass in jail."

"Go for it, rookie, and see how long you have that badge."

"That's enough," Don said sharply.

"Where the hell did you get this guy?" I asked Don.

"I said 'that's enough'. What do you want, Tidsdale?"

"I would like to take a look at the crime scene."

"You can't," Latimer said with a hint of authority.

"It's looking like he can," Don said before I had a chance to tell Latimer that he couldn't stop me.

"You're not going to let him in the house?" Latimer said looking at Don.

I looked at Don while completely ignoring Latimer. Don knew that it wouldn't take me long before I could get a judge to allow me to examine the crime scene. All I had to do was to get Moore to tell the judge that I was working for him as part of Carlson's defense team and that the police would not give me access to all the evidence including the crime scene. Don was well aware that the defense council, including its investigator, have a right to all the evidence including the crime scene, once forensic was done gathering evidence.

"Are you sure you're working for Moore?" Don asked.

"Yes. Go ahead and call him. I'll wait," I said as I leaned back against the porch railing.

Don was looking at me. We had a pretty good understanding of each other. I had made it a point to be as honest with him as I could be without giving him any confidential information. Our relationship over the years had proved to be a good one, although I wouldn't call us friends. I had helped him on several cases, and as a result, he had helped me from time to time. He knew the value of having someone who knew his way around the system, and who didn't always have to play by the same set of rules as the police.

"Okay. I would appreciate it if you didn't touch anything just in case the forensic guys have to come back," Don said.

"No problem. I'll wear gloves," I said.

I reached into my inside coat pocket and pulled out a sealed packet that contained a pair of rubber gloves. I took the gloves out and put them on.

Latimer looked from Don to me, than back to Don. It was clear that he didn't like the fact that I was going to enter the crime scene. I really think that he was afraid that I might find something that would prove Carlson didn't kill his wife.

If I did that, he would not only look like the fool he was; but he might have to actually go to work to find the real killer. There was also the possibility that I would find something he should have easily found. Since he had made up his mind about the guilt of Carlson, he didn't bother to look for any other evidence. Either way, it was clear that he didn't like the idea of me rummaging around in the house, but I didn't care what he liked or didn't like.

Latimer shook his head and stormed off the porch to his car. I half expected Don to call him back, but he didn't.

"That guy's got a lot to learn," I said to Don as I watched Latimer cross the street.

"Yeah," Don said, with a deep sigh.

"Are you going to stick around while I go through the house?"

"I suppose I better. Besides, I was planning on going through the house anyway."

"Good. I'd like your input on what you think. I already know what Latimer thinks."

"Like you said, he has a lot to learn. I hope he learns some of it soon or he won't be a detective very damn long," Don said.

I didn't comment, although I could think of several things to say. None of them would further my cause or my standing with Don; so it was better to keep quiet. Instead, I turned and went into the house. Don followed me inside.

Mr. Moore arrived at the police station where Carlson was being held and asked to see his client. The desk sergeant led him to an interrogation room where he waited until Carlson was brought to him from his holding cell.

"How are you holding up?" Moore asked.

"I don't like it here. Isn't there some way you can get me out of here?"

"You haven't been arraigned yet. I talked to the DA this morning. He thinks there is enough evidence to have you arraigned for murder. He has scheduled it so that we go before the judge this afternoon."

"I don't believe this. I don't understand. How can they charge me with murdering my own wife? I didn't do it," he insisted with a note of frustration and anger in his voice.

"Listen, Jim. You have to admit that it doesn't look good. You were found with a gun in your hand, and the blood on your shirt and hands was that of your wife. So far they can't find any evidence that there was someone else in the house before the police arrived. I know it is all circumstantial, but I've seen cases made on a lot less."

"Does that mean you think they will find me guilty?" his voice showing how scared he was that he might be spending the rest of his life in a prison.

"No, not at all. You have to try to relax and give us time. I have one of the best private investigators in the city working on it."

"Tidsdale?"

"Yes."

"I talked to him this morning. He asked me a few questions then left."

"I hope you answered them."

"I did. He said that he was working for you, but what's he going to do for me?"

"He's going to find out who killed Jennifer," Moore said with a note of confidence he wasn't sure he truly believed himself.

Carlson looked at his attorney. He didn't know what more there was to say.

"I brought you an electric razor, toothbrush and toothpaste, and a comb. I want you looking as professional as possible. I don't want you looking like a bum off the street when you're arraigned. Even though it is not supposed to make any difference how you look, it does. I wish that I could have you arraigned in a suit, but I did well just to get them to let you shave and clean up a little.

"When you're in front of the judge, I want you to stand up straight. Don't look down at the floor, but keep your eyes on the judge. Don't look around the court room. I don't want you to say anything to anyone except the judge, and only when he asks you how you plead. Then you will say that you are not guilty in a clear and firm voice. Don't yell it out and don't whisper it. Say it as if you mean it."

"I'm not guilty," Carlson said with a hint of anger in his voice.

"That's good. That's just how I want you to say it."

"What happens after that?"

"That will depend on what the charge is. The ADA in charge of your case will be present at the arraignment. After you plead not guilty, he will ask the judge for remand, or ask for an amount for bail that they want the judge to approve. Then I will ask for a lesser amount and hope we get it."

"You don't know what the charge is?" he asked, worried about what it might be.

"Not yet. The ADA hasn't said what charge or charges he will present to the judge, yet."

"What happens if I can't post bail?"

"We'll worry about that when the time comes." Moore said with a reassuring grin. "Right now I want you to get ready to stand in front of the judge. The jailor will take you to a room where you can shave, comb your hair and get a clean set of coveralls. We'll go before the judge shortly after lunch. The guards will take you to the courtroom when it is time."

"Where will you be?" he asked with a worried look on his face.

"I will be in the courtroom when it is time for your arraignment. Until then, I will find out who the ADA is in your case. I will be talking to the ADA to see what he has on you and try to negotiate your bail before you are charged."

"Okay."

"Now go with the guard and get cleaned up as best you can. I'll meet you in court."

Carlson nodded that he understood and watched as Moore stood up and left the interrogation room. Within a couple of minutes, the officer came in and took Carlson to a washroom near the holding cell so he could get ready for his arraignment.

CHAPTER ELEVEN

As soon as I got inside the entryway of Carlson's house, I began looking around. I was in no hurry. I wanted to be sure that I didn't miss anything, even the slightest of clues. Carlson's life might very well depend on it. Since it was such a brutal murder, I would not be surprised if Carlson was charged with first degree murder.

The first thing I noticed when I stepped inside the entryway was the drops of blood on the floor. Several of them looked like they had been stepped on and some of them appeared to have been smeared, but that was understandable. The first policemen that arrived on the scene had to take the gun away from Carlson first. Until they had the situation under control, they couldn't worry about a few drops of blood. In the process of taking Carlson into custody, they probably stepped in the blood. Some of the blood may have even smeared when they took him to the floor to cuff him.

I also noticed that the drops of blood seemed to run the length of the hall from the front door to the stairs that went upstairs. I took a minute to look back out on the porch for drops of blood, but found none. I returned to the entryway and began following them.

"There's a blood trail here that seems to run from upstairs to the door. My understanding is that Carlson never went to the door. I don't see any blood on the porch. Did you find any blood outside?" I asked.

"No. We didn't find any sign of it outside the house. It appears to stop at the door."

"How do you explain that?"

"I don't."

"Whose blood is it?"

"We're not sure, yet. We don't have the report back from the lab. We should be getting it this afternoon."

"Would you see to it that I get a copy of the report?"

"Sure."

"Did Carlson have any cuts on him?"

"No, but he had blood all over his hands, chest and neck, as well as on the gun."

"How did he account for all the blood?"

"He said that he held his wife for a few minutes before he came to his senses enough to called 9-1-1. From the looks of him, that could have been true.

"Did the blood on his clothes show any signs of splatter? I would expect to see some splatter if he had shot her.

"No. I did get a chance to see the shirt he was wearing, but just for a moment before the lab took it for analysis. I didn't see any blood splatter. There was no mention of blood splatter on the shirt by the officers on the scene, either."

"Your hotshot partner was here before you got here. Did he say anything about the bloody shirt?"

"All he said was that it was soaked with blood. No mention of splatter."

"Did they take samples of the blood in the front hall and on the stairs?" I asked.

"Yes."

"I'd like to know if the blood samples are Mrs. Carlson's blood, or someone else's."

"Sure. I'll fax you a copy of the forensic reports as soon as I can."

"It could prove that there was someone else in the house at the time of her death."

"I'm looking into that possibility, as well," Don said.

"Carlson told you in his interview that he had been working in his shop in the basement. Have you been in the basement?"

"Yeah. Carlson could have been working on a wooden bench for the front porch like he said. We found sawdust that looks like it matches the wood on his bench. His electric sander was lying on the bench, too. It was still plugged in as if he left it there with plans to return, or as if he was in a hurry to leave his shop. All his other tools looked like they were stored in their assigned places."

"The sander was the only tool out?"

"Yes."

"What do you mean by all his other tools were stored 'in their assigned places'?"

"I've never seen a woodworking shop so clean. Everything had a place and everything was in its place, except the sander. There was a light dusting of sawdust on the workbench and around the immediate area; otherwise, the place looked like it had just been cleaned. Not a thing out of place."

"He said he had been working on a bench in the basement?"

"He did, but I can't get over the idea that it was just a little too perfect. I'm a woodworker myself. My shop never looks that clean. If he was sanding, there would be sawdust all over the place. Everything in that shop looked as clean as if it had just come out of the box," Don said.

I found what he had to say interesting. I'm not a woodworker; but all the woodworking shops that I have seen in my life were dusty, and there was sawdust all over the place. Unless Carlson was a clean freak, which he might be, his shop should show some signs of use.

"Let's take a look," I said.

I followed Don to the basement. When we entered the workshop, I quickly got the idea of what Don was saying. Except for the workbench and the floor close to it, there wasn't a single thing out of place. I had never seen a floor so clean and free of dust and dirt in a woodworking shop before. The only tool that was not in its place was the sander on the workbench next to a piece of wood that Carlson had apparently been sanding.

There was something else I noticed, but didn't know if Don had. The amount of sawdust on the floor in front of the workbench seemed excessive when compared to the sawdust on the workbench. Plus, some of the sawdust on the floor appeared to be from a different kind of wood than the piece of wood on the workbench. The sawdust was a darker color as if it was from walnut or cherry rather than the white pine board on the workbench. If Carlson was such a neat freak as the rest of the shop indicated, that didn't add up. He would have cleaned that up before sanding or working on something else. I decided not to say anything to Don, at least for the moment.

As I was about ready to leave, I noticed a waste basket in the corner. It had sawdust and small pieces of wood in it. They were from a couple of different kinds of wood. I noticed there was some from a little darker wood than the piece of wood on the bench. I had no idea what that meant, but one thing was becoming clear. There was some doubt in my mind as to the innocence of Mr. Carlson.

Another thing that caught my attention was the fact that there was only one board for the bench in sight. I had to think about that. With the board on the workbench being almost ready for assembly, where were the rest of the boards needed to make a bench. For that matter, where was the bench.

"I think I've seen enough down here for now. I would like to take a look around upstairs."

"Sure," Don said, then turned and started for the stairs.

It was time for Carlson's arraignment. He was led into the courtroom by the bailiff. He was wearing a clean, fresh orange jumpsuit and his hands were in cuffs. He was clean shaven and his hair was combed. Except for the orange jumpsuit, he looked every bit the typical businessman. As he entered the courtroom, he held his head up and stood straight. He was led to the railing in front of the judge's bench where he was immediately joined by Mr. Moore. Mr. Moore smiled a reassuring smile.

"Everything will work out," Moore assured him in a whisper. "Tidsdale is at your house now looking for evidence that will support your claim of what happened."

Carlson looked at Moore, but the look on his face didn't give the impression that he was reassured. The expression on his face was more like that of someone who was worried about what Tidsdale might find, or maybe he was just worried about what was about to happen to him. Moore took it as if Carlson was just nervous about the arraignment, which was easy to understand.

The bailiff began reading the charges filed against Carlson. Carlson's jaw dropped when the bailiff read the charge of "Murder in the First Degree" with an alternate charge of "Murder in the Second Degree".

"How do you plead, Mr. Carlson?" the Judge asked.

There was complete silence as Carlson looked at the judge. His eyes were big as if he was in shock. He had frozen at the sounds of the words "Murder in the First Degree". His mouth went dry and he couldn't speak. Although he knew there was a good chance that he would be charged with first degree murder, it didn't seem real until the charge was actually read out loud in the courtroom.

"Mr. Carlson, how do you plead?" the judge asked again with a hint of impatience in his voice.

Again Carlson didn't answer. He simple stared at the judge as if he didn't understand what was happening to him.

"My client pleads not guilty, your honor," Moore said looking up at the judge.

"A plea of not guilty to the charges has been entered. Since this is a capital offense of murder carried out with extreme violence, the accused is remanded to jail without bond," the judge said, then struck the gavel to let all present know that the proceeding was over.

The striking of gavel caused Carlson to jump. He suddenly became aware of what had just happen. He turned and looked at Moore just as the bailiff reached out and took him by the arm. He continued to look at Moore as the bailiff led him away, still unable to believe what had just happened to him.

CHAPTER TWELVE

Don followed me up the stairs to the main level of the house. Instead of heading on up to the second level where Mrs. Carlson had been found, I went into the living room and began looking around. The first thing I noticed was that the drapes were closed. It made the room fairly dark even though the sun was out. The other thing I noticed was that the drapes had fairly heavy sheers behind them. There were decorative tiebacks for the drapes, but the drapes were not tied back. I walked over to the drapes and discovered that there were no draw strings normally used to open and close the drapes. That gave me the idea that the drapes were normally open all the time. If that were the case, why were they closed now?

"Don, were the drapes just as they are now when you arrived?"

Don looked at the drapes before he replied, "Yeah. I think so. Why?"

"Doesn't it seem a little strange that drapes with fitted tiebacks would be closed when there are heavy sheers and no draw strings?"

"Maybe they close them at night."

"Yeah," I replied, but didn't totally agree.

The tiebacks on the drapes were not the type designed to allow the opening and closing of the drapes easily, especially with the arrangement of the furniture. They were closed for some reason and I wondered why. Were they closed to prevent the outside world from seeing what had taken place inside? My guess? Probably.

I looked around the room, but didn't see anything that seemed to be out of place. It was clean and neat. There wasn't any dust on any of the end tables or coffee table. It looked as if it had been cleaned recently. With both the Carlsons working, I wondered if they had a cleaning lady come in to clean the house. It was something that I would have to ask Carlson.

I had seen enough for now, so I left the living room and went through the dining room. There didn't seem to be anything out of place there. It was clean, too.

I continued on into the kitchen. The kitchen looked like it had not been used. There were no dirty dishes and the dishwasher was empty. Every kitchen tool was carefully put in its place. I couldn't help but notice that the kitchen was as orderly as the workshop in the basement.

It wasn't until I was looking at things on the counter that I noticed the knife block. Each slot had a knife in it and they all matched, except for one. The handle was the same color as the others, but shaped slightly different. It was obviously not part of the set. I could see where it would not be too difficult to miss the difference in the one knife. There was also the fact that they weren't looking for a knife as the murder weapon. I pulled the odd knife from the knife block and looked at it. It was clean and sharp. There was no sign that it had been used recently.

That got me to thinking. With all the care that had been taken to have everything in its place and for everything to match perfectly, that one knife seemed to stand out like a sore thumb. It may have been my suspicious nature, but it just didn't fit. Where was the knife that belonged in the knife block? I decided that I would keep the knife to myself, at least until I had a chance to see the autopsy report and the blood report. I put the knife back in the knife block for now.

The only other rooms on the main floor of the house were a den and a half bath. I went to the den and stood in the doorway while looking around the room. It had all the indication that it was the den of an accountant, a very tidy accountant. It was my guess that it was Carlson's home office.

"Have your people gone over this room?"

"Yeah. They didn't find anything to indicate that anything had been disturbed."

"In other words, they concentrated on the bedroom where the body was found and the blood trail to the front door."

"Pretty much. Latimer said he looked over the room. He found no reason to believe there was anything in the room that was part of the murder scene. Do you think there is?"

"I don't know," I replied. "It is obviously an office. Is it Carlson's office or his wife's?"

"Carlson's, I believe."

"That's what I thought. Maybe I'll look at it later."

"Probably a good idea," he said.

I took a quick look in the half bath, but found nothing of interest there. There was a complete set of clean towels hanging on the towel rack, and the bathroom looked as if it had not been used since it was last cleaned. I turned and looked up the stairs. I had an idea what I was going to find and was not in any big hurry to see it. But if I was going to get to the truth, I would have to see where Mrs. Carlson was murdered.

Carlson was pacing back and forth in the holding cell. He still couldn't believe that he had been charged with first degree murder. He was also worried about what Tidsdale might find in his house. With the way things were going for him, he couldn't be sure that someone hadn't planted evidence that was sure to convict him. He suddenly stopped pacing when he heard the voice of the officer coming toward his cell.

"You've got company," the officer said. "I'm getting tired of running back and forth for you."

"Who is it?" Carlson asked, not one bit interested in the complaints of the officer.

"Jacob Rinehart."

"Who's Jacob Rinehart?"

"He's a lawyer. Say, I thought you had a lawyer."

"I do."

"You want to talk to him?"

"Might as well. Moore might have hired him to assist him in my defense."

"Okay."

The officer put cuffs on Carlson and led him down the hall to an interrogation room. Once he was secure, the officer left the room.

Within a couple of minutes, a tall man in a dark suit walked into the room. He smiled at Carlson, then sat down across the table from him.

"I'm Jacob Rinehart. I'm an attorney for Mile High Design, where your wife worked. I'm sorry to hear about her untimely death," he said, but it didn't sound like he was all that sorry.

"I know where my wife worked. What do you want with me?"

"Since your wife was a valued employee, we want to help you."

"Why would you want to help me? You don't even know me."

"Actually, we do know you, Mr. Carlson. But more importantly, we knew your wife and liked the work she did for the company."

"I don't understand. How do you think you can help me?"

"It's really quite simple. Since it would be a conflict of interest for us to offer our services directly to you, we have come up with another way that we could help. Let me get to the point of why I'm here."

"Please do."

"When we found out that you were charged with first degree murder, we felt that it was our obligation to help you. We can't get directly involved. However, there is one way we can help."

"Excuse me, but how did you find out so fast that I was charged with first degree murder?"

"We had a representative in the courtroom to keep us posted on the outcome of your arraignment. Anyway, we want to help."

"I'm listening."

"This trial is going to be very expensive, especially with a defense attorney of Mr. Moore's caliber. And by the way, he is the best. We would like to help with the expenses."

"And just how do you plan to do that if you can't get directly involved?"

"We know that your house is almost paid for. We would like to buy it from you at its current market value to give you the money you would need for your defense. Then when this is over, we would sell it back to you at a very good rate of interest when you are found not guilty."

"You must have a lot of confidence that I'll be found innocent."

"We do, but if the outcome should go against you, we would be able to recover our money by selling the house."

"Why would you want my house?"

"The fact is, Mr. Carlson, we don't. Your wife's supervisor thought it would be a good gesture for all the good work your wife has done for us since she came to work for us six years ago. We look out for our employees and their families. I have a form here that if you sign it, we would immediately transfer the money to your account so it would be available for Mr. Moore's use in your defense."

"I'll have to think about it."

"I understand. I'm sure Mr. Moore would go along with it. It will provide him with the money he will need to mount a good defense."

"I still would like to think about it."

"Fine, Mr. Carlson. I'll be by to see you in a day or so," he said as he stood up and left the room.

Carlson sat there staring at the door as it closed. The offer seemed a bit strange, but it was one way for him to raise the money he would need. That, along with his other investments and savings could go a long ways toward paying his defense bills.

Carlson's thoughts were interrupted when the officer came in and said, "Time to go back to the holding cell."

His comment caught Carlson off guard. He had been so engrossed in his thoughts that he hadn't seen or heard the officer come in. He stood up, turned around and waited while he was cuffed. He was then taken back to the holding cell.

* * * *

Rinehart left the police station without the signed form. He was disappointed that Carlson would not sign it, but it was not something that was totally unexpected. He had taken a chance and it didn't work. Rinehart returned to his office to plan his next move.

CHAPTER THIRTEEN

Being careful not to step on any of the dried drops of blood on the stairs, I slowly worked my way up the stairs to the second floor of the house. Taking notice of each spot of blood, I wondered how they got there. It seemed to me that there was a lot of blood, far more blood than I would have expected under the circumstances.

The spacing and size of each drop of blood indicated that someone had probably been bleeding. It didn't appear to be secondary blood such as blood that had dripped off Carlson hands, the gun he apparently had been carrying, or the clothes he was wearing as he went down the stairs after finding his wife murdered in their bedroom. Most of the blood on him had been on his clothes, although there had been some on his hands and the gun. There was also the fact that most of the drops of blood were close to the banister indicating that whoever was bleeding, was bleeding from his arm or hand, or at least from that side of his body. There was also some blood smeared on the hand railing.

I stopped near the top of the stairs, knelt down and looked at a couple of the bloody drops very closely. There were a couple of things about the drops of blood and the pattern they left on the steps that didn't set well with me. I couldn't say what it was that made me suspicious at first. Then I realized that three of the drops of blood on the top couple of steps appeared as if they were from someone going up the stairs, not down. A quick look at one of the few places where the blood was smeared on the banister seemed to confirm my suspicion. The blood appeared to be smeared upward rather than down.

"You find something?" Don asked, as he watched me studying the blood drops.

I didn't answer Don right away. Instead, I looked back down the stairs letting my eyes follow the blood trail. It was then that I noticed that the drops of blood seemed to get closer together going down the stairs.

"Maybe. Take a look at this," I said as I pointed at the drops of dried blood near the top of the stairs, "and here where the blood is smeared on the banister."

Don knelt down and took a closer look at the drops of blood, then looked at the blood on the hand railing. He then turned and looked up at me.

"Based on the pattern of the drops of blood, these drops look like they fell from someone going upstairs, not downstairs," I said. "And the blood smears on the banister look like they were also made by someone going upstairs. My guess would be that the blood is from a cut on someone's right hand or arm, and that they received that cut at the front door. At least that would explain why there's no blood on the porch."

Don turned back and looked very carefully at the drops of blood again before he responded.

"That's what it looks like to me," Don said as he looked up at me, again. "I can't believe that the forensic team missed that. I'm getting them back out here and have them look at every drop of blood. I'd like to know if this is Mrs. Carlson's blood or someone else's, or maybe both."

"Looking at the pattern of blood drops from the top all the way down the stairs, it looks like the bleeding was worse at the bottom of the stairs than up here. That would indicate that whoever was going up the stairs had managed to get the flow of blood slowed considerably."

"It does," Don replied after looking at the complete pattern of blood drops. "That would indicate that whoever was bleeding was injured downstairs after he got in the house, and he was able to slow the bleeding on the way up the stairs. I'll check with forensic and see if they came to the same conclusion. If not, I'll have them back out here. It will help if we can find out whose blood it is. I may know that by this afternoon."

As soon as Don stood up, we continued on into the master bedroom. I stopped just after entering the room and looked around the room. The mattress was pulled halfway off the box springs, and the sheets and pillow cases were missing. I figured that the sheets and pillow cases had been taken to the lab to be analyzed by the forensic experts.

"Was the mattress pulled off the bed like that when Mrs. Carlson's body was found?"

"Yeah, I think so. It looks like Mrs. Carlson had put up a struggle with her attacker. I'll get copies of the crime scene photos for you. I don't have any while Mrs. Carlson was still here. They were all taken after I got here."

"How come?"

"Latimer forgot to take them."

"Great," I said with a note of sarcasm.

"Mrs. Carlson was lying off the side of the bed," Don said as he pointed to where her body had been according to what Latimer had told him. "She was face up with her left arm outstretched toward the bed and her right arm sort of tucked under her."

"How do you know that without photos of her?"

"Latimer told me how the body was positioned. I did find places in the blood that looked like someone had knelt down beside her. It would have been consistent with the body in the position Latimer described to me. Carlson had said that he knelt beside her and held her for awhile before he called 9-1-1. As you can see, it was a mess in here."

"I see. Any idea who the bloody footprints belong to?"

"Not yet. They don't match any shoes that belong to Carlson, at least that we have found so far. We didn't find any shoes in the garbage or out in the trash. I had every garbage can in a three block radius checked. That's what has me thinking that maybe there was someone else in the house either at the time of the killing or very shortly after," Don said."

"They're not from any of your people?"

"No. I'm sure of that. The hard part is they appear to be the same size shoes that Carlson wears. We just haven't been able to find the shoes if they are his."

I stepped a little farther into the room and looked around. There were nightstands on both sides of the bed. The one on the side of the bed opposite of where Mrs. Carlson's body had been found still had the telephone on it. There was also an alarm clock and a book on the nightstand. The nightstand next to where Mrs. Carlson's body was found had been moved out away from the wall and bed. From the way it was sitting, it had probably been moved during the struggle. Another alarm clock, a lamp that matched the one on the other table, and another telephone had been knocked off the nightstand and were lying on the floor.

Since the telephone was in plain sight and very close to where the body had been, I had to wonder why Carlson had not simply picked it up and called for help from there. From my time on the phone with Carlson while the police were coming in, it was obvious that he had called me from the hall near the front door. I had to wonder where he had called the police from.

That brought to mind another thought. I wanted to see his phone records. I wanted to know in what order he called Mr. Moore, 9-1-1, and me. I also wanted to know how far apart the calls were made. That would provide me with a timeline of those three events.

"Don, does Mrs. Carlson have an office here at home?"

"I don't know, but she might."

"I'd like to see the other rooms on this floor."

"Okay. There are two more bedrooms and two baths on the second floor."

I found the Master bath was fairly clean. There were no signs of blood or anything else that would lead me to believe it was connected to the murder scene except for the fact that it was connected to the bedroom. The only thing that seemed to be out of place was it appeared that there was a hand towel missing from the towel rack next to the sink. I had to wonder where it was. Had the towel been taken by a third party to cover an injury and hopefully stop the bleeding? That might explain why there were no blood drops leading down the stairs. It would help to know if the blood on the stairs was from someone other than Mrs. Carlson.

"Did the forensic team go over the master bathroom?"

"Yes. They said they found no indication of blood anywhere. They also said that I would have to wait for the results of fingerprints found in the bathroom to know if anyone other than the Carlsons had used the bathroom."

I followed Don down the hall to a second bedroom. It looked like it might be a guest room. It was clean and neat. The bed was made up and the curtains were drawn back. I did notice a stack of magazines in the corner. They were accounting magazines and they were old editions. I assumed that Carlson kept them for future reference, but there was really nothing to make me believe that it was anything other than a spare room.

We went on down the hall to the third bedroom. The door was locked. I thought that it was a little strange.

"Was this door locked when your people were here?"

"I don't think so. Latimer said that there was nothing of interest in that room. He indicated that he had searched it before I got here. He probably locked it."

"Did he give you any idea what it was used for, or tell you anything about it?"

"No, as a matter of fact he didn't. He didn't have very much to say after I chewed him out for having the body removed from the bedroom before I got here and before the crime scene photos were taken."

"Let me ask you a question. With Latimer already having found Carlson guilty of murder; don't you think it might be a good idea to find out what is in that room for yourself?" I asked, hoping that he would agree with me and let me open the door.

"You don't trust him, do you?"

"Hell no. And if I were you, I wouldn't trust him, either. He's too new at this, and way to arrogant. He's also very sloppy in his investigation. Then there's the fact that he didn't follow procedures. It makes me wonder if he even looked in this room. We only have his word that he searched the room."

I watched the look on Don's face. He looked as if he might have made a big mistake in not checking out everything for himself. The fact that he had a lot to deal with when he first arrived on the scene was no excuse for not checking it out for himself. I sure would have.

"Open the door," Don said sharply.

It didn't take but a few seconds for me to get the door open. The lock was very expensive, but there was a gap in the door frame that allowed me to slip a credit card in and slide back the door bolt. As soon as the door bolt slid back, the door opened and I stepped inside.

"You do that almost too easy," he said as he followed me into the room.

I didn't bother to comment. The third bedroom had been converted into an office. From the looks of the desk and the material on it, it was Mrs. Carlson's home office. There were several bookshelves on one side of the room. A very up-to-date computer on the desk gave me the idea that she probably did a lot of work at home. There were also several file folders on the desk and a large file cabinet in the corner.

I walked over to the desk and looked down at the file folders. I didn't recognize the names on any of the folders, except for one. It was the name of a business that I knew belonged to one of the biggest crooks in town. I had to wonder if that had anything to do with Mrs. Carlson's murder. Again, I didn't say anything to Don about the files. I was sure that he would check them over and come to his own conclusions.

I decided that it was time for me to leave. There wasn't anything else that I could do in the house right now, not with Don standing there looking over my shoulder. It was time for me to check out a few other ideas I had. I could come back later, alone.

"I think I'll be going for now. I might want to come back after I have a talk with Carlson. You leaving, too?"

"No. I think I'll have a look around. Never know what I might find," he said.

"I'll talk to you later."

Don just nodded, then sat down at the Mrs. Carlson's desk and looked at the files on the desk. I left him to nose around. I only hoped that if he found anything of interest, he would let me know about it.

It was late in the afternoon when Mr. Moore arrived back at the jail to visit with Carlson. Once again Moore was taken to an interrogation room. He only had to wait a few minutes before Carlson was brought in.

"When the hell are you going to get me out of this place?" Carlson demanded.

"I can't get you out. You're just going to have to be patient. There's no bail for a charge of first degree murder. I told you that."

"But I didn't murder her," he insisted.

"We are working on it. This is not something that can be resolved in a couple of days."

"It isn't fair. I'm sitting here in jail and my wife's murderer is running around free."

"It isn't fair, but there's nothing I can do about it. Do you want another attorney?"

It was clear that Mr. Moore was getting a little tired of Carlson's demands and his constant complaining.

Carlson looked at Moore as if he had suggested something completely out of this world. His mouth fell open as if he was expecting Moore to quit on him and let him fend for himself.

"No. I don't want another attorney," he said softly.

"Jim, you have to trust me. We are doing everything we can. It is just going to take time."

"I know. It takes a lot of money, too."

"We can worry about that after we get you out from under all this." Moore said.

"I'll be able to pay you."

"I know."

"You know? You know about Jacob Rinehart?"

"Who's Jacob Rinehart?" Moore asked, with a surprised look on his face.

"He said he was an attorney with the company my wife worked at. He said that they would help me by buying my house to help pay my legal expenses, and that I could buy it back when I was set free?"

"I don't know any Jacob Rinehart."

"He said you would agree with the deal."

"I'll do no such thing. Did you sign any agreement?" Moore said with a worried look on his face.

"No. He had one all drawn up, but I told him that I wanted to think about it."

"Well, don't sign anything without talking to me first. I don't even want you talking to him again. I'm going to have Tidsdale look into this. I have to go and get hold of Tidsdale as soon as possible. I'm also going to have the police stop him from visiting you again. I don't know what he's up to, but it smells fishy to me."

Moore got up and headed out the door. He was no more than outside the police station when he placed a call to Tidsdale on his cell phone.

CHAPTER FOURTEEN

I no more than stepped into my office and the phone began to ring. The answering machine was just about to take the call, when I picked it up.

"Tidsdale Investigative Agency."

"This is Albert Moore. Something has come up and I want you to look into it immediately."

"What's the problem?"

"Jim Carlson was visited by a man who claims to be an attorney. I've never heard of him before. I want you to find out what he's up to."

"What's his name?"

"Jacob Rinehart. Do you recognize the name?"

"No. What do you think he's trying to do?"

"I don't know, but he told Carlson that he works for the same company that Mrs. Carlson worked for. He wanted Carlson to sign over his house and he would pay for Carlson's defense. This guy, whoever he is, never contacted me."

"I'll see what I can find out about him and get back to you."

"Okay," Moore said. "I have to call the police station and make sure that Carlson doesn't have any more visitors except for you and me."

"You mean this guy walked into the police station, and they let him talk to Carlson?"

"Yes. He probably said that he was working for me, but I don't know that for a fact."

"I'll give my friend at the police station a call and have him make sure it doesn't happen again without notifying you first."

"Good. I was so upset and in a hurry to get hold of you that I didn't take the time to find Detective Wright to tell him about it."

"That's okay. I'll take care of it."

"Thank you."

I hung up the phone and immediately placed a call to Detective Wright. He was in. I explained what happened. He assured me that he would make sure that it didn't happen again.

"By the way, since I have you on the phone, do you know Jacob Rinehart?"

"No. I don't think so. Is he someone of interest to you?

"He is now. He's the guy that talked to Carlson."

"I see your interest in him. I'll see what I can find out about him.

"Thanks. I'll talk to you later," I said then hung up.

I had to wonder what this guy, Jacob Rinehart, was up to. It sounded a little like he wanted free rein of Carlson's house for some reason. The first thing I needed to do was find out who he was and who he worked for. The second thing was to find out why he was so willing to "help" Carlson. The best and first place to start was the phone book.

The phone book proved to be no help at all. There were several Rineharts in the book, but none with the first name of Jacob. There was, however, one with the initial J. Since I didn't have a City Directory, I decided that it might be best if I drove by the address listed in the phone book. I left my office and headed out for Aurora, a large Denver suburb.

Carlson sat quietly in the holding cell. Everything that had happened so far had not given him anything to be hopeful about. The hours passed by slowly. The quiet made it almost unbearable for him. There was nothing to get his mind off his troubles, not that there was much that could do that. All he could think about was that his life was going to end in a jail cell in some miserable state correctional facility.

Carlson laid down on the bunk, put his hands behind his head and stared up at the ceiling. It was going to be another long lonely night in a dark and dingy holding cell. He couldn't help but think that he was going to spend the rest of his life in such a place. A place where he would be told what do and when to do it.

CHAPTER FIFTEEN

I drove out to the suburb and found the address that was listed in the phone book. I stopped near the corner and parked at the curb so I could watch the house for a little while. I had no idea what I was looking for, but it wouldn't hurt to watch the place for a few minutes while I thought about what might be going on.

The house was a small single story home with a one car garage. It looked as if it could use a good coat of paint; and the lawn needed some attention. There were a number of toys in the yard that would indicate that there were small children living there.

A look around at the other houses in the immediate area gave me the impression that it was a neighborhood where I was more likely to find a blue collar worker than an attorney. The homes were small and probably dated back to the late nineteen-forties or -fifties. They were all of similar design with only minor differences. Most of them were in need of some care. They all had one car garages, none of them attached to the houses.

I had only been there a few minutes when a service truck for a company that did carpet cleaning pulled into the drive and parked off to one side of the garage. A man in his mid-twenties got out of the van and headed for the house. He was wearing coveralls with the name of the company on the back. He walked up to the door and let himself in. I had the feeling this was not the man I was looking for. This guy was a working stiff, not some fancy corporate lawyer. If he was a lawyer, he was either a very poor one that needed to subsidize his income by cleaning carpets, or he had a great disguise.

A quick look at my watch told me that I probably had time to go downtown and check out Mile High Design. If I got lucky, I might find Jacob Rinehart's name listed on the directory in the lobby.

I started my car and was about to drive away, when I decided to have a talk with this guy. I shut off the engine, got out of my car and walked up to the door. My knock on the door was answered almost immediately. A young woman with a small child in her arms answered the door.

"May I help you," she asked with a pleasant smile.

"I certainly hope so," I said with a smile. "I'm looking for Mr. Jacob Rinehart."

"There's no Jacob Rinehart living here."

"I'm sorry to disturb you. Is there a possibility that Jacob Rinehart is related to you and that you might know where he does live?"

"Not that I know of, but my husband might know. Come in. I'll get my husband."

"Thank you," I said as I stepped inside the home.

While she went to get her husband, I took a moment to look around. I could see the entire living room and part of the dining room. There was a small boy coloring in a book at the coffee table in front of the TV. He looked up at me for a second then returned to his coloring book.

The house was small but very nice inside. Apparently Mrs. Rinehart was a good housekeeper even with two small children. There were family pictures on the walls and some toys for a toddler on the living room floor. It was a comfortable looking home that was nicely cared for.

Just then a tall young man came into the living room followed by Mrs. Rinehart. He was the same man I saw enter the home only a few minutes ago. I smiled and stuck out my hand to him.

"I'm Frank Tidsdale."

He stuck out his hand and shook mine and said, "Joe."

"As your wife may have told you, I'm looking for a Jacob Rinehart. Do you happen to know him?"

"No. Don't know any Jacob Rinehart."

"I'm sorry to have bothered you."

"That's okay. I'm sorry that I couldn't help."

I nodded at the young woman, then turned and left. I returned to my car and decided that I still had time to check out Mile High Design.

Darkness came over the holding cells in the police station as the sun began to set. Carlson lay on the bunk and listened to the sounds of the coming night. He suddenly heard the sounds of someone coming toward his cell. He looked up to see the officer stop at the door to the cell and look in.

"It's time," the officer said.

"Time for what," he asked as he sat up and swung his legs off the bed.

"Time for you to be transferred to the county lockup. The county jail."

"I thought I would stay here until my trial."

Carlson was a bit confused. He wondered if his attorney knew he was being transferred. He also wondered what it would be like in a real jail cell.

"We don't keep prisoners here very long after they have been formally charged. We send them to the county jail where they have showers and better food service. They're better equipped for longer stays."

Carlson didn't like the sound of that, but stood up, turned around and put his hands behind his back. He began to worry about the move, but he had no idea how things worked. He would have to take the officer's word for it. After all, he had no choice.

"Does my attorney know that I will be transferred to the county jail?" he asked not wanting to upset the officer.

"Mr. Moore knows how things work around here. He knows that you will be at the county jail. We usually transfer prisoners earlier in the day after they have been arraigned, but things got a little busy around here today. We're running a little late."

As soon as Carlson was cuffed, the officer took him and led him out of the holding cell. They walked down a long *hall and left the precinct through a big steel door to a waiting van. He was placed in the back of the van. He couldn't help but think how loud the closing of the van door sounded.*

After about a twenty minute ride, the door opened. He was greeted by two very large men in Sheriff Uniforms. They took him by the arms and led him through a big steel door into the area of the county jail where the cells were located.

As he was led down the hall, he could see several prisoners in the cells. The uniformed officers stopped at a cell and waited for the door to open. Once it was open, Carlson was guided into the cell and then the cuffs were removed.

"Make yourself at home. This will be your home until after your trial," one of the guards said. "You will find that except for visitors, your day will be pretty routine. You do what you're told and things will go better for you. You understand?"

"Yes. Will my attorney know where I am?"

"I'm sure he will be notified where you are," one of the guards said.

The guards then turned and walked away leaving Carlson with his thoughts. He looked around the cell and found it to be just a little larger then the holding cell he had been in. It was strange, but he began to wonder if the cells in the state prison were any bigger. That thought caused him to sit down and think about what might happen to him, what the future held for him. He began to wonder if he even had a future. From the looks of where he was, he had his doubts.

Carlson laid down on the bed and curled up in the fetal position and began to cry softly. It took him a while, but he finally fell asleep.

CHAPTER SIXTEEN

I arrived at the Hammond building where Mile High Design was located. With the lateness of the hour, there were plenty of places to park on the street. I parked about a half a block from the entrance, left my car and went inside. It didn't take me but a minute or so to find the building's directory. It was on the wall just to the left of a bank of elevators.

The directory told me that the Mile High Design was located in the top two floors of the twenty story building. I also found that Carlson's accounting firm was located on the floor just below the architectural firm. There were also an insurance office and another office that was listed simply as "Security" on the same floor as Carlson's office.

At first, I didn't think much of it. Almost all of the high rise buildings in the downtown area had security of some sort. But then it occurred to me that the security offices of buildings like this one were almost always located on the ground floor. Just then, my thoughts were disturbed.

"May I help you, sir," someone said from behind me.

I turned to see a security guard standing behind me. The name tag and the patch on the front of his uniform told me that he was one of the security guards for the building.

"Yes. I'm a little surprised that your security office is near the top of the building. Most of them are on the ground floor."

"That's not our security office, sir. Our office is right over there," he said as he pointed to a glass door just off to the left of the front entrance.

"Do you know whose security office that is?"

"It's a private security company."

"Oh."

"What is your interest in the security company?"

"Nothing really. I was looking for the name of the head man for Mile High Design when the word "security" caught my eye."

"Wilbur Steinman is the owner and president of Mile High Design."

"I see that on the directory."

"Mr. Steinman isn't in right now. He checked out about an hour ago. You'll have to come back in the morning if you want to see him."

"Thank you for your help," I said as I turned and started for the front doors.

As I left the building and turned to go down the street to my car, I glanced back toward the lobby. The guard was standing next to the big plate glass windows watching me, most likely to make sure that I was actually leaving.

I got in my car and began to wonder about the security company on the eighteenth floor. It seemed strange that it was located directly below Mile High Design. It didn't have a name on the building's directory or the name of anyone who worked there. It was almost as if they didn't want anyone to know that they existed. The only reason I could think of for that was that they worked exclusively for one company or one person. I had to wonder if that one company was Mile High Design. I also had to wonder if Jacob Rinehart worked for Mile High Design, or for the security company. If he worked for the security company, was the security company a front so that he could not be directly connected to Mile High Design? It seemed like a possibility, but a rather slim one since I had no idea who Jacob Rinehart was, let alone who he worked for.

This was going to take a bit of looking into if I was going to find out anything without being discovered. In any case, it was going to have to wait until tomorrow. There was nothing much I could do tonight. It was time to go home and get a good night's sleep and start again tomorrow.

As I was driving home, I remembered that I had not gotten a chance to see the autopsy report, the report on the gun, or any of the lab reports. A quick glance at my watch showed me that it was a little late to get copies of the reports tonight. I would have to wait until tomorrow to see them. Moore would most likely have copies of all the evidence the DA had by then and I could get them from him.

I went home and placed a call to Jackie. We talked for several minutes before we hung up. I got a little something to eat and went to bed.

Carlson was suddenly awakened by screams coming from one of the cells down the hall from him. He was scared enough being in jail in the first place without terrifying screams waking him in the middle of the night. He pushed himself back in the corner of the bed, as far away from the cell door as possible. He pulled his blanket and pillow up around him as if it would protect him. His heart was beating fast and he could hardly breathe.

Then he heard the clamoring of a steel door opening down the hall followed by the crash of it closing. He could hear the sounds of feet racing down the hard floor of the hall. Within seconds, two guards ran past his cell. Between the screams, he could hear a cell door being opened then what sounded like people fighting.

Carlson couldn't see what was going on, but the sounds of it frightened him even more. He was shaking all over. From the other side of the cell block, he began to hear others yelling from their cells.

"Police brutality," one prisoner yelled.

"Shut up down there," one of the guards yelled back.

As suddenly as it had begun, there was quiet in the cell block again. Carlson wasn't sure if it was because the man who started screaming suddenly stopped, or because of the guard yelling for everyone to shut up. He wondered if the guard had beaten the man unconscious to quiet him, or if something else caused him to quiet down.

Still curled up in the corner of his bed, Carlson listened in an effort to hear what was going on. Now that it was quiet, he could hear one of the guards talking softly to someone. From what he could make out, it sounded as if the guard was trying to reassure the prisoner that he was all right and that it was just a bad dream.

It wasn't long before he could hear the sounds of footsteps coming toward him. One of the guards stopped in front of Carlson's cell and looked at him for a minute.

"Are you okay?" he asked after seeing Carlson curled up in a ball in the far corner of his bed.

When Carlson didn't answer, he spoke again.

"Are you okay, Mr. Carlson?"

"Yes, sir," he replied, his voice shaky with fear.

"Everything is okay. The guy just had a bad dream. It happens in here sometimes."

"Is he all right?" Carlson asked, afraid that the man had been beaten to shut him up.

"He's fine. You'll see him in the morning at breakfast. This place can be a little scary at night when you've never been in a jail before," the guard said with a reassuring smile.

Carlson understood all too well what he was saying. He was scared half to death of this place.

"Thank you," Carlson said.

The guard nodded as if he understood what Carlson might be feeling at this moment.

Carlson moved out of the corner, rearranged his bedding, then laid back down. It still took him a long time before he was able to go back to sleep.

CHAPTER SEVENTEEN

It was raining again when morning came. I could hear the sound of it on my bedroom window. Reluctantly, I swung my legs over the side of my bed and sat up. As I ran my hand through my hair, I began to think about Rinehart. Who was he and what was his interest in Jim Carlson? One thing was for sure, I wasn't going to find out sitting on the edge of my bed.

I got up, took a shower and got dressed. As I went into the kitchen, I noticed that it was a rather gray and dismal day outside. I had no more than sat down to have my breakfast when the phone began to ring. I got up and answered the phone.

"Tidsdale."

"Mr. Tidsdale, this is Albert Moore."

"What can I do for you?"

"I was wondering if you had been able to find out anything about Jacob Rinehart."

"Not yet. I'm going to the office where Mrs. Carlson worked this morning. I'm hoping they will be able to tell me who he is, since he indicated that he worked for them."

"Will you let me know what you find out?"

"Of course. You're paying me."

"I wanted you to know that they moved Jim to the county lockup. It's a matter of routine."

"I figured that he would be transferred since it will be a while before he goes to trial. Is there anything else," I asked.

I got the feeling that Mr. Moore had something more to say, but wasn't sure how to say it. He was not the kind of man who should play poker. Even over the phone, I could tell he had something else on his mind.

"Actually, there is," he said, then didn't say anything for what seemed like a rather long time.

"Are you going to let me in on it, or do I have to guess?"

"Sorry, but I'm a little worried about Carlson."

"How so?" I asked.

"You've seen Carlson in jail, right?"

"Yeah."

"I'm worried about him. He seems very depressed and almost suicidal. Everything the police have so far seems to point to him as the killer, and he knows it."

"That's not unusual. Most cases start out that way. If the police didn't think they had enough evidence, he wouldn't have been arrested. Sometimes it takes a while to find the real evidence and the truth. I don't see this case as any different."

"I understand, but I need you to find something that will help convince Carlson that we believe he is innocent. Right now he needs someone to believe in him. Nothing I say seems to do that for him."

"All I can say is that I'm working on it."

"I know you are. It's just that I'm worried about him."

"I can understand that. I'll give you a call after I've had a talk with the owners of the firm Mrs. Carlson worked for. I also plan to look into who the contractors are that do most of their work, and who their major clients are."

"I don't understand. What good will that do?"

"I want to know if they are on the up and up."

"Oh. Call me if you find out anything. I might be able to help you find out about the makeup of the corporation."

"That might help. I'll be in touch," I said, then hung up.

After hanging up, I sat there for a minute to think about what he had said about Carlson. I could understand how Carlson might feel really depressed, if he was not guilty. At this point, I had not made up my mind whether he was guilty or not. There was a lot of evidence against him, but it was mostly circumstantial.

I also took a moment to think about what I had said to Mr. Moore. The thought that there might be something that was not on the up and up going on in the firm that Mrs. Carlson had worked for had simply crossed my mind while I was talking to him. It was nothing that I had even considered until that very moment. Certainly nothing that I had any proof of.

Then again, maybe I had considered it before. When I first found out about Jacob Rinehart, I had to wonder why he was so eager to get his hands on Carlson's house. He said that he worked for Mile High Design, but did he? He said that he wanted to help with legal expenses, but did he? Maybe he just wanted free access to the house, but why? What was in the house that he would want? Or what did he think might be in the house?

Since I had been in the house and found out that Mrs. Carlson had an office at home, I began to wonder if she had come across something that she shouldn't have seen. It could have been almost anything. Maybe she saw a memo that she shouldn't have seen about something that was illegal, or might be construed as illegal. Maybe she had found out that the company was doing business with a contractor that cut corners, or purchased materials that were inferior and skimmed the money saved.

Maybe she overheard a conversation that led her to believe there was something crooked going on. If someone found out that she knew, or they thought she knew that things were not on the up and up, they might have been afraid that she would tell someone. If she told the right person, it could cause problems. If it was something she saw like a memo or a file, they might be worried that she had made copies of what she found and took it home. If it got out, it could cause a lot of trouble for those involved. That, of course, depended on what 'it' was. Any one of those situations could easily be a motive for killing her.

My mind was running all sorts of possibilities through my head. It was a really big stretch to think that there was something illegal going on at Mile High Design, but it was something that might not hurt to take a little time to check out.

At this point, I had no solid motive for Mrs. Carlson's death. Every idea I could come up with needed to be explored if for no other reason than to clear it out of my head.

If Carlson had not killed his wife, then who else would have a motive? Finding someone with a motive would go a long way toward showing that Carlson might be innocent.

The more I thought about it, the more it seemed like a good idea to look into Mile High Design's top personnel and into the background of the contractors who did the work. The best place to start was to find out who the contractors were and who owned Mile High Design. When I finished there, I would stop in and see Don. I wanted to know what evidence they had on Carlson.

I got in my car and headed for Mile High Design. It would not be very hard to find out who owned the business. The big problem was to find out who they owed money to. The old saying of "follow the money", seemed like a good idea at the moment, even if I didn't know what money.

Carlson had sat in his cell early in the morning with nothing to do but think about what was going to happen to him. He began to wonder if he would end up screaming in fear just like the guy last night. Over all his mediocre life, he had hardly given a second's thought about what it would be like to be in jail, especially for any length of time. But why would he? He had always tried to be an honest law-abiding person, and what good did it do him. Now he was accused of murder. He was in a jail and it was beginning to look like he might be there for the rest of his life.

He looked around the cell that was his home, at least until the trial was over. The walls were made of concrete and painted in a dull medium green. All he could think of was that it was the most depressing color he could ever remember seeing.

The wall opposite the beds, if you could call them that, was bare except for a small metal shelf at one end where a roll of toilet paper, soap and other toiletry items had been placed. In the corner near the shelf was a stainless steel sink and stool combination. The sink was up above the stool. It made it seem so unsanitary to have the sink so close to the stool.

On the outside wall was a long narrow window. The window had thick heavy glass with a wire mess running through it. There were no bars on the window, but then it didn't need them. The window was so narrow that a person would not be able to squeeze through it. The glass was clear allowing him to see out. Even though he could see out the window, there was nothing to look at except the brick wall of another building. It did let in a little light, however.

The other inside wall had heavy steel frames attached to it that served as bed frames. There were two frames, one above the other. On the frames were mattresses, if you could *call them that. They were more like sacks. They were only about three inches thick and rather hard. The upper bunk had just a bare mattress rolled up at the foot of the bed. The lower bed had a mattress with a heavy cotton mattress cover over it, and a wool blanket that was not very soft for the prisoner to cover himself with when he laid down to sleep.*

The front of the cell was made of steel bars with heavy steel hinges on the door and a heavy steel lock. There was a small place where a food tray could be slid into the cell. It made Carlson think that he would be spending all his time in the cell except for when he had a visitor.

He couldn't help but think that he would rather be dead than to live in a place like it for the rest of his life. His only ray of hope was that Tidsdale would be able to find some evidence that he didn't kill his wife. Up to now his future looked pretty grim.

Carlson got up and walked over to the cell door. He took hold of the bars and looked out into the hall. It was so quiet. There was not a sound. He had to wonder if he was there all alone.

Suddenly, he heard a noise. The steel bars of the door at the end of the cell block opened and the guard came walking down the hall. As he stopped in front of Carlson's cell, Carlson stepped back away from the cell door.

"You ready for breakfast?"

"Yes."

"Okay," the guard said as he stepped up to the cell door then motioned for the guard at the end of the hall to open the door.

Carlson turned around and put his hands behind his back.

"You don't need to do that here. Just come with me."

Carlson turned back around and looked at the guard for a moment then stepped out of his cell. The guard led him to the opposite end of the hall from the door he had come in. At the end of the hall was another door, a solid steel door.

As they walked toward the end of the hall, Carlson wondered if he was the only person who was going to eat. He thought about asking, but decided against it.

The guard opened the door and motioned for Carlson to enter. Carlson entered a room that had steel tables and benches bolted to the floor. It looked like a small cafeteria. There were about six other men in orange jump suits standing in line with steel trays in their hands. He figured the other men had come from a different cell block.

"Get in line if you want to eat."

Carlson looked at the guard, then walked over and got in line. He filled his plate with food, then went and sat down alone at one of the tables. He ate his breakfast in silence, only occasionally looking around the room. After he finished, he was taken back to his cell to sit and wait for a visitor or for lunch time to come.

CHAPTER EIGHTEEN

I arrived at the Hammond building where the Mile High Design business was located. The first thing was to find out who was in charge. I checked the directory in the entrance to the building. It listed a Wilbur Steinman as the President and a William A. Stevenson as the Vice President. Neither of the names meant anything to me, but than I would not have expected them to. After all, I had not had any dealings with the company in the past.

The offices were located on the top floor of the building. I pressed the button to call for an elevator. While I waited, a man in a dark suit walked up and stood off to the side. He smiled and nodded politely when I glanced over at him, but didn't say anything.

When he turned and looked at the light panel above the elevator, I quickly looked him over. I noticed that there was a bulge under the left arm of his expensive suit coat. It was obvious to me that he was carrying, and it was not a small weapon. I quickly sized him up. He was fairly tall and seemed to be very well built. He was a guy that probably worked out on a regular bases. He looked like he might be able to handle himself if it came down to it.

Just then the bell rang and the elevator door opened. Since he was standing closer to the door, I motioned for him to go on ahead. I followed him into the elevator and watched to see which floor he was going to get off at. He reached over and pressed the button for the eighteenth floor, the same floor that the security company was located on, and the same floor that Carlson's accounting office was on. There was something very familiar about him, but I couldn't place him.

"What floor?" he asked.

"Twenty please," I replied, then watched his face for any reaction.

The man didn't respond or show any sign that he was the least bit interested in where I was going. He simply turned and pressed the button for the twentieth floor.

When the elevator started to move, I stepped back in the corner where I could keep an eye on the man. He didn't say a word all the way to the eighteenth floor. When the elevator stopped and the doors opened, he simply walked out of the elevator without so much as glancing back at me. I watched him turn and head down the hall in the direction of the security company. I was not sure if he went to the security company because the door of the elevator closed before he got that far down the hall.

The elevator began to move again. I put the man out of my mind for the moment as I began to wonder what I was going to find when I got to the twentieth floor. There was not much time to think about it, as the elevator door opened.

It was mid-morning when the guard came walking up to Carlson's cell again. He looked in and found Carlson lying on his bed with his hands behind his head looking up at the bottom of the bunk above him. Carlson slowly turned his head and looked over at the guard.

"You interested in getting out of here for a little while?" the guard asked.

"Where would I be going?"

"You are allowed thirty minutes in the exercise ground twice a day. You can refuse if you want, but it is the only chance you have to get out of that cell and get some fresh air. Take it or leave it. It makes no difference to me."

"I'll take it. I'll take it."

Carlson swung his legs over the side of his bunk and stood up. The guard motioned for his cell door to be open then stepped back. Carlson walked out of his cell and looked at the guard.

The guard motioned for Carlson to walk toward the end of the hall where he had gone for breakfast. Just before they got to the door to the mess hall, the guard pointed to a small steel door off to the side.

Carlson walked up to the door then stepped to one side while the guard opened it. The guard stepped back and motioned for Carlson to pass through the door.

As Carlson entered, he looked around. He found himself in an open outdoor area surrounded by a tall cyclone fence with razor wire running through the fence and rolled razor wire running all the way around the top. There was also a guard tower in one corner of the fenced off area. The entire area looked to be about twenty feet wide and fifty feet long. Around the edge was a narrow paved walkway, while in the center there was grass. Carlson was not sure what he *was supposed to do, so he looked back at the guard standing in the doorway.*

"You can walk or run around the paved part for exercise, or you can do pushups, or just lay on the grass in the sun if you want. You can do whatever you want in here, but whatever you do, do not touch the fence. I might suggest that you don't lay on the grass in the sun today as it is still wet from this morning's rain."

"How long do I have?"

"Thirty minutes. I will be back to get you when your time is up."

"Thank you," Carlson said, then watched the guard go back inside and shut the door.

Carlson heard the door being locked. He then took a couple of minutes to look around and to make a decision as to what he wanted to do. He had never had a set amount of time to do exercises. Without thinking, he simply began to walk around the outer perimeter of the exercise yard. With each lap, he began to walk just a little bit faster. He couldn't believe how good if felt to be someplace where he could walk and breath in the fresh air, even if he was still confined to a fairly small space.

It seemed like it had only been a few minutes when the guard returned and called him to come back inside. The last thing he wanted to do was to go back inside, but he knew that he had no choice. Besides, if he refused to go back in he might not be allowed out in the exercise area again. Reluctantly, he went back inside.

The guard took him to his cell where he was immediately locked in. Carlson sat down on the edge of his bed and listened to the footsteps of the guard as he walked away. Once again he was alone. It felt strange, but he found himself actually looking forward to the next time he could get out of his cell, even if it was just to walk around the exercise area.

CHAPTER NINETEEN

I stepped off the elevator into a large well decorated lobby. The walls were covered with large pictures of buildings that I was sure had been designed by Mile High Design. Directly across from the elevator was a fairly long reception desk. There were two women sitting behind the desk. The younger of the two looked up and smiled.

"May I help you, sir?" she asked politely.

I walked over to the desk before I responded.

"Yes. I would like to talk to Mr. Steinman, if I may."

"Do you have an appointment, sir?"

"No, but I'm sure he would like to see me. Just tell him that Mr. Tidsdale, a private investigator, would like to talk to him about Mrs. Carlson."

The mention of Mrs. Carlson's name seemed to get the attention of both of the women. The pleasant smile faded from the younger woman's face and she seemed a bit nervous. The older woman looked up at me. The expression on her face seemed to indicate that she was surprised to hear me mention Mrs. Carlson's name.

"I'll tell him, Mr. Tidsdale," she said, her voice breaking up a little.

While I waited, I glanced over at the older woman. She was still looking at me, but quickly looked away.

"Mr. Steinman will see you, sir."

"Thank you."

"Go down the hall to the right. You will be greeted by his personal secretary."

"Thank you," I said as I turned and started down the hall.

I had taken no more than about six steps when a tall middle aged woman in a gray business suit stepped out into the hall. She looked every bit the part of a serious business woman. The look on her face gave me no idea what she was thinking. A sort of smile came over her face as I got closer, but it was anything but a friendly smile.

"Right this way, Mr. Tidsdale," she said without any emotion.

I didn't bother to respond. I simply followed her through the large oak doors into a very nice and obviously expensive office.

The office was very nice, although not as nice as Mr. Moore's office. One wall was made almost entirely of glass and looked out over the city. In front of the windows was a long oak table surrounded by ten or twelve black leather office chairs. Another wall was covered almost entirely by oak bookshelves with each shelf full of books. The other two walls were white with a number of oil paintings of what appeared to be the Rocky Mountains. If I had to guess, they were probably originals. It was clear that no expense had been spared to decorate the office.

In front of the bookshelves was a large oak desk with a high back, black leather chair behind it. There were three black leather chairs in a semi-circle in front of the desk. Mr. Steinman was sitting behind the desk looking at me as I looked around the room. When I looked at him, he was smiling at me.

"Well, what do you think, Mr. Tidsdale?"

"Pretty impressive."

"Yes, it is. Won't you have a seat?" he said as he pointed to one of the black leather chairs in front of his desk.

"Thank you," I said as I sat down.

"Now, Mr. Tidsdale, how may I help you?" he asked as he looked more seriously at me.

"As I told one of your receptionists, I'm a private investigator. I'm looking into the untimely death of Mrs. Carlson."

"I see," he said without any change of expression. "And who are you working for?"

"I'm working for Mr. Albert Moore, Jim Carlson's attorney."

"What is it you think I can do for you?"

"I would like a little background into Mrs. Carlson. You know, the usual things like work history, what type of employee she was and who she was close to here in the office. Generally anything that might give me some idea of the kind of person she was and how she got along with the other employees. That sort of thing."

"I see," he said again, then just sat there looking at me.

I got the impression that he was not feeling very comfortable giving me that kind of information. I had to wonder why. What possible difference could it make to him? It certainly wouldn't make any difference to Mrs. Carlson.

"Well, Mr. Tidsdale, about all I can tell you is that she was a very good and loyal employee. She was a hard worker and fit in with the rest of the staff very nicely."

"Could you tell me who she might have been close to?"

"I wouldn't know that. You see, I rarely worked that closely with her."

"What department did she work in?"

"She worked in the Interior Design Department."

"What did she do there?"

"She worked with our clients to design floor layouts to fit the client's desired use of the building."

"Who is the head of the department?"

"That would be Norman French".

"I would like to talk to him, if I may."

"I'm sorry, but that will be impossible. You see, he retired last week and now lives in England, I believe."

"He retired last week? Isn't that pretty sudden for him to have made such a move so quickly?"

"I believe he had been planning the move for some time."

"How about the person who would be her supervisor if she were still alive?"

"That would be Julie Townsen, but I don't think she knew Mrs. Carlson. She was moved here just two days ago from our LA office."

"Would it be all right if I talk to some of the people in her department that were here when Mrs. Carlson did work here?" I asked.

I was getting a little frustrated with the runaround I was getting. It was fast becoming apparent that he was hiding something and I wanted to know what it was.

"I'm afraid that won't be possible. I can't have my employees spending time on the job to answer the questions of a private investigator," he said with a smug smile on his face.

That answered that for me. There was no way I was going to get anything useful out of him. I wondered if he would treat the police in the same way. I had to come up with something to get Don to obtain a warrant and start questioning all the employees. That might prove to be a bit of a problem since I had nothing to connect Mrs. Carlson's death to Mile High Design at this point.

"I just have one more question for you. Do you have an employee by the name of Jacob Rinehart working here? I understand he is a lawyer."

That question seemed to come as a surprise to him. I noticed that the muscles in his jaw seemed to tighten and he took a deep breath. It took him a second to get his thoughts together. There was little doubt that I had struck a nerve, but I wasn't sure what it meant.

"No. Ah, no," he stuttered a bit. "We don't have any attorney by that name working here."

"Thank you," I said as I stood up. "Thank you for all your help."

"You're welcome," he said without getting up.

As I walked out of the office, I could see his reflection in a glass panel. He was picking up the phone while watching me leave. It was clear that I had shaken him up a little, but I had no idea as to why. A good look into Mr. Steinman and his company was definitely in order now.

As I got on the elevator, I turned and looked toward the reception desk. The young woman at the desk was watching me rather closely. The look on her face gave me the impression that she might want to talk to me, but was afraid to talk to me here. I had to come up with a way to see her without anyone from the company knowing that I was talking to her. She was still watching me when the elevator doors closed.

As the elevator descended, I was thinking about the young woman. Suddenly, it stopped on the eighteenth floor. The same man that had ridden up in the elevator with me earlier got on. He didn't say anything, but I noticed that he took a much closer look at me this time. There was no doubt that this guy was a professional. There was also no doubt in my mind that I should know him, but I still couldn't place him.

When we got to the ground floor, I stepped off the elevator and left the building. I glanced over my shoulder to see if he was going to follow me. He quickly turned to look the other way as if he was looking for someone, but it was clear that he was planning on being my tail. He was one guy that I didn't want following me.

I went around the corner where I had parked my car, got in and left. When I drove by him, he watched me drive away. He had plenty of time to get my license plate number. With that information, he could find out where my office was without a great deal of difficulty. I had registered my vehicle using my office address instead of my home address.

I would have to be on my toes with this guy. I had no idea what the guy's plans were or what his instructions might be, but I would be very watchful.

Rinehart had not recognized the man in the elevator that went up to Mile High Design. He wondered who he was, but it was his job to be suspicious of anyone he didn't recognize going upstairs. After all, he was the security for Mile High Design. However, it was normal working hours and he didn't feel that there was anything for him to be concerned about.

Rinehart had been sitting at his desk for a while when his private phone began to ring. He immediately knew who was calling since the line was a direct line to Mr. Steinman's office at Mile High Design. He picked up the receiver and listened.

"Frank Tidsdale is just leaving my office. He asked a lot of questions about Mrs. Carlson. He could be a lot of trouble if he talks to the wrong people. Do something about it," the voice on the other end said.

"I'm on it," was all he said before he hung up.

Rinehart immediately got up, left his office and hurried to the bank of elevators. When he got there, he looked to see which one was coming down. He then moved in front of it to wait for the door to open.

As soon as the door opened he saw Tidsdale in the elevator. He stepped into the elevator but didn't say anything. Rinehart simply stepped aside and waited. He took a minute to size up Tidsdale. Since Tidsdale was a little smaller than he was, he didn't think it would be very difficult to intimidate him into getting off the case. He also knew that he would have no problem finding Tidsdale's office now that he knew his name.

When the elevator reached the ground floor, he hesitated a moment allowing Tidsdale to leave the elevator first. He followed Tidsdale out the front door then stopped and watched to see where he went.

When Tidsdale looked back over his shoulder, Rinehart turned and looked down the street the other way as if looking for someone. He turned back in time to see Tidsdale get in his vehicle. As he drove by, Rinehart took note of his license plate number and wrote it down as soon as Tidsdale was out of sight. He thought it might come in handy to find out where Tidsdale lived.

Rinehart returned to his office and looked up the address for Tidsdale Investigations in the phone book. He was not familiar with that private investigator, but he didn't feel that it would be necessary to know anything about him before confronting him. After all, he was just another PI as far as Rinehart was concerned.

CHAPTER TWENTY

I went to my office and placed a call to Donald Wright. It took a few minutes for him to answer my call.

"Detective Donald Wright, how may I help you?"

"It's me, Frank Tidsdale."

"What is it, Frank. I'm a little busy," Don said rather abruptly.

"I was wondering if you know a guy by the name of Jacob Rinehart?"

"You asked me about him before and I said I didn't think so, but since we talked I remembered him. I don't really know him, but I've heard of him. He's supposed to be the head of security for Mile High Design. Why? You got something on him?"

"No, not yet anyway. You said that he's "supposed to be head of security", what do you mean by that?"

"I don't have any proof, but I think he's more of an enforcer than the head of a security agency. I'm told he works for Mile High Design, Inc, now, but he once worked for Sargossa."

"You mean Donato Sargossa?"

"That's the one. He was pretty good at breaking knee caps and skulls, as I recall. We've had no problems with him for the past two or three years. What's your interest in him?"

"That's it," I said realizing that I had heard of Jacob Rinehart.

"What's it?"

"I didn't recognize the name until you mentioned Sargossa. He followed me out of the Hammond building where Mile High Design is located."

"Sargossa?"

"No. Rinehart."

"What were you doing at Mile High Design?"

"Trying to find out a little about Mrs. Carlson. I got the runaround from the president of the firm, a Wilbur Steinman. He as much as told me that he would not allow his people to talk to me. He was less than cooperative. When I was leaving his office, he got right on the phone. I think the call was to Rinehart because he joined me on the elevator when I was on my way out."

"Frank, you be careful around him. He's mean and he knows how to handle himself."

"I'm sure he does. By the way, he also carries a gun."

"Yeah, I know. He has a .45 caliber auto registered to him and a permit to carry it. Is there anything else? I've got an appointment with the lab."

"Not right now, but you might let me know what you find out from them."

"I will."

"By the way, did you ever look into the order in which Carlson placed his calls the night his wife died?"

"Yeah. He called Moore first then 9-1-1, then you. All the calls were placed in a matter of five or six minutes. Does that help you any?"

"It might, but it doesn't at the moment."

"I have to run," he said.

"Talk to you later."

I hung up and leaned back in my desk chair to think about Rinehart. I had never had any personal run-ins with him, but I had seen a photo and read about him in the papers a number of years ago. He had never been convicted of anything that I knew of.

Now that I knew who he was, my thoughts turned to the young receptionist that had watched me leave. If my impression of her was right, she wanted to talk to me, but I had no idea what about. Getting a hold of her might not be the best thing for her. If Mile High Design had anything to do with Mrs. Carlson's death, contacting the young receptionist might put her in danger.

It might be hard for me to contact her since I didn't know what her name was or anything about her. I also had the problem of having Rinehart watching me, and I had no idea how many other guys he might have working for him to make sure the employees towed the line.

It was at that moment I came up with an idea. I reached over and picked up my phone. I placed a call to Mile High Design. The phone rang just twice before it was answered.

"Mile High Design, how may I help you?"

The woman who answered the phone sounded like the young woman I had talked to earlier. I wasn't sure if I should say anything because I wasn't sure I had the right person, but I really wanted to talk to her.

"I hope this doesn't sound too personal, but I would like to speak to the young woman who was at the reception desk this morning."

"That would be me, sir."

"May I ask what your name is?"

"I'm not sure I want to give out that information."

"I understand. Are you where anyone can hear you?"

"Not at the moment," her voice sounding like she wasn't sure she wanted to say anything.

"Good. I was there this morning. You looked like you wanted to say something to me when I was leaving, but didn't think you could without drawing attention to yourself."

"Are you the private investigator that was here this morning?" she asked in a soft whisper.

"Yes."

"I'm not supposed to give out my name, but it is Julie Mathews. I have to go. Someone is coming."

"Thank you. I'll talk to you later," I said then hung up.

I quickly wrote down her name on a slip of the paper. The sudden knock on my door quickly got my attention. I slipped the paper inside my desk drawer.

"Come in," I said as I closed the drawer, reached under the edge of my desk and pressed a button that turned on a recorder. I looked up as the door opened to see who it was.

Rinehart walked into my office. I was not all that surprised to see him because I had more or less expected to meet him sometime, somewhere. I just hadn't expected it to be so soon, and in my office.

"What can I do for you, Mr. Rinehart?" I asked, but remained seated at my desk.

"I see it didn't take you very long to find out what my name is."

"No. Not long at all. I also know that you are security for Mile High Design. What is it I can do for you? Do you need an investigator?"

"No, I don't need an investigator," he said rather sharply. "You were in the office of Mr. Steinman this morning asking a lot of questions about some of our employees."

"That is only partly true. I was asking about one former employee. I might add that Mr. Steinman was not a great deal of help."

"That is because personnel matters are private and not open to scrutiny by the public."

I could see no reason to discuss why I was there, or what information I wanted. First of all, I was sure he already knew, or at least had a good idea. Secondly, it wouldn't make a bit of difference to him. I was sure that he had his instructions which were probably to get me to leave Mile High Design's employees alone.

"So you came all the way to my office to tell me that personnel matters are private. Seems like a waste of time. You could have told me that over the phone."

"You don't seem to understand," he said firmly. "I thought you would be smarter than that."

"Oh, I understand all right. But you understand this. I'm investigating the death of one of Mile High Design's employees. I will continue to do that, with or without Mr. Steinman's help. Do you understand that?"

"I understand," he said with a sinister grin. "I wish you luck. You're going to need all the luck you can get."

"Is that a threat, Mr. Rinehart?"

"Let's just say that it would not be in your best interest to bother the employees."

With that said he simply turned around and left my office. I knew it was not over between us, and so did he. I knew that we would meet again if I didn't drop the case, but next time it would not be so civil. I reached under the edge of the desk and shut off the recorder. I would save that tape because it just might come in handy at some future date.

Rinehart left Tidsdale's office. As he stepped out of the building, he was pretty sure that Tidsdale would not scare easily. If he didn't, it was going to take a lot more to get him to drop his investigation. He could have had it out with Tidsdale while he was in the office, but there was too much of a chance that they would be interrupted, or he would be seen. It was going to take some planning to get Tidsdale to back off. Rinehart had not missed the thought that he might even have to kill Tidsdale.

Rinehart returned to his office. Once inside, he picked up the direct line to Steinman's office. It wasn't but a couple of seconds before the phone was answered.

"Well, did you get him to drop it?"

"I doubt it. He's a very stubborn man," Rinehart said.

"I want him out of the picture. Do you understand?"

"I understand, but it won't be easy. He has a lot of friends."

"And just how do you know that?" Steinman asked with a sharp tone in his voice.

"I didn't recognize him until I was in his office talking to him. He has a lot of friends on the police force."

"And just how do you know that?

"I remembered him. He's an ex-cop. He has a dozen or more pictures of cops he's worked with in his office."

"Well I don't care if he's an ex-governor. I want him out of the way, permanently. Do you get what I'm telling you?"

"Yes sir, but it won't be easy. And this will cost you plenty. I wasn't hired to kill people for you. Break a few bones and mess them up a little, but no killing."

"You get paid for your services, and that includes whatever I demand of you."

The phone suddenly went dead. Rinehart looked at the phone as he hung it up. The thought crossed Rinehart's mind that he would like to go up to Steinman's office and beat the hell of him just for the practice, but that thought quickly passed. He knew that Steinman had enough on him to send him to jail for the rest of his life. He also knew that if he did as he was told, he would stay out of jail and live very comfortably. He had to admit that Steinman paid him well for what little he had to do, most of the time.

Rinehart set out to find a way to get Tidsdale off the case without killing him. He knew that it was risky, but assault had a much lesser penalty than murder. He would tail Tidsdale and look for a chance to work him over real good, preferably in private. That way it would be his word against Tidsdale's if he was charged. If that didn't stop him, he would be left with no choice but to kill him.

CHAPTER TWENTY-ONE

I tipped back in my chair and took a moment to think. Detective Wright had told me that Rinehart had worked for Sargossa and might still work for Sargossa. I began to wonder if Rinehart still had connections to Sargossa. I also began to wonder if Sargossa had connections to Mile High Design and what the connection might be. The one thing I knew for sure was if there was a connection it would not be easy to find. If Sargossa had a hold over Mile High Design, it would most likely be through intimidation and debt. I had to wonder if Steinman owed money to Sargossa. Even if he did, there would certainly be no official record of it.

However, I did come up with an idea for a motive for the death of Mrs. Carlson. I wondered if Mrs. Carlson might have accidentally found something that would show a financial connection between Steinman and Sargossa. If she did, the big question was did she know that Sargossa was a mob boss? The more I thought about it, the more I felt it was important that I search her home office.

There was one way that I was sure I would be able to find out if Sargossa had any kind of a hold over Mr. Steinman or Mile High Design. I knew a guy that made his living on the edge of the law. He had done work for Sargossa in the past and might know what was going on. I reached out, picked up my phone and dialed a number. The phone rang only twice before it was answered.

"Yeah," a voice on the other end said.

"Tidsdale. Are you where you can talk?"

"Just a minute."

I could hear what sounded like several people talking in the background, but couldn't hear what they were saying. I heard a door close followed by silence.

"What's up, Franky?"

"You still got connections with Sargossa?"

"Some. Whatcha' need?"

"I need to know if Sargossa has any connections with Mile High Design. It's an architectural firm in the downtown area. If he has connections with them, I'd like to know what kind of connections."

"I'm not sure about any connections, but it wouldn't surprise me none. I can probably find out."

"See what you can come up with, but don't take any risks."

"Sure."

"Do you know a Jacob Rinehart?"

"Sure. He's a bone breaker for Sargossa."

"I hear he has a security agency and works for Mile High Design."

"He does, sort of."

"What do you mean, 'sort of'?"

"I'm not sure about this, but since he left Sargossa I've seen them meet a few times. The word is that Rinehart is keeping an eye on Mile High Design for Sargossa. For what reason, I don't know. The word is that Rinehart still works for Sargossa, but their being very secretive about it. Let me do a little nosin' around and see what I can dig up for you."

"Thanks, but keep your head down."

"No worries about that, Franky. I always keep my head down. Be in touch."

"Thanks," I said then hung up.

The next thing on my agenda was to pay a visit to Carlson's house. I needed to find out if there was anything there that might give me a clue as to why Mrs. Carlson was murdered.

Albert Moore sat behind his desk as he placed a call to the DA's office. It didn't take long before his call was directed to the Assistant DA in charge of Carlson's case. Her name was Marsha Russell. She was a very ambitious woman who was out to make a name for herself in the DA's Office. She had a reputation as a hard woman to deal with, and didn't care whose toes she stepped on to get what she wanted. And what she wanted was a big promotion.

"Ms Russell, I'm Albert Moore. I'm calling to find out what evidence you have against Mr. James Carlson."

"We have enough to charge him with first degree murder."

"That may be so, but I have not had the opportunity to see what evidence you have. I'm sure you are aware that as his defense attorney, I have the right to see all the evidence against my client. And you have an obligation to see to it that we have access to that evidence in a timely manner. I would like to know what that evidence is. By failing to allow me access to the evidence, you are jeopardizing your case and causing my client to remain in jail longer than necessary.

"I can assure you, Mr. Moore, that we are getting all the evidence together and will get it to you as soon as possible," she said.

"I suspect that will be within the next few hours?"

"I'm not really sure."

"I am sure that you know as well as I that withholding evidence from the defense attorney is serious and frowned on by the courts."

"You don't have to tell me about the law," she replied with a sharp tone in her voice.

"In that case, I might suggest that you make every effort to get the results of all lab work and any other evidence you *have to me before the day is out, or I will be left with no choice but the ask the judge for a dismissal of all charges. Do I make myself clear?"*

"Yes. You make yourself perfectly clear," she said sharply. "But - - -."

Mr. Moore hung up the phone before Ms Russell had a chance to say anything else, or before she could offer any lame excuses for the delay. Moore was not interested in any reason she might offer for the delay. He wanted Carlson out of jail as soon as possible.

CHAPTER TWENTY-TWO

I left my office on my way to Carlson's house when I realized that I was being followed by a dark blue BMW sedan. There was no doubt in my mind that it was Rinehart. It was obvious that he was not very good at tailing someone. If he had been, I would not have discovered him so quickly.

The last thing I needed was to have him follow me to Carlson's house. Since he had made an attempt to buy Carlson's house, whoever he worked for must think that there is something of importance in that house. I had to wonder what it was, and who he was working for now. Was it Sargossa or Steinman? Either way, I didn't want him following me.

At the moment, I didn't want him to know that I knew he was following me, either. I needed to get rid of him without him suspecting anything. It occurred to me that a stop at the police station to have a talk with Don would be one way to get him off my back. Besides, I needed to talk to Don about what he had found out from the lab and what he found the other day when I left him in Mrs. Carlson's home office.

I took a right at the next corner and headed toward the police precinct Detective Donald Wright worked out of. The way I had chosen to go was not likely to arouse suspicion and make Rinehart think that I was on to him.

When I came around the corner, I turned into the parking lot and parked in the visitor's parking space. I could see out of the corner of my eye, the BMW pull over to the curb and stop. I avoided looking in his direction as I walked in the front door of the building. Once inside, I stopped and looked out the window next to the door. It was tinted and he would not be able to see me. Rinehart sat there for about three or four minutes before he pulled away.

When I turned around, I could see the desk sergeant looking at me. I smiled as I walked up to his desk.

"Got a problem?" the desk sergeant asked.

"Not now. Could you tell me if Detective Donald Wright is in?"

"Yeah, he's in."

"I would like to speak to him, please."

"I'll see if he's busy."

I watched him as he called Don's office. I couldn't hear what he was saying, but from the look on his face it looked good.

"Detective Wright will see you. Down the hall, third door on the right."

"Thanks," I said as I started down the hall.

When I got to the third door on the right, I knocked.

"Come in."

I opened the door and stepped into Wright's office. It was not a big office, but it was nice. Don was sitting behind a desk. Latimer was sitting in front of the desk looking at me. He made no effort to say anything to me, but then I didn't expect him to.

"What can I do for you?" Wright asked.

"I would like to talk to you about the Carlson case. More importantly, about the lab reports and the report on the gun that Carlson had on him."

"Have a seat," Wright said.

As I sat down, I noticed that Latimer made no effort to leave. I got the feeling that he was planning on staying.

"Here are the reports on the gun and the autopsy," Wright said as he handed me the reports then leaned back to give me a chance to look at them.

The very first thing I noticed from the autopsy report was that the cause of death was two gun shot wounds from a large caliber gun, namely a .357 magnum pistol. That certainly would explain the amount of blood, the blood splatters on the walls and the lack of cartridges at the scene. A gun like that tended to cause a lot of damage.

The second thing I noticed was that the report indicated that Mrs. Carlson had been severely beaten before she was shot. The only thing I could deduce from that was that someone had probably beaten her in order to get some information out of her. I had to wonder what she knew, or what someone thought she knew, that would justify such a beating to get her to talk. I had to wonder if she had told them what they wanted to know. I didn't think so, especially since someone seemed to still be looking for something. The report had indicated that she had not been sexually abused. The rest of the report showed nothing else of interest.

It suddenly occurred to me that there was no mention of a knife in the autopsy report. Did that mean there was no knife involved in her murder, or simply that there were no wounds on Mrs. Carlson caused by a knife? Maybe the missing knife from the kitchen had nothing at all to do with her murder. That did nothing to explain the blood trail in the front hall and on the stairs. If she had been shot in the bedroom, where did all the drops of blood on the stairs come from? I still had not seen the lab reports on the blood found on the stairs and in the front hall.

I looked up at Don but didn't say anything. I wasn't sure if it was because I was still thinking about the knife, or if it was because Latimer was sitting there watching me.

I turned my attention to the report of the gun that had been taken from James. It was a small caliber gun, a .25 caliber pistol to be more accurate. It was obviously not the murder weapon. That would be good news to Carlson and Moore. But the real question was where did the gun come from? Carlson had said that neither he nor his wife owned a gun. I had to wonder if Mrs. Carlson had purchased the gun without telling her husband. That would be something to look into.

I again looked up at Wright. I didn't really want to talk to him in front of Latimer, but it didn't appear that Latimer was going to leave the room.

"Don, do you have the lab reports on the blood, especially the blood found in the front hall, on the stairs and on the banister?"

"I'll have those reports later this afternoon. They're running DNA test on them before they release them."

"I would like to have that information as soon as possible."

"I'll fax a copy to you and one to Moore as soon as I get it."

"You think that will help you any?" Latimer said with an arrogant grin.

I slowly turned and looked at Latimer before I spoke.

"I don't really know. I do know that the report on the gun proves that it was not the murder weapon. That shoots your theory all to hell that Carlson had the murder weapon in his hand when they arrested him."

It was easy to see by Latimer's expression that he didn't like what I said, but then I didn't give a damn what he liked or didn't like. He had made a fool of himself and I was sure that everyone in the precinct knew it by now.

I couldn't help think about how much else he had bungled by not paying attention to procedures and to the evidence. Had he really searched the other rooms in the house for evidence? I had my doubts. Did he bother to try and find out if there was a second person involved in the murder? I seriously doubted that, too.

I had intended to tell Wright that I needed to take a look at the crime scene again, but with Latimer there I decided against it. I would just go to the house and let myself in.

"I have some things to check out," I said to Wright. "I'll talk to you later."

I got up and left the room. As I headed for the front door, I couldn't help but think about Latimer. He seemed so dead set on Carlson's guilt that it made me wonder if there was something else going on here that I wasn't seeing. I gave up that thought when I thought of him having to work with Wright. Latimer might overlook things, but I was pretty sure that Wright wouldn't overlook anything.

With that idea firmly planted in my mind, I walked over to my car. As I opened the door, I looked over the top of my car for the BMW that had been following me earlier. There was no sign of it.

I got in my car and taking an around about way in order to make sure no one was following me, I drove over to Washington Park. I parked my car about two blocks away from Carlson's home and walked the rest of the way. I entered the property from the alley behind the house, making sure that no one saw me enter the house through the backdoor.

Rinehart watched as Tidsdale drove into the police parking lot. He pulled over and stopped next to the curb. Since it would be too easy for Tidsdale to spot him, he decided to drive on around the corner and park. He spent the next ten minutes sitting in his car thinking about what he should do. The one thing he didn't want was for a cop to walk up and ask him what he was doing there.

Believing that Tidsdale didn't have much to work on at the moment, Rinehart figured that he had plenty of time to "convince" Tidsdale to back off. Believing that, he pulled away from the curb and headed back to his office.

Once he arrived at his office, he sat down to think. As much as he tried to think about how to get Tidsdale to stop his investigation without killing him, he couldn't help but think about Steinman.

The way Steinman had talked to him earlier that morning had been slowly grating on him. If it was not for what Steinman knew about him, he would let Tidsdale keep digging. It would serve Steinman right, but he knew he couldn't do that without Steinman pointing the finger at him.

It suddenly came into Rinehart's mind that maybe he should have a talk with his real boss. He reached over and picked up the phone and placed a call to Donato Sargossa. The phone rang a couple of times before it was answered.

"Yeah," the person answering said.

"Rinehart. I would like to speak to the boss."

"Just a second."

Rinehart waited for almost ten minutes before anyone came on the line.

"Jacob, my boy. What's on your mind?"

"I would like a meeting with you, sir."

"You would? Is it important?"

"I believe it is."

"Okay. I'll pick you up in front of the downtown Marriott in fifteen minutes."

"I'll be there," then the phone went dead

Rinehart immediately drove to the Marriott. He knew that he had better be there in fifteen minutes and not one second later if he wanted to talk to the boss.

He arrived at the hotel just a couple of minutes before Sargossa's Cadillac pulled up to the curb in front of the hotel. The backdoor of the car opened and Rinehart climbed in, then the car pulled away.

"Well, my boy. What seems to be the problem?"

"Steinman wants me to kill Tidsdale just to get him out of the way."

"I take it you don't think it's necessary."

"If you say it is, I'll do it. But I'm not going out on a limb for the likes of Steinman."

"What do you think? Is Tidsdale a problem for us?"

"I think Tidsdale could be a problem, but right now I don't think he knows anything. I really think that if we kill him now, it will cause more problems than we need. Killing him would be almost as bad as killing a cop."

"What makes you so sure?"

"He's an ex-cop and has a lot of friends on the police force. If we kill him now, we'll have almost every cop in the metro area looking for his killer. I don't think you want that kind of attention."

"You're right about that. Why does Steinman want him dead?"

"He thinks he could cause trouble, and maybe he could. But if we kill him now, we'll be looking for more trouble than what we might ever see otherwise."

"Is Steinman going to be a problem?"

Rinehart looked at Mr. Sargossa. He was pretty sure what he was asking.

"I think Steinman is worried about what might happen to him. If things start to point to Mile High Design being involved in the death of Mrs. Carlson, it could be a problem for him. If that occurs, Steinman could be a problem for us."

"You think he would talk?"

"Yeah," Rinehart replied after thinking on it for a minute. "If he thinks it will save his own skin, he'll probably squeal like a pig under an electric fence."

Sargossa sat back in the seat and rubbed his chin as he thought about what he had been told. He then looked at Rinehart for a moment or so before saying anything.

"I want you to keep an eye on Tidsdale. If you think he is getting too close, do what you have to do to get him to back off. If he doesn't back off, you will have to kill him, but only if you have to. Do you understand?"

"Yes, sir. What about Steinman?"

"I'll put someone on him to make sure he doesn't do anything stupid. I'll make sure Steinman knows who is really running the show here."

"Thanks."

"Take us back to the Marriott," Sargossa said to the driver.

Nothing more was said between Rinehart and Sargossa. Rinehart was left off at the Marriott. He was feeling a little better about not having to keep an eye on both Tidsdale and Steinman, and that Sargossa would let Steinman know who was the boss. He got in his car and returned to his office.

CHAPTER TWENTY-THREE

Once I was inside Carlson's house, I stood at the backdoor and listened. I wanted to make sure that there was no one else in the house. It was as quiet as a tomb. I moved from the back entry into the kitchen. As far as I could tell, nothing had been touched since I had been there. There were no indications that the forensic unit had dusted for prints, looked for evidence, or had even been in the kitchen. It was apparent that no one had noticed the odd knife in the knife block.

The knife that I had found earlier was still in the knife block. I looked around as I wondered what had happened to the knife that actually belonged there. Had it been damaged in some way and tossed out? It was possible, but my mind wouldn't let me think that way for very long. They were very expensive knifes, the top of the line. No one would just toss out one of those knives. More than likely, it would have been replaced with a new knife that matched the set. Of course, there was always the possibility that the Carlsons had not had a chance to replace it yet.

Being very careful not to make any unnecessary noise, I began looking in the kitchen drawers for the missing knife. After searching all the drawers and cabinets, all I found was one knife that matched the odd knife in the knife block. I was unable to find the knife that belonged in the block.

I had this theory floating around in my head that the blood in the front hall and on the stairs might have been the result of someone being cut, and probably with the missing knife. The problem I had was simple. I had nothing to back up that theory, not a thing. The fact that there were no cuts on either Mr. or Mrs. Carlson went a long way toward my thinking that it was someone else's blood. Someone had been bleeding and the blood drops were more typical of those caused by an injury from a knife or some other sharp object than from a gunshot wound. There was no blood splatter on the stairs or in the front hall like there would have been if a gun had been used. The fact that there was no blood splatter in the front entryway helped support my theory. Until I had the results of the blood tests, I would just have to file away my theory in the back of my mind, at least for now.

I continued to look around as I worked my way through the dining room and the living room to the stairs. I went up the stairs and went past the master bedroom to Mrs. Carlson's office. The door was locked, but I had no difficulty getting it open.

Once in the room, I walked around behind the desk and sat down in the desk chair. I took a moment to look around the room. I had no idea what I was looking for, but I couldn't get it out of my mind that there was something here that would help explain why Mrs. Carlson was murdered. The PC unit of Mrs. Carlson's computer was gone, but I more or less expected that. Wright would have taken it, or had it removed for his computer experts to see what they could get off it.

It looked like the best place for me to start looking for any evidence was in the desk. I began by opening the center drawer. There were the usual small items one almost always found in a desk. Things like paper chips, pens, pencils, etc. There were also a couple of legal pads and some typing paper. In other words, there was nothing there that I didn't expect to find.

I started working down the desk drawers on the right side. I found nothing of interest in the top drawer. In the bottom drawer I found several file folders. Each one was clearly labeled. In each folder were receipts that fit into the category listed on the folder's label. Again, there was nothing unusual. That is until I came to the last folder.

The last folder did not have a label on it. I almost overlooked it because it didn't have a label and didn't look like it had anything in it. My first thought was that it was just an extra folder. But not to look in the folder would mean that I had not done a complete job of searching the desk. I pulled the folder up and looked in it. Inside was a single piece of paper only about four inches wide and six inches long. It was a hand written store receipt. It was all that was in the folder.

I took the receipt out of the folder and looked at it. It was a receipt from the Lakewood Gun Shop in Centennial, Colorado. It showed that Mrs. Carlson had purchased a .25 caliber pistol almost ten days ago which included five lessons at the Lakewood Gun Club, an indoor pistol range, to learn how to use the new gun. The receipt described the gun and also had the serial number written on it.

The gun that Carlson had been holding when the police broke into his house and arrested him had been a .25 caliber pistol. I didn't know what kind of gun it was, nor did I know the serial number, but I would have bet a week's pay that it was the same gun. Since Carlson had said that neither he nor his wife owned a gun, my guess was that Mrs. Carlson bought it without telling him. What did she know that would cause her to buy a gun and not tell her husband? I was afraid I might never get an answer to that question.

I noticed that there was a small desk style copy machine on a table in the corner. I took the receipt and made a copy of it. I then returned the original to the folder and put it back in the desk where I had found it. I wrote on the copy a note describing where I had found the original receipt along with the time and date that I found it. I then signed it and put the copy in my pocket.

I continued to search the rest of the desk, the two file cabinets and the credenza behind the desk. There was nothing else that seemed to be important, or that offered even a hint of why Mrs. Carlson had been murdered.

It was my guess that Don had taken her PC unit to have his computer people see if they could find anything on it that would help him find her murderer. I wasn't sure if he had taken any discs or CD's, but I had not found any in the office. I was pretty sure any CD's or discs would have been taken by the police as well.

After sitting back down in the chair behind the desk, I began to just look around the room while I thought about Mrs. Carlson. She had to be a pretty smart woman to be in the job she had. If she was smart, and if she knew her way around computers, she would probably have been smart enough not to leave anything on her computer that could be harmful to her or her husband. She wouldn't have left discs or CD's lying around either, if they had information on them that she didn't want anyone to find.

That thought gave me an idea. Hers was not the only office in the house. Hers was not the only computer in the house, either. Was it possible that she put whatever it was she found on her husband's computer? Would she even think to do that? I doubted that she would put anything she wanted kept secret on any computer in the house. If she put what she found on a disk, maybe she didn't leave it on the computer at all. If she put what she found, that is if she had found anything at all, on a disk or CD, where would she hide it? It would have to be someplace other than in one of the home offices. My reason for thinking that was I had not found one single disk or CD in her office. It was easy to assume that Wright would have taken any disk or CDs he found in the house.

I know I was running a lot of "IF's" through my head, and I had nothing solid to go on at this point. I had found nothing that would provide me with a motive for Mrs. Carlson's murder.

It was after noon when I left Mrs. Carlson's home office. There were several things that I needed to do, so it was time to get out of there. I could always come back later and search Carlson's office.

On my way out of Mrs. Carlson's home office, I stopped at the door and looked around the room. The last thing I wanted was to leave some indication that I had been there. Once satisfied that all was as it should be in her office, I went downstairs and took a quick look in Carlson's office. His computer was also gone. I then left the house the same way I had come in.

I returned to my car and drove back to my office.

Carlson was lying on his bunk reading a book that he got from one of the guards when a guard walked up to his cell. Carlson looked up wondering what he wanted now. He had already been out to the exercise yard.

"You've got a visitor. Your attorney is here to see you," the guard said.

Carlson immediately put down the book and moved over next to the door. The guard had the door opened. The guard led Carlson to one of the private rooms where prisoners met with their attorneys. Moore was sitting at a table waiting for him.

"I didn't expect to see you for a couple of days."

"Well, I have some good news for you. The gun that was taken from you when you were arrested was not the murder weapon. That weapon was a major part of the DA's case against you."

"I tried to tell them that, but no one would listen to me."

"I know, but now they have lost a major part of their reason for holding you. The test for gun residue was negative also. That's another point in our favor. There is one other thing. The Assistant DA has not been forthcoming in getting their evidence against you to me in a timely manner, which is required by law. I think she is holding up giving me what evidence she has because she knows she doesn't have enough for a case against you. She's probably hoping to find something to show you killed Jennifer.

"I'm trying to schedule a motion hearing with the judge for the first thing in the morning. I'm going to ask him to drop all charges against you and release you from jail."

"If the judge releases me, can they charge me again?"

"Yes, they can. But the judge will probably make them come up with some much stronger evidence in order for them to recharge you. Judges tend not to like it when their time is wasted by overzealous ADAs looking for promotions."

"So, I will be out of jail until they find something else to connect me to Jenny's murder. Right?"

"That's right. Well, that is if the judge grants our motion."

"Has Tidsdale found anything to prove I didn't do it?"

"I have not been in touch with him since earlier this morning. But at that point, he didn't have anything that would help. He did, however, have a couple of promising leads and was looking into a few things."

"Do you think he can prove I didn't kill my wife?"

"I think so."

"When do you think I will get out?"

"If I can get a hearing in the morning, and the judge agrees with my motion to have the charges dropped, you could be out of here by lunch time tomorrow."

"That would be great," Carlson said with a grin.

"Jim, I don't want you to get your hopes up too much. The judge is tough, and I still don't know all the evidence the ADA has. At the motion hearing, she could surprise us with something we don't know anything about."

"Like what?"

"I don't know. Just keep it in mind that getting you out of here tomorrow may not happen."

"Without the murder weapon, it makes it harder for them, right?"

"Yes, it does. Look, you try to relax. Be assured that both Tidsdale and I are working to get you out of here."

"I'll try."

"I have to go. I'll talk to you after the motion hearing. Try to get a good night's sleep."

Carlson nodded that he would try, but he was feeling a bit concerned about the motion hearing. His luck had not been running very well lately. All he could think about was the ADA coming up with something that would keep him in jail.

Carlson's thoughts were disturbed by the sound of the door closing. He looked around and noticed that Moore had left the room. He sat there waiting for the guard to take him back to his cell.

After a few minutes, the guard came in and got him. He returned Carlson to his cell, then left him alone.

CHAPTER TWENTY-FOUR

I grabbed a little something to eat on my way back to my office. When I arrived I found two faxes in the fax machine. They were from Detective Wright and were the lab reports on the blood found in the Carlson house. I sat down at my desk and ate my lunch while I read them over carefully so as not to miss anything. The conclusion was very clear. The blood found in the front entry way, on the stair steps and on the handrail was from an unknown person. The DNA testing, with cross match to the state's DNA data bank, did not provide any help in finding out whose blood it was. It did, however, confirm that the blood was from one person, and was not that of either James Carlson or his wife, Jennifer.

That bit of information provided proof that there was someone other than the Carlsons in the house at the time of Mrs. Carlson's death. It also left some reasonable doubt with regard to Carlson's guilt. But on the other hand, it didn't completely eliminate him as being involved in his wife's death. From what I had been able to tell from the blood, there appeared to have been some sort of altercation at or near the front door.

The reports left me with more questions than the reports answered. One thing was sure. There was someone walking around the Denver area with a very nasty cut, probably on his lower arm or hand. It sure wasn't a minor cut based on the amount of blood left on the stairs and in the entryway. It probably would have required several stitches.

I decided it was probably a good idea to call Wright and see if he was checking hospitals in the area for someone coming in with a nasty cut on his arm or hand that required stitches. I reached over and picked up the phone. It was only a couple of minutes before Wright came on the line.

"I take it you got the lab reports?" Wright asked.

"Yes. I did. I was wondering if you got out of them the same thing I did. That being someone had a pretty serious cut, and it wasn't either of the Carlsons."

"Yeah. I've put the word out to all the hospitals. I asked the hospitals to check their records for anyone who came in with a cut that required stitches since the day of the murder. We'll have to wait and see what comes of it."

"Will you let me know?"

"Sure."

"One other thing. Did your people take Mrs. Carlson's computer?"

"Yes. We also took Carlson's computer and all the discs and CDs we could find. So far we have found nothing of interest on them, but we're not done looking at them," he said. "By the way, how did you know they were missing?"

"The usual way," I said with a grin to myself.

"That's what I thought. Since you were there, did you find anything of interest?"

"No, I didn't. I got a lead I'm going to try to follow up on this evening. I'll let you know how it works out."

"Okay. You be careful out there."

"Will do," I said then hung up.

I sat back to think for a moment before I reached over and picked up the phone book. I began looking for a phone number for Julie Mathews, the young receptionist at Mile High Design. I found her number, then wrote it down along with her address. A quick look at my watch told me that she would still be at work. It would probably be six or after before she would get home. It would take her maybe forty-five minutes to an hour during rush hour to get to Thornton, where she lived. That was no problem for me. I had someone else that I wanted to have a little talk with first.

I locked up my office and went to my car. I was going to head to the Lakewood Gun Shop in Centennial. It was probably a forty minute drive this time of day.

As I drove out of the underground parking garage of the building where I had my office, I noticed a dark blue BMW parked about a half block down the street on the other side. There was someone setting in the driver's seat, but with the glare on the windshield I couldn't see who it was. I had to chuckle when I saw it because I was sure that it was Rinehart. The BMW had a small dent in the left front fender. It was in the same place and about the same size as the one I had seen on Rinehart's car when he tried to tail me before.

If this was Rinehart, and I was sure it was, he had to be pretty stupid. He might have been pretty good at breaking bones and intimidating people, but at tailing someone he had a lot to learn. And I didn't want to be the one to teach him. The first thing he should learn was not to use a car that would stand out like an elephant in a china shop.

Since I didn't want him knowing where I was going, I would have to ditch him as soon as possible; but I didn't want him to know that he was being ditched. I had no idea how well he knew the Denver area and its back alleys, but I think I had read or heard some place that he was raised in the Denver area. The best way for me to ditch him would be for me to let him keep an eye on my car while I went off and did what I needed to do.

I turned out on the street and headed for the local library. I obeyed all the speed limits and all the traffic signs as I drove along as if I didn't have a care in the world, even if Rinehart was someone to worry about.

When I got to the library, I pulled into the parking lot and found a parking space. I parked my car and got out. As I did, I glanced over the top of my car to see where Rinehart had parked. He parked in a location that made it easy for him to see my car.

I smiled to myself as I turned and walked into the library. Since the library was large and covered several floors, it would be easy for me to ditch him inside the library if he decided to follow me inside. I went inside to an area where I could see out. I needed to know what he was going to do.

Rinehart did not get out of his car. It didn't surprise me. He probably didn't know his way around a library, especially one as big as the Denver Library. He would have no idea what I would be looking for in the library. As a result, he would have no idea what part of the library I would be in.

As soon as it was clear that he was going to sit in his car and watch my car, I left the library by the door on the other side of the building. Keeping the building between me and the parking lot, I walked a couple of blocks down Broadway to the Rent-A-Wreck car rental. It was one of those places that rents old cars by the day, week or month. I rented a Plymouth Aries and headed for the Lakewood Gun Shop.

Rinehart sat in his BMW about a half a block from the entrance to the underground parking garage in the building where Tidsdale's office was located. He had been there since shortly after noon waiting for Tidsdale to return from wherever he had been. He had been kicking himself for not staying with Tidsdale at the police station, but had finally seen him when he drove into the underground parking area less than an hour ago.

He had no idea how long he was going to have to wait before Tidsdale decided to leave again. The thing that was running through his mind was where had he been all morning. He had no idea that Tidsdale had been rummaging around in Carlson's house.

Sitting in his car, Rinehart had all the time in the world to think. He hated surveillance more than just about anything he did. It was usually long hours spent sitting around drinking coffee and most often resulting in finding out nothing, but it sometimes had to be done.

Just as he was about to take another sip of coffee, he saw Tidsdale's car come up out of the underground garage and stop for traffic. Rinehart wondered where he was off to now as he reached down and started his car. He was ready as soon as Tidsdale decided which way he was going to go. It seemed to him that Tidsdale was taking a long time trying to decide.

Suddenly Tidsdale's car pulled out on the street and headed away from him. Rinehart was glad of that as he would not have to make a U-turn in order to follow him.

Rinehart stayed a nice easy distance behind Tidsdale. All the time he was wondering where he was going, and who he was going to see. It pleased him when Tidsdale drove past the Police Station.

"At least he wasn't going there, again," Rinehart said to himself.

He couldn't believe how casually Tidsdale was driving. He didn't seem to be in any big hurry. Rinehart felt a little more comfortable when Tidsdale didn't turn down the side street that would have taken him to Carlson's house. Rinehart didn't know that he had already been there.

Rinehart was two cars behind Tidsdale when he stopped for a red light. He could see Tidsdale through the cars in front of him. He still had no idea where Tidsdale was going.

They went several more blocks, before Rinehart noticed that Tidsdale had turned on his turn signal and moved over into a turn lane. Rinehart looked around. The only thing he could see was the Denver Library. Rinehart turned on his turn signal and moved into the turn lane. There was now only one car between them. As soon as traffic had cleared enough, Tidsdale pulled across the oncoming lanes onto the street along side the library, then turned into the library parking lot.

As soon as the car immediately in front of Rinehart turned and the intersection was clear, he turned and followed Tidsdale into the library parking lot. He had seen Tidsdale park, so he pulled into a parking space closer to the entrance to the parking lot, but close enough to Tidsdale's car that he would be able to keep an eye on it.

Rinehart watched as Tidsdale left his car and walked into the library. He thought about following him into the library, but decided against it. It would be too easy for Tidsdale to spot him in the library. There were too many open spaces, plus he had no idea what part of the library Tidsdale would be in once he got inside.

As a result, Rinehart decided that the best thing for him to do was to sit in his car and keep an eye on Tidsdale's car. He knew it could be a long wait, but what choice did he have if he wanted to find out what Tidsdale was up to.

Rinehart tipped the seat back to make himself as comfortable as possible. He relaxed for what he was sure would be a long wait.

CHAPTER TWENTY-FIVE

It didn't take long for me to get to the Lakewood Gun Shop from the library, maybe twenty-five minutes. It was a nice looking gun shop with a large selection of weapons. There were at least four people working at the counters, but they were not the ones I wanted to talk to. I wanted to talk to the manager or owner. I walked up to one of the counters where there was a young man looking like he was waiting for a customer.

"May I help you, sir," he asked with a pleasant smile.

"Yes. I was wondering if the manager or owner is in?"

"Yes, the owner is in. Is there anything I can do to help you?"

"No. I don't think so. I'm investigating a murder, and I'm here to talk to him about one of his customers."

"Oh," he said as the look on his face quickly turned serious. "I'll get him for you."

"Thank you."

I took a minute to look around the shop while I waited for the owner. The shop was full of rifles, shotguns, and pistols in all different makes, models and calibers as well as almost any accessory that a hunter or target shooter could want. While I waited, I listened to one of the salesmen as he showed a young man a .357 magnum. The young man was in his mid-twenties and seemed to know a little about guns. The salesman was explaining that if he purchased the gun he would get five free lessons at their indoor range. He recommended that the young man take advantage of them as it was included with the purchase so the buyer could become comfortable with the new gun. That immediately caught my attention. I remembered seeing on the receipt I found in

Mrs. Carlson's desk that the purchase had included the lessons. I wondered if she had actually taken advantage of them.

My thoughts were disturbed when a tall man wearing kaki slacks and a blue polo shirt with the name of the gun shop in white over the left breast pocket came across the store toward me. The man was clean shaven and looked like a businessman.

"Yes, sir," he said. "How may I help you?"

"I'm Frank Tidsdale and I'm looking into the death of one of your customers."

"One of my customers?"

"Yes."

"You're not with the news media, are you? Not that I would expect you to tell me the truth if you were."

"I am not with the news media. I'm a private investigator working for an attorney," I said as I reached in my sport coat pocket and got out my ID.

I showed him my private investigator's license and my concealed weapon's permit. He looked at it, then looked up at me.

"What kind of a weapon do you carry, Mr. Tidsdale?"

"I carry a 9 mm most of the time."

"Nice gun. What do you carry for a backup?"

"A .38 caliber with midrange load wad cutters."

"I would think that would be a good choice for someone in your line of work. Now, how may I help you?"

"One of your staff sold a .25 caliber auto to a Mrs. Jennifer Carlson along with five lessons at your indoor range. I would like to speak to that salesperson, please."

"As a matter of fact, I sold Mrs. Carlson the gun. It was all on the up and up, I assure you."

"I'm sure it was," I said with a smile. "I'm not here to look into your sales practices. You may have read in the paper that Mrs. Carlson was murdered."

"I didn't see it. I'm sorry to hear that. What happened?"

"We don't have all the details yet. What we do know is that she was not killed with the gun she purchased from you. What I am interested in knowing was did she give you any indication as to why she wanted the gun?"

"Not in so many words. All she said to me was that she felt that she should have some protection in the house as there had been several break-ins in her neighborhood. Now that's what she said, but I got the impression that there was more to it than that."

"How so?"

"I can't say for sure, but she seemed especially nervous when she purchased the gun. When I asked her about it, she said it was because she was not very familiar with guns. But when she was handed the gun, she immediately checked it to make sure it was not loaded. She took hold of it like someone who had handled guns before."

"One other thing. Did she take you up on the free lessons?" I asked.

"She only came twice. I have instructors that help people get familiar with their new gun and how to handle it safely. The instructor that helped her told me after her first lesson that she handled and shot the gun as if she knew how to shoot. He also said that she was "a darn good shot", as he put it. He said he had never seen a first timer so at ease with a new gun. He said he was sure that she had handled guns before."

"She never came back for any other lessons?"

"No. In fact, I've never seen her since. I can check with the staff to see if any of them have seen her."

"I don't think that will be necessary. Thanks for your help." I said as I stuck out my hand.

"Come by anytime," he said as he shook my hand. "When you're ready for a new firearm, we hope you will think of us."

"I will, and thanks."

I turned and left the Lakewood Gun Shop. I got in my rental car and drove back to the Rent-A-Wreck rental lot and turned in the car, then headed back to the library. I had no idea if Rinehart would still be there or not, but it didn't matter. The only thing I was concerned about was that he didn't follow me to my next stop in Thornton.

Rinehart sat in his car watching Tidsdale's car. Every once in a while he would look over at the library and wonder what Tidsdale was doing in there that was taking him so long. Time passed slowly for Rinehart. He was beginning to think about calling it a day. He had been there for well over an hour, and he was getting tired of sitting in his car. He even thought about going inside to make sure that Tidsdale had not slipped out of the library.

The more he thought about it, the more he began to think that Tidsdale had given him the slip. He grew angry at the thought that some two-bit PI could give him the slip so easily. Yet, he was pretty sure that he wasn't dealing with a two-bit PI. He knew that Tidsdale had been a cop for about ten years before he became a PI. Tidsdale was probably as professional a PI as any in the Denver area. Rinehart also knew that he was going to have to use his head if he was going to keep tabs on him.

But right now, he needed to know where Tidsdale was. He decided that he would go into the library and act as if he was there to do some kind of research while he was actually looking for Tidsdale. That way if Tidsdale saw him, he could even speak to him without causing any suspicion.

Rinehart got out of his car and started for the library entrance. Just as he pulled open the door to go inside, he saw Tidsdale walking toward the door. It was clear that Tidsdale had already seen him so there was no sense in trying to hide that fact. It pissed him off a little that he had not had more patience in waiting for Tidsdale to come out. If he had waited just five more minutes, he was sure that Tidsdale never would have known he was there.

"Well, Tidsdale, I see you use the library for research, too," he said with a smile that he really didn't mean.

"On occasion. It becomes a rather handy place when you need information on a particular company," Tidsdale said as he stopped.

"What company?"

"What do you care? It could be the company you work for, then again it might not be," Tidsdale said with a grin, then left the building.

Rinehart slowly turned and watched as Tidsdale walked out of the library and across the parking lot to his car. He couldn't say for sure, but he had a feeling that Tidsdale had known all along that he was being followed. It would not do any good for him to hurry out to his car so that he could follow him. If he didn't know he was being followed before, he would now. It was time to return to his office and regroup.

As he drove back to his office, Rinehart thought about Tidsdale and how he had been made to look like a fool. He didn't like that one bit. It was time for him to take a more drastic approach to get Tidsdale off the case before he came up with something. He couldn't help but think that a good beating would go a long way toward getting Tidsdale to back off, and for him to get even for being made to look like a fool. He would want to get Tidsdale someplace very private so he could work him over real good without being disturbed. It would take some time to work it out.

CHAPTER TWENTY-SIX

I took the Interstate over to Thornton. There was no one following me as far as I could tell. I certainly didn't see the BMW. If Rinehart was smart, he would find himself a different, less conspicuous, car to use when tailing someone. But I had my doubts that Rinehart would think to make such a change. He was too full of himself to even think of getting a more common looking car, at least when he wanted to tail someone. Even though I was sure of my assessment of him, I still continued to watch for anyone in any kind of vehicle that might be following me.

It was getting on toward supper time and I still had a little time before Miss Mathews would most likely get home from work. I pulled into a convenience store and parked off to the side. I was in a location where I could see anyone coming or going from the store. I got out of the car and went inside and got a cup of coffee, then returned to the car to wait until I was reasonably sure that Miss Mathews would have gotten home.

As I sat in my car watching what was going on at the intersection, I thought about what I had been told by the owner of the Lakewood Gun Shop. I wondered why Mrs. Carlson had acted like she had not handled a gun before when it was obvious that she had. I knew there no telling why some people do what they do, but in their own mind there was always a reason. One thing was for sure, and that was she had never gotten a chance to use the gun on her assailant.

That brought to mind the blood in the entry way and on the stairs. Had she answered the door with a knife in her hand? If she did, why did she have the knife in her hand in the first place? Was she starting to fix something to eat when someone came to the door? Had she tried to defend herself with what she had, namely the knife? If she had been successful at cutting her attacker, who was it. There were still a lot of unanswered questions about what actually happened in the Carlson house.

I took a deep breath, then glanced at my watch. It told me that I might be able to get hold of Miss Mathews about now. It was a couple of minutes after six. I took her number out of my pocket and dialed it on my cell phone. The phone was answered almost immediately.

"Hello."

"Hello. Is this Julie Mathews?" I asked.

"Yes. Is this - - -," she started to ask, but I cut her off."

"Yes. No names please. Can you get away?"

"Yes."

"Good. Would you be willing to meet me in person?"

"Well, I - - - ah."

"It will be at a very public place, I assure you."

"Okay," she said nervously.

"I want you to leave this very minute and go directly to the Black Eyed Pea Restaurant at the I-25 exit to highway 44 in Thornton."

"Okay," she replied, then I hung up.

I drove across the street to the parking lot of the Black Eyed Pea Restaurant and parked my car where I could see anyone driving into the parking lot, then I waited. I knew it wouldn't take her long to get to the restaurant from where she lived if she left right away. It was less then ten minutes when I saw her drive into the parking lot. She must have done as I told her and left immediately.

As she parked her car, I got out of mine and began walking toward her. I didn't know if she would be followed, but I didn't want to take any unnecessary chances. I watched her get out of her car and walk toward the front door to the restaurant. I followed her in. While she stood waiting for the hostess to seat her, I walked up beside her.

"Good evening, Miss Mathews," I said quietly in the hope of not startling her.

She turned sharply, looked up at me, then took a deep breath. My attempt to not startle her had apparently failed.

"I'm sorry," I said. "I didn't mean to scare you like that."

Just then the hostess showed up.

"Two?" she asked with a smile.

"Yes. Would it be possible to have a booth away from the incoming traffic?" I asked.

"Certainly," she said with a smile. "Right this way."

Julie and I followed the hostess to a booth. I could tell by the look on the hostess's face that she thought Julie and I were involved. The booth the hostess led us to was located along a wall near the corner of the room. The window looked out over the parking lot. We were seated and given menus, then the hostess left. Where I was sitting, I could see most of the parking lot and anyone who came into the restaurant.

"I'm sorry that we have to meet like this, but I got the impression that you wanted to talk to me when I paid a visit to Wilbur Steinman. Am I correct in that belief?"

"Yes," she said softly as if she was afraid to say anything.

"I had already been told that the employees of Mile High Design would not be allowed to speak to me. I take it you were told not to speak to me?"

"Yes."

"I thought so. I didn't want to get you in trouble by talking to you where anyone from Mile High Design would see us."

"After you had been there, we were told by our supervisor that we were not to speak to anyone about Mrs. Carlson. They mentioned you as one that we were not to talk to. They made it clear that if we did we would be immediately fired. They also told us not to talk to the police without one of their attorneys present."

Just then the waitress showed up. We gave her our order, then waited for her to leave.

"Well, it seems that I rattled someone's cage by my visit to Mile High Design."

"What do you mean?"

"You know that Mrs. Carlson was murdered, right?"

"Yes."

"What have you been told about her death?"

"We were told that she was murdered by her husband during a violent domestic argument. The newspaper reports of her death didn't come out and say that, but they hinted at it."

"I take it you're not buying that story?" I asked.

Just then our meals arrived. We leaned back while the waitress set our meals on the table in front of us. I couldn't help but think that Miss Mathews was very concerned about what had happened to Mrs. Carlson, but wasn't sure what she should say.

"Is there anything else I can get for you?" the waitress asked.

I looked across the table at Julie, then looked up at the waitress and smiled.

"I don't think so. Thank you," I said, then watched her walk away.

I turned back and looked at Julie. She was looking down at her meal. I got the feeling that she might not be very hungry right now. It was easy for me to understand. The talk of murder at the dinner table does tend to take away one's appetite.

"You should probably eat some of it," I said. "What you don't feel like eating now, you can take home to eat later if you wish."

She smiled at me, then said, "I don't know how many people in Mile High Design knew Mr. Carlson, but I don't believe he could hurt a fly, much less kill his wife. He's a very gentle man."

"What can you tell me about Mrs. Carlson?"

"She was a hard worker, nice to everyone, and was always in a good mood. That is until the last week or so."

"What happened?"

"I don't know, but she became quiet and reserved. Hardly talked to anyone unless it was necessary, and she always seemed suspicious of everyone. She was jumpy, too."

"You have no idea why?"

"No. She never talked to me about it. I tried to get her to talk to me about it once, but she said it was better if I didn't know."

"What do you think she meant by that?"

"I don't know, but it kind of scared me a little."

I leaned back to think about what she was saying. Something happened that caused the sudden change in her. What was it? Of course, that was the number one question and I couldn't answer it. There had to be something or someone somewhere that would give me the answer.

Neither one of us did a very good job of finishing our meal. She was afraid, and I was deep in thought about what was really going on.

I made some ridiculous excuse to the waitress for not finishing our meal, paid the bill and walked Julie to her car. After I made sure that she was secure in her car, I stood back and watched her as she drove out of the parking lot.

I then went to my car, got in and left the parking lot. As I turned out onto the street, I wondered if it might be prudent to at least follow her home. I had a feeling that if anyone had seen us talking, she could be in danger.

I caught up with her at the next intersection and followed her to her apartment building. I watched as she parked her car and went into the building. I sat in my car and waited to make sure that she got in without difficulty. Once she was in her apartment, she waved at me from the window so that I knew she was safe inside. I took a few minutes to look around. There didn't seem to be anything out of place or anyone watching the building, so I left and drove home.

While Rinehart was in his office, he got a call from Steinman. Steinman told Rinehart that his personal secretary had told him that Julie Mathews had appeared to be nervous all afternoon, and was especially so just before she left work. Steinman suggested that he have a talk with Julie to make sure that she didn't talk to anyone and Rinehart agreed.

Rinehart arrived in the parking lot where Julie Mathews's apartment was located at about six-thirty. He parked off in a corner of the lot where his car would be hard to see. It didn't take him long to find out which apartment belonged to Miss Mathews. He knocked on the door and waited, but there was no answer. Rinehart knocked again, and again there was no answer.

After looking around to make sure there was no one in the hall to see him, he reached into his inside coat pocket for his lock picks. Looking around again to make sure there was still no one around to see him, he quickly picked the lock and let himself into her apartment.

Once inside, he took a pair of surgical gloves from his pocket and put them on. He looked around the apartment. There was still enough evening light coming in the living room window to allow him to see without turning on a light.

The apartment was furnished with medium priced furniture. There was a television that was not real new, a brown sofa and two green chairs. There was a cheap coffee table and one end table, a floor lamp and one table lamp. It looked like it had been furnished with either used furniture, or with furniture she had gotten from her family. It was obvious that Miss Mathews did not have a lot of money.

Rinehart went through the two bedroom apartment. In the first bedroom was a bedroom set including a single bed, a dresser, a dressing table and a bedside table with a lamp.

There were a lot of family pictures on top of the dresser. The walls were decorated with things that one was most likely to find in a schoolgirl's room, but that made sense to Rinehart. He knew from the company's records that Julie Mathews's job as a receptionist at Mile High Design was her first job after she finished a secretarial course at a junior college out in the plains of eastern Colorado.

He checked out the other rooms in the apartment. It was quickly becoming clear that she lived in the apartment by herself, and that she had not lived there very long. He knew that from the bulletin board in the break room where Julie had posted a note asking for someone to share the apartment along with expenses, like rent and utilities.

Rinehart had no idea where Miss Mathews was at the moment or when she would be returning. Since she lived alone, he decided that he would wait for her. He had checked out the small deck off the dining area. If she came home with someone, he could make his escape out that way. It was now time to wait for her to come home.

It was starting to get dark before he saw Miss Mathews drive into the parking lot. He was glad that the parking lot was well lit. He also noticed that she had been followed by a car that was familiar to him. It was Frank Tidsdale's car. He watched as Miss Mathews parked her car. It was a relief to see that Tidsdale had simply stopped and watched her enter the building. He didn't get out of his car and follow her in.

Rinehart quickly moved to the bathroom and stood behind the open door where he could see part of the living room. She would also have to walk past the bathroom to get to her bedroom. He could hear the front door being unlocked, opened, then closed and locked again.

Julie walked across the living room to where the floor lamp stood. She turned on the light then walked over to the large front window. She looked down at the parking lot and waved to Tidsdale. Tidsdale flashed his headlights to let her know that he had seen her. She smiled as she pulled the drapes shut.

Although Frank Tidsdale was probably fifteen years her senior, she thought that he had been very nice to her. Having dinner with him had been more like a date, even if they did talk about the death of Mrs. Carlson. But, then she hadn't had very many dates in her young life.

Julie headed for her bedroom with the idea of getting into something comfortable for spending a quiet evening alone with a good book. But that was not to be.

Just after she passed the door to the bathroom, Rinehart quickly stepped out and grabbed her from behind. He put one hand over her mouth while wrapping his arm around her narrow waist. She struggled, but only for a couple of seconds. Rinehart was much too strong for her.

"I see that you talked to Tidsdale after you were told not to," he whispered in her ear. "You shouldn't have done that."

She tried to talk to him, to tell him that she didn't tell him anything, but he would not take his hand off her mouth.

With his arm still around her and his hand over her mouth, he picked her up and carried her into her bedroom. Her feet were dangling only inches above the floor all the way into the bedroom.

Once in the bedroom, he pushed her face down on the bed then fell down over her forcing her face into the thick comforter. Taking his hand off her mouth, he placed it on the back of her head and pushed down hard. He held her down against the covers as he slowly suffocated her.

At first she struggled for a breath of air, but before long she stopped moving. He continued to hold her down after she stopped moving to make sure that she was not going to suddenly come around and scream.

When he felt that she was dead, Rinehart got off her and stood beside the bed looking down at her. There were no *signs of life in her. He then rolled her over on her back and checked for a pulse. There was none. She was dead.*

He looked around the room then went to her closet where he found a flannel nightgown with flowers on it. He took the flannel nightgown and laid it on the bed. Rinehart undressed her and put the flannel nightgown on her. He then placed her in the bed and covered her with the comforter. When he was done, he looked at her. She looked so at peace. She looked as if she was sleeping, except for the fact that her eyes were open. He reached down and closed her eyelids.

When he was satisfied that he had not left any trace of his presence, he left the apartment, wiping off the doorknob and lock before leaving the building. He got in his car and drove back to downtown Denver to his office.

CHAPTER TWENTY-SEVEN

It had been a long day and I was tired. I sat down in front of the television to catch a little of the local news before I hit the sack. There was nothing special on. It seemed that the news was just a repeat of last night's news, and the night before that, and the night before that and so on. The only things that seemed to change were the names and places. Even the weather report hadn't changed much.

I was about to call it a night and get some sleep when my phone began to ring. I thought about letting my answering machine take the call, but I was kind of hoping that Jackie would call to say "goodnight". I reached over and picked up the phone.

"Hello."

"Frank?"

"Yeah."

"This is Donald, Donald Wright."

"What's up, Don?"

"Do you know a Julie Mathews?"

"Sure. I was with her tonight for dinner. Why? What's your interest in her?"

"She was found dead in her apartment this evening by the Thornton police. I recognized her name from the list of employees at Mile High Design when it came over the wire."

"Damn. I knew I should have taken her to a safe place tonight."

"What's that mean?

"It means that she talked to me about Mrs. Carlson. The employees of Mile High Design were told not to talk to me, or the police, under a threat of being fired."

"Do you think that her death has anything to do with Mrs. Carlson's?" Don asked.

"I believe it does. The only problem I have is that I can't prove it."

"You want to let me in on what you believe? I might have some ideas on how we can prove it."

"Sure."

I spent the next few minutes telling him about my meeting and dinner with her. Since I had not found out anything that I thought would help him figure out who had killed Mrs. Carlson, there wasn't much I could tell him that would be of help in his investigation. The gag order imposed on the employees of Mile High Design by Steinman gave me reason to believe that they had something to hide. Don seemed to agree.

I also told him about Rinehart following me earlier in the day and my ditching him. I also told him about my visit to the Lakewood Gun Shop.

"Do you think Steinman has something to do with both of the murders?" Don asked.

"To be honest, I can't say. He might, but then he might not. The orders for the hits might have come from Steinman, or from Sargossa. My problem is I can't find anything concrete that connects Sargossa to Mile High Design except for Rinehart. Even that connection is pretty thin."

"I have to agree. Anything else you can tell me?"

"No. How was Julie killed?"

"It appears that she was suffocated, probably in her sleep since she was wearing a nightgown. I'll know more after an autopsy and the forensic guys get done."

"Will you let me know what they find out?"

"Sure, as soon as the Thornton Police get their reports to me. They promised to send me copies."

"How was it that the Thornton Police found her so quickly after I left her?"

"They got a call from one of her neighbors. He had heard that she wanted to find someone to share her apartment and expenses and went to talk to her about it. When she didn't answer the door and he saw her car in the lot, he got concerned and called the police.

"Thanks for calling," I said.

"No problem. If you think of anything else, give me a call."

"I will," I said, then hung up.

I leaned back in the chair and began to think about a nice young woman, who had probably never hurt anyone in her whole life, having her life snuffed out when she was just starting to live. It made me angry, but I had no one to take my anger out on. The more I thought about it, the more I was convinced that Rinehart had something to do with it. I just couldn't prove it, yet.

At that moment, I made the decision to find out who had murdered Julie and why. And, if there was a connection between Julie's death and the death of Mrs. Carlson, I was going to find it come hell or high water. I was convinced that there was a connection; I just didn't know what the connection was. All I had to do now was to prove what I already believed. And that job would start first thing in the morning.

Once Rinehart was back in his office, he picked up the phone and dialed the number for Mr. Sargossa at his home. The phone was immediately answered.

"Yeah," a heavy male voice said.

"Rinehart. I need to talk to Mr. Sargossa, please."

"One minute. I'll tell him you're on the phone."

Rinehart waited for several minutes before Mr. Sargossa came on the line.

"Jacob, my boy. Do we have a problem?"

"I'm not sure, but we could have."

"What happened?"

"It would appear that one of the Mile High Design employees has been talking with Mr. Tidsdale. He had followed her home and waited outside her apartment to make sure that she got home safely. She waved at him from her apartment window, then he flashed his headlights and drove off."

"That's what makes you think she talked to him?"

"Yeah. Why else would he see her home safely?"

"I see your point. Who was the girl?"

"Julie Mathews. She worked as a receptionist in the entrance to Mile High Design," Rinehart replied.

"What makes you think that a lowly receptionist would know anything that would interest Mr. Tidsdale?"

"I've heard rumors that she was a good friend of Mrs. Carlson. They often went out to lunch together and took coffee breaks together. I can only assume that they talked about work from time to time."

"I see where that could be a problem. I take it you have taken care of the problem?"

"I have, sir."

"Good," Sargossa said.

"What do you want me to do about Tidsdale?"

"I think it would be a good idea if you were to use your special talents to convince him to drop his investigation and forget about the receptionist and Mrs. Carlson," Sargossa said.

"I don't think it will work. He has a lot of friends on the police force."

"Killing him could prove to be a bigger problem, as you so clearly pointed out on our last visit. Have a talk with him and stress the importance of his dropping this case and dropping it quickly. If he is smart he will drop it."

"What if he won't?"

"If he shows any signs at all that he has not given up on it, then you have my permission to kill him. But do it in such a way that makes it look like an accident. I don't want anything to happen to him that would make it look like he was killed to get him to drop the case. Do I make myself clear?"

"Yes, sir," Rinehart said just before the phone went dead.

Rinehart tipped back in his desk chair to think about what he had been told. It was time to get Tidsdale's attention. He had planned to catch Tidsdale somewhere private and work him over. He felt that Tidsdale's apartment might not prove to be a very good place. There was too much of a chance of a neighbor hearing it and calling the cops. He had the same feeling about Tidsdale's office, unless he could catch him there at night when the offices near his would be empty. That meant only one thing. He would have to follow Tidsdale until the opportunity presented itself. He would start following Tidsdale first thing in the morning so he could get some idea of what his routine was like.

For now, Rinehart decided that he would go home and get some rest. It could take him a while to figure out where and when to confront Tidsdale.

CHAPTER TWENTY-EIGHT

Morning came with the crash of thunder and the sound of rain pelting my window. It woke me up at least an hour before I had planned to get up, but I knew that I would not go back to sleep. There was no sense in lying there watching the lightening and listening to the rain when I had some things I wanted to do.

I got up and took a shower, dressed, then sat down for breakfast which consisted of a toasted bagel with peanut butter on it and a cup of coffee. After breakfast, I drove to my office. Once there, I sat down and went over my mail. There was nothing that I needed to take care of immediately. In fact, most of it was junk and ended up in the trash.

I decided that Mr. Moore would probably be in his office, so I gave him a call to let him know what progress I had made to date, which seemed like very little. The phone rang a couple of times before it was answered by one of the secretaries. She immediately transferred my call to Mr. Moore.

"Good morning, Mr. Tidsdale."

"Good morning, Mr. Moore. I'm calling in to give you a progress report."

"Good. What do you have to report?"

"I won't waste your time with telling you about the lab reports and the ballistics report as I'm sure you've already seen them."

"I have."

"I found a receipt that shows where Mrs. Carlson purchased a .25 caliber pistol from a gun shop in Centennial about a week before she was murdered. If you have seen the ballistics report on the gun Carlson had in his hand when he was arrested, you know that the .25 caliber pistol that Carlson had was not the murder weapon."

"I do know that."

"I found out something that I didn't expect to find in talking to the owner of the gun shop where the gun was purchased. He told me that Mrs. Carlson handled the gun like she knew how to use one. Has Carlson had anything to say about Mrs. Carlson's ability to handle a gun? I know he said that neither of them owned a gun, but we now know that was not true."

"No. He hasn't said anything about Mrs. Carlson's ability to handle a gun. As for Mrs. Carlson owning a gun, he has stated flatly that neither of them own a gun, and stands by it. I would have to assume that he didn't know about her purchasing a gun."

"That's certainly possible. Next time you talk to him, see if you can find out if she knew how to handle a gun and where she might have learned."

"I'll be seeing him this afternoon and I'll ask him. The lab and ballistics reports leave a great deal of doubt about his guilt. I'm working on a motion to have the judge release Jim from jail based on the fact that the evidence did not support the arrest warrant in the first place."

"Might I make a suggestion?"

"Certainly. You are a part of his defense team. What's on your mind?"

"Hold off on getting him out of jail."

"Why's that?" Moore asked, sounding surprised by my request.

"One of the receptionists for Mile High Design was murdered last night."

"I'm sorry to hear that, but what does that have to do with Mrs. Carlson's murder?" Moore asked.

"To be honest, I don't know. What I do know is that I have been asked to drop the investigation by a man that has connections not only with Mile High Design, but with the

Sargossa crime family. The girl was killed after she had talked with me about Mrs. Carlson."

"What are this man's connections to Mile High Design?"

"He is the head of security for them. He's also a bone breaker for Sargossa."

"I see." Moore said.

There was a long few minutes of silence before Moore spoke again. I got the impression that what I had said caught him off guard, and he needed a minute to digest it.

"Do I understand that you are saying Mile High Design is in bed with the Sargossa crime family?"

"It's beginning to look that way. If what I think is true, Mrs. Carlson might have found out something that she wasn't supposed to know. That may have been what got her killed."

"What do you think she found out?"

"That's my problem, I don't know. The young woman that I talked to wasn't able to tell me. What she did say was the Mrs. Carlson went from being a very open and friendly person to a scared, quiet woman almost overnight."

"I see, but why do you want me to keep Jim in jail?"

"I have two trains of thought on that. Either one, I think, puts him in danger of being murdered, too."

"So what you are saying is that you want to keep him in jail for his own protection?"

"At least until I can find out what is going on, and why his wife was murdered."

"How long do you think it will take you to find out?"

"I don't know. So far I can't prove anything." I said.

"That doesn't give me anything concrete to tell Jim."

"I know, but maybe you could make up some excuse. You could tell him something like – ah - the judge would not be available to hear your motion for a couple of days," I suggested. "You lawyers can always come up with some song and dance to delay things. Use your imagination. Be creative."

"I'll do my best," he said with a slight chuckle. "He doesn't know that I was planning on visiting him this afternoon. I guess I could wait a day or so before I go see him."

"Good. That should give you plenty of time to think of something."

"What's your next move?"

"You don't want to know," I said.

"I understand," Moore said then immediately hung up the phone.

I smiled to myself as I thought about what must be going through his mind about now. I'm sure he was convinced that whatever I had planned would probably be something illegal. It would be best if he had no knowledge of what I was planning.

I was about ready to leave my office when my phone began to ring. I reached over and picked it up.

"Tidsdale Investigative Agency."

"Franky?"

"Yeah," I said with a smile, knowing immediately who it was.

"Can you talk?"

"Sure."

"I got that information you wanted."

"Good. What have you got for me?"

"Rinehart is on Sargossa's payroll."

"Are you sure?"

"Yeah. He's also on Mile High Design's payroll. From what my sources tell me, Rinehart's real job is to keep an eye on Sargossa's interest in Mile High Design. One of my sources says that Steinman owes Sargossa a lot of money, and he's paying it back by having Sargossa's construction companies build the new city buildings."

"Any idea why Steinman owes Sargossa money?"

"It seems that Steinman likes to gamble, but he isn't very good at it. He made the mistake of gambling in one of Sargossa's secret clubs and lost a lot of money. Some of it not his own."

"What do you mean "not his own"?"

"The word is that some of the money belongs to the company. You know, Mile High Design."

"It's Steinman's company. How can that be a problem?"

"Steinman doesn't own the company. It's owned by a corporation out of San Francisco."

"So he's been embezzling money from Mile High Design to pay for his gambling?"

"That's the word."

"Any idea where this club is located?" I asked.

"It's actually in a private home in the hills above the city. It's by invitation only."

"I would think. I wonder why Steinman was invited to gamble there?"

"You can bet it was so Sargossa could get their hooks in him."

"I'm sure you're right. Anything else for me?"

"Not right now, but I'll keep nosing around. If I come up with anything, I'll call again."

"You take care out there," I said.

"I will, but you better be watching your back. Rumor has it that Rinehart has been looking to get you to drop your investigation."

"It's no rumor. He's already asked me to drop it."

"Does he know that you haven't?"

"I'm not sure, but I would think so."

"Well, watch your back. If I know him, he will be looking for a chance to work you over.

"I'm sure you're right, but it won't work," I said.

"If it doesn't, he'll be looking to kill you."

"Thanks for the warning. I'll keep my eyes open."

"If I hear anything else, I'll get in touch."

"Thanks," I said, then the phone when dead.

I spent the next few minutes thinking about what my friend had said. Rinehart was no amateur. He was in good physical condition and was good with his hands. The one thing I didn't know was how good he was with a gun. I knew he carried a pretty good sized caliber gun, but that didn't mean that he knew how to use it. The size of a gun has no relationship to the shooter's ability to use it. In any case, I would have to be alert all the time.

With the new information, I decided that it might be time to pay another visit to Steinman. If I presented him with what I knew, he probably wouldn't talk to me; but he might get scared enough to make a mistake.

I went down to the underground garage and got in my car to go to the Hammond Building.

Rinehart got up early in the morning and left for the building that Tidsdale's office was in. On his way, he stopped for a couple of doughnuts and a large cup of coffee. There was little doubt in his mind that he would be there for a very long time. He drove into the parking area under the building, and looked around until he found a parking space where he could see both the entrance to the parking garage and the elevator to the offices in the building.

He hadn't been there very long before Tidsdale showed up. He watched as Tidsdale parked in his reserved parking space and got out of his car. It was quiet in the parking garage at that early hour. Rinehart thought about having a little heart to heart with Tidsdale now, but was afraid that someone else who worked in the building might come to work early and see him working Tidsdale over. If he wanted to make sure that no one saw him, he would have to wait for a more opportune time.

It seemed that the longer he waited, the more he wanted to beat up Tidsdale. He knew that he would have to work Tidsdale over pretty good if he was going to get him to back off. And then there was some doubt that it would even work.

Rinehart sat in his car eating doughnuts and drinking coffee for what seemed like forever. But it was only an hour or so before he saw Tidsdale come out of the elevator. He watched as Tidsdale walked to his car and got in. Rinehart wondered where he was off to now.

CHAPTER TWENTY-NINE

As I pulled to the corner after driving out of the garage, I saw in my rearview mirror that same dark blue BMW that had been tailing me the last time I had come out of the garage. I sat waiting near the exit to the garage until the light in front of me turned green. When I pulled away from the light, the BMW pulled out onto the street and stayed a couple of cars behind me. I smiled to myself thinking that Rinehart was at it again. He still hadn't learned to get rid of that fancy car when he was going to tail someone.

As I drove toward the Hammond Building where Mile High Design was located, I thought about losing Rinehart in the traffic. I didn't really want him to follow me to Mile High Design. But after thinking about it for a moment or two, I decided against ditching him. I would let him follow me, but instead of going to Mile High Design, I would go to Carlson's office and see what I could find there that might be of interest. I could always pay a visit to Steinman some other time when Rinehart was not on my tail.

There was a strong possibility that he would go to Mile High Design to make sure that Steinman didn't talk to me. If he did, he would quickly find out that I had not gone there. If that occurred, he might go to Carlson's office looking for me. Rinehart may not be the best at tailing someone, but he was not stupid. He would know that since I was representing Carlson that the next most likely place for me to go in that same building would be Carlson's office. Rinehart would expect me to go there to see if I could find some evidence that might point to Carlson being involved in his wife's death, or for something that would indicate that he was not

involved in her death. Either way, it would look normal to
him.

I had planned to pay a visit to Carlson's office anyway.
I just hadn't gotten around to it. It struck me as a good time
to take a look around. I had no reason to think that Carlson
had anything to do with Mrs. Carlson's death, but there were
a few unanswered questions floating around in my head that
needed answers. A look in Carlson's office might get me an
answer to one or two of them.

When I arrived at the Hammond building, I pulled
around the corner and parked in front of the building. I got
out of my car and went inside. Glancing back over my
shoulder, I saw Rinehart drive by the front of the building
and turn at the next corner. It was my guess that he was
going around to park in the underground garage where he
could park and get to the elevator that would take him to the
top floor quickly.

I went to the elevators and was able to get one right
away. I punched the button that would take the elevator to
the floor where Carlson's office was located, then the button
that would take it on up to the top floor.

As the elevator started to rise, I thought about Carlson.
It had crossed my mind again that Carlson might have had
something to do with his wife's murder, but I didn't know
what. If he didn't, did he know why she was murdered? I
had no answer to that question, but if I was lucky I might
find something in his office that would answer it, or at least
lead me in the right direction.

When the elevator stopped on the floor that Carlson's
office was on, I got off. I then reached around and pressed
the button to close the door quickly so the elevator would
continue to go up. As soon as the door closed, I turned and
went down the hall to Carlson's office.

Rinehart reached down and turned the ignition to start his car as he watched Tidsdale drive out onto the street. Giving Tidsdale a little more room than he had in the past, he followed him out of the garage. Rinehart had no idea where he was going, but he would stick to him like glue.

He followed Tidsdale until he turned the corner in front of the Hammond building where Mile High Design was located. Rinehart stopped at the corner and watched as Tidsdale parked his car. It crossed Rinehart's mind that he was going to pay Steinman another visit. He wondered if Tidsdale had anything on Steinman at that moment.

As soon as Tidsdale went into the building, Rinehart drove around to the underground garage where he parked his car. He hurried to the elevator, pressed the call button and waited for it. It seemed to take forever. Once it arrived, he got in and pressed the button for the top floor. When the door didn't immediately close, he pressed the button several more times before the door began to close. He felt the need to get to Steinman before he had time to say anything to Tidsdale.

Rinehart arrived on the top floor of the building and stepped off the elevator. He looked at the woman at the reception desk. She was looking at him as if she was surprised to see him.

"May I help you, Mr. Rinehart?"

"Has anyone come up here in the past five minutes or so?"

"No," she replied, but wondered why he seemed so excited.

"You're sure?"

"Yes. I'm sure. I have been here every minute for the past thirty minutes or more. No one has gotten off the elevator during that time."

Rinehart looked around then looked back at the woman. His mind was racing to figure out where Tidsdale had gone if he had not come here. Had Tidsdale known he was being followed and simply come in the building and waited for him to go by, then left again? Was it possible that he had gone to Carlson's office? It was possible, he thought, but what would he want from there?

It took Rinehart a few minutes to think about the past few days. He had to wonder if Tidsdale knew he was following him. How would he have known?

"Damn," he said as the thought of his car being the reason Tidsdale knew where he was passed through his mind.

"Pardon me, Mr. Rinehart. Did you say something?"

He glared at the woman, then turned on his heels and left without responding to her question. He hurried into the elevator and pressed the button for the garage.

When he got to the garage, he got in his car and drove to the exit. He was sure that Tidsdale had managed to ditch him. Stopping at the exit to the underground garage, he looked both ways in an effort to figure out where Tidsdale had gone. Unable to come up with where he might have gone, Rinehart decided that he would drive around the block and see if Tidsdale's car was still parked out in front. If it was, then he had probably gone to Carlson's office. If it wasn't, Rinehart had no idea where he might have gone. Either way, Rinehart had figured out that Tidsdale was able to tell he was being followed at every move. He also figured it was probably due to his BMW. Rinehart decided that he would go rent a less conspicuous car, then go to Tidsdale's office and park in the garage to wait for him to return.

Rinehart turned the corner and headed for a place where he had rented cars before. As he drove by the front of the building, he saw Tidsdale's car still parked there. It was a little satisfying to know that Tidsdale had gone to Carlson's office. At least, he had not ditched him.

He knew the owner of a car rental place not very far from the Hammond Building. It was a place where he could rent a less conspicuous car quickly and return to the Hammond Building in a very short time. He would also be able to leave his car there while he followed Tidsdale.

CHAPTER THIRTY

Since I didn't have a key to Carlson's office, I looked around to see if the hall was clear. It was, so I simply picked the lock using my lock picks. Once inside, I closed and locked the door.

I stood just inside the room and looked around. There didn't seem to be anything out of place. I couldn't help but think that Carlson was a neat freak. Everything had a place and everything seemed to be in its place, at least as far as I could tell.

The office was fair sized, but not what one would call large. I was sure he didn't need a real big office. He probably met with most of his clients at their place of business. There was a good sized desk with a very up-to-date adding machine on the corner of it. Behind the desk was a large computer desk with bookshelves above it. There was a computer, a printer, a large monitor, and stacks of CDs.

There was a table with six chairs around it that looked comfortable. There was a smaller adding machine at one end of the table. Carlson would probably sit where the adding machine was when his clients came to him. The one thing that I didn't see was file cabinets. I had never been in an accountant's office that didn't have a zillion file cabinets neatly lined up against at least one wall of the office. I had to wonder if Carlson kept all his records for his clients on CDs.

I did notice a door on one wall. It seemed like I may have been a little too quick to make a judgment. I went over to the door and found it locked. I picked the lock and went into the room. It was lined with file cabinets along every wall except for where the windows were located. Each file cabinet was clearly marked, except for one. It had no markings at all. Every file cabinet had a lock and they were all locked. It was clear to me that it would take a long time to pick the lock on every file cabinet and go through each and every one of them. I had no idea if it would provide any information that would help in my search for who killed Mrs. Carlson, but it might.

At this point, I was willing to spend whatever time it took to find something that would help me figure out who killed Mrs. Carlson and why. Although I had plenty of suspicions, I had no proof.

Just then, I heard the outside door to Carlson's office rattle slightly. I was sure that it was probably Rinehart looking for me, and it almost sounded like he was picking the lock.

I silently closed the door to the file room and locked it. As I waited for him to enter the office, I drew my gun from under my sport coat, then slipped down in the corner beside one of the file cabinets. From where I was, he would not be able to see me unless he came into the file room and walked around the first row of file cabinets. I waited to see what he was going to do.

"I don't see anyone in here," I heard a voice say.

I quickly realized that it was not Rinehart who had opened the door. I stood up, slipped my gun back in its holster and went to the door. I opened it and looked into office. It was one of the building's security guards and a woman in a very nicely tailored suit. The security guard had a hand full of keys.

"Can I help you," I asked as if I was supposed to be there.

"Who are you," the guard asked.

"I'm Frank Tidsdale. I work for Mr. Carlson."

"I didn't know he had anyone working for him."

"I just started. Is there something I can help you with?"

"We got a report that someone was in Mr. Carlson's office. I came to investigate. Can you prove that you work for him?"

"Sure. Why don't you give Mr. Moore a call? You can use this phone," I said as I pointed to the phone on Carlson's desk.

"Who's Mr. Moore, and why would I call him?"

"Mr. Moore is Carlson's attorney. I'm sure that you are aware that Mr. Carlson is being held in jail on charges of murdering his wife. It might be a little hard to get hold of him."

"Yes, but what does that have to do with you?"

"I actually work for Mr. Moore on Carlson's behalf. I'm an investigator on Carlson's defense team."

"That doesn't give you permission to search Mr. Carlson's office."

"Actually, it does. Now, you can either call Mr. Moore, or you can get out of here while I do my job."

The guard stood there looking at me for a minute. I could see in his eyes that he didn't trust me. I could also see that he wasn't sure of what he should do.

"Look, I've got a hell of a lot of work to do, and I don't need you standing over my shoulder while I'm doing it. Pick up the damn phone and call Mr. Moore, or get the hell out of here," I said sharply.

The guard looked at me then went to the phone. As he reached for the phone, I handed him one of Moore's business cards. The guard called the number. It didn't take but a minute for him to find out that I did in fact work for him on Carlson's defense team.

The guard hung up the phone and said, "Sorry, Mr. Tidsdale. We can't be too careful."

"Fine. Now would you please leave me to do what I have to do?"

"Yes, sir."

He turned around and motioned for the woman to leave then followed her out the door. The guard shut the door and I let out a sigh of relief. I wasn't sure if Moore would back me if I was in Carlson's office. There was little doubt in my mind that Moore would be asking me about it the next time I talked to him.

I stood there thinking about what I might find in Carlson's office. It would make it a whole lot easier if I had the keys to the file cabinets, but I had no idea where they were. I felt I needed to pay a visit to Carlson. I checked to make sure that the file room was locked, then left the office making sure that the door was also locked. I left the building the same way I had come in, through the front door.

Once I was in my car, I headed for the county jail where Carlson was being held. I kept an eye out for anyone following me. There was a rather plain looking car about two or three cars back that seemed to be going to the same place I was going. I wasn't a hundred percent sure who it was, but I had to smile at the thought that Rinehart was finally getting smart by getting a less conspicuous car to use to follow me. It wasn't until I got to the county jail that I got a glimpse of the driver.

Rinehart returned in the rented car to the Hammond Building where Carlson's office was located. He found Tidsdale's car still parked in front of the building. After finding a parking space about a half a block away from Tidsdale's car, he leaned back to watch and wait. He had no idea how long it would take Tidsdale to finish his search of Carlson's office, but he needed to keep a close watch on Tidsdale.

Rinehart began to wonder what Tidsdale might find in Carlson's office. He began to wonder if he might have made a big mistake by not searching Carlson's office when he had the chance. He had no idea how much Mrs. Carlson might have told her husband about what she had discovered. He wasn't even sure that Mrs. Carlson had discovered anything that would be damaging to anyone other than Mr. Steinman, and even that was questionable. There were no names revealed in the memo. It had simply been addressed to the president of Mile High Design and there was no return address. The relationship between Sargossa and Steinman was not contained in the letter, but it did indicate ever so slightly, without actually saying it, that Steinman might be misappropriating funds to pay off someone for something.

He couldn't help but think about how stupid Steinman was to have had the memo lying around on his desk with some of the cost analysis, material cost sheets and other documents for the new city buildings.

As best as Rinehart could figure, Mrs. Carlson had apparently gone into Steinman's office to pick up the documents she needed for her part in the project and had picked up the memo along with other papers by mistake.

Rinehart knew that Steinman wasn't even sure that Mrs. Carlson had even seen the memo before he got it back. He discovered it missing within minutes of its disappearance and retrieved it from her office still in among the rest of the papers. Steinman began to suspect that she had seen it when she began acting strangely. It was the fact that she would hardly talk to him and became very quiet that caused Steinman to believe she had seen it and may have figured out what it was all about.

If it became public knowledge, or had been presented to the proper authorities, it would have meant an investigation into Mile High Design's financial practices. If that occurred, the connection between Sargossa and Steinman might become known, which would have caused problems for not only Steinman but for Sargossa as well. It would have also brought to light the fact that Steinman was embezzling money from the company. That would have meant the end of the business and most likely jail time for Steinman. Steinman would do almost anything to prevent that from happening, including talking to the authorities. Rinehart could not let that happen.

Just then, Rinehart saw Tidsdale leaving the building and going to his car. Rinehart started his car and followed Tidsdale at a safe distance. It wasn't long before Tidsdale turned into the County Jail parking lot. Rinehart pulled over to the curb and stopped.

He watched as Tidsdale parked his car and went into the County Jail. There was little doubt that he was going in to talk to Carlson again. Since Tidsdale had talked to Carlson just a short time ago, he wondered if Tidsdale had found something of interest and was looking for more information from Carlson.

Rinehart knew that it would do no good to go search Carlson's office now. Anything that would shine a little light on why Mrs. Carlson was murdered had most likely been found already. It was time to do something about Tidsdale. He would keep a close eye on him and wait for an opportunity to convince Tidsdale to close his investigation before things got any worse for him.

CHAPTER THIRTY-ONE

I told the guard on duty at the entrance to the county jail that I wanted to visit with Jim Carlson. I surrendered my guns and was led back to a private visiting room. The room looked a lot like one of the interrogation rooms at the police station where Carlson had first been interviewed by Detective Wright.

It took about five minutes for the guard to bring Carlson into the room. I couldn't help but notice that Carlson looked tired, and he seemed to look older. It was my guess that his time in a jail cell was wearing on him. I waited for Carlson to sit down and for the guard to leave the room. I also waited for the guard to close the door behind him before I spoke to Carlson.

"How are you holding up?"

"I'm okay. Mr. Moore said he was trying to get a motion hearing to get me out of here. He said that the evidence didn't support the arrest warrant."

"I'm sure he's doing his best."

"I wish he would hurry it along. I don't like this place."

"I can understand that. I'm sure he is working on it. Sometimes it takes a little time to get a judge to hear the motion. They're pretty busy," I said.

I used the small talk to get him to relax. I needed him to be able to think past his imprisonment.

"That's what he said. He told me it might take a couple of days and that the ADA could object to my release. He still thought that he had a good chance of getting me released, maybe without a bond."

"That's good," I said, then took a deep breath before continuing.

"Jim, I came to ask you a couple of questions. I want you to think about what I ask before you answer. Okay?"

"Yeah, sure."

He looked a little puzzled by my statement. The look on his face gave me the impression that he was wondering what kind of questions I was going to ask him that would require him to think about the answer.

"I want to know if your wife had spent any time alone in your office in the past week to ten days? By alone, I mean without you or anyone else present for more than just a few minutes."

Carlson looked at me, then closed his eyes apparently to think. I wasn't sure if he was thinking about why I asked the question, how he should best answer it, or if he was trying to remember if his wife had been in his office alone.

"I'm not sure, but she could have been. She might have been in my office when I had to go to the restroom, but not any longer than that would take. Yes. Yes, she was," he added suddenly with a surprised look on his face as if he had just remembered it.

I wasn't sure if this was an act, or if he had actually remembered something. It could have been my suspicious nature that caused me to wonder if I was getting the truth, or a lie. It also could have been the fact that I didn't know Mr. Carlson very well.

"When was that and how long was she alone?"

"She came down to go to lunch with me. She waited in my office while I went to the john. I don't think I was gone more than five minutes. Well, maybe a couple of minutes longer than that, but not much. Is that important?"

"When was that?" I asked ignoring his question.

"I - - ah - - think it was three or four days before she was - - murdered," he said choking a little on the word 'murdered'.

"Did she often meet you in your office before going to lunch together?"

"Not real often, maybe two or three times a month, except during tax season. I'm pretty busy during tax season."

"Did your wife's attitude or disposition change any in the days before her death?"

"I thought it did, a little anyway. She seemed to be withdrawn and didn't want to talk about her work. She often talked about what she was working on at home, but not recently."

"Did she give you any reason for the change?"

"She said that she was under a lot of pressure to get her part of the project finished."

"I take it you are talking about the new city buildings?"

"Yes. That was the project that she had been working on."

"Was she acting like she usually did when she was under a lot of pressure?"

He again looked at me as if I had asked him a really strange question. I got the feeling he was thinking that I was looking for something specific, but he didn't have any idea what it was.

"Now that you mention it, no. I don't ever remember her going off to her office at home and shutting herself in for so long at a time. She did it almost every night for almost a week before," he paused for a moment before continuing. "I thought that she was just doing some of the work at home in order to catch up."

"Did she often work at home?"

"No. Not often. But she did sometimes."

"Did she often lock the door to her office when she worked there?"

"No. Not usually."

"What do you do when she is working at home?"

"I sometimes work in my shop in the basement. It relaxes me. It gets me away from my accounting duties. Sort of clears my head. On occasion I work in my home office if I need to, but I try to keep my business at the office as much as I can."

"Do you do any accounting work for Mile High Design?"

"Wait. What are you getting at with all the questions about my wife, and my relationship with Mile High Design?" Carlson asked, the tone of his voice getting sharp.

"I don't want you to worry, but I'm looking for some reason for someone to want to murder your wife. Someone other than you."

"And what happens if you don't find one? Will you be looking at me?"

"Let's face it; Jim, the police are already looking at you. I'm looking for other possibilities. Other suspects. Other reasons for someone to want her dead. Right now, you are the only one the police have."

"And you agree with them?"

"I'm a little more open minded about it than they are," I replied, avoiding a direct answer as I had still not made up my mind about him.

"Oh."

"Back to my questions. Do you do any work for Mile High Design?"

"I have been the accountant on a few of their projects over the years."

"Are you the accountant for the city project?"

"No."

"Why not?" I asked.

"I think the city's accountants and attorneys are handling that part of the project."

"Is that normal?"

"Not usually, but with the city it sometimes works out that way," he answered without any hesitation.

"I would like to have the keys to your office and your file cabinets."

"Why do you want them?"

"I'm looking for a reason for your wife's murder."

"In my office?"

"Yes. If she found something that was, shall we say, incriminating to someone in her office, she might have hidden it in your office rather than try to get it out of the building, or take it home."

"Oh. But she wouldn't have had access to my file cabinets. I always keep them locked."

"I still want the keys to the file cabinets. I can assure you that nothing will be said about anything that might be found in your files that doesn't have a direct impact on who killed your wife."

He looked at me as he thought about what I was asking. For all I knew, he might have been trying to decide if there was anything in his files that would cause him problems if someone found out.

"Okay," he relented. "The keys to the file cabinets and the file room are located in my desk. They are in a key box located by opening the top drawer on the left side of my desk. Open the drawer part way then reach up under the desk top. You will find the key box glued to the bottom of the desk top inside the drawer. The keys are in it."

"Okay. What about the key to your office?"

"The police have the one that is on my keychain. They took my keys from me when I was taken to the police station."

"Okay. I've got a couple of quick questions that might help me with a couple of things that have been bothering me. The first is do you have a cleaning lady?"

"Yes."

"When was the last time she was there?"

"The morning before Jennifer - - was - -.

"It's okay," I said as I waited for him to gather his emotions.

"A couple of different types of sawdust were found in your woodworking shop, but there was only one piece of wood found on your workbench. Can you explain that?"

"Yes. I cut a piece of wood from some scraps, then sanded the edges and drilled a couple of holes in it to hold some of my very small wood files, then I went on to sand the rung for my bench. I didn't clean up after making the file holder."

"Okay. Is there anything you need?"

"Yeah. I need to get out of here."

"I'm sorry, but that is out of my hands. Mr. Moore is working on that."

I stood up and walked to the door. I knocked on the door and a guard opened it.

"I'm done for now."

The guard didn't say anything. He simply nodded and pointed in the direction I was to go to get out. I walked down the hall to the room where they stored the inmate's personal possessions and asked for Carlson's keys. The guard checked with Carlson to see if he could give me the key I asked for before taking it off the key ring and giving it to me. I signed for the key, then signed out. I was given back my guns and I left.

I had no idea what I might find in the file cabinets in Carlson's office, but I knew it would probably take a long time to go through all of them. I also wanted to take a good look at the rest of his office for anything that he or his wife might have hidden there.

I returned to my car and drove to my office. I noticed that the same nondescript car I had seen earlier appeared to be following me. Since I had gotten a glimpse of Rinehart in it when I arrived at the county jail, there was no doubt about who was following me. I didn't figure it was going to make much difference if he followed me or not. If I let him follow me now, he might get the idea that I had not spotted him. That might give me a little better chance of ditching him when it became necessary. At this point I had nothing to hide.

I made a brief stop at my office to get some rubber gloves and take a quick look at my mail. There was nothing of interest except for a couple of bills. Most of the mail was junk and quickly got tossed in the circular file.

Once I was finished, I returned to my car and headed back to Carlson's office. I figured that I would be spending the rest of the afternoon and most of the evening going through his files.

After parking my car where it wouldn't be towed, I went into the building and took the elevator to the floor where Carlson's office was located.

Tidsdale hadn't been in the county jail building very long when he returned to his car and drove off. Rinehart wondered who he had gone to see. He was pretty sure that it was Carlson. Rinehart followed Tidsdale to the underground garage of the building where his office was located. He parked in a space where he could keep an eye on Tidsdale's car and the elevator. He thought about going in and having another more serious "talk" with Tidsdale in his office, but there were too many people around at that time of day. Instead, he sat in his car and waited.

He was hoping that Tidsdale would stay in his office until the building had pretty much cleared out for the evening. If that didn't happen, he would continue to follow him until he could catch Tidsdale alone someplace where he could work him over in private.

It was about three-thirty in the afternoon when Tidsdale came out of the elevator and walked to his car. Rinehart watched him carefully, wondering where he was headed. Tidsdale had only been in his office for a short time. Tidsdale started his car and left the underground garage with Rinehart staying back so he would not be seen. Once Tidsdale was out on the street, Rinehart pulled out of the garage and began following him.

He followed Tidsdale to a coffee shop where he watched him get a large cup of coffee, then return to his car. It was only when Tidsdale pulled up in front of the Hammond Building where Mile High Design was located that he wondered if he was returning to Carlson's office, or if he was going to talk to Steinman. Rinehart couldn't take the chance that he might be going to talk to Steinman. Rinehart was sure that if Tidsdale had anything at all on Steinman and confronted him with it, especially if it looked like he *might end up in jail, Steinman would sing like the proverbial canary. He couldn't let that happen.*

Rinehart quickly rounded the corner and drove into the underground parking garage. He parked in his assigned parking place and ran for the elevators. It took several minutes for the elevator to get to the garage. When it did, he got in and pressed the button for the top floor of the building where Steinman's office was located.

It seemed to Rinehart that the elevator took forever to get where he wanted to go. When he stepped off the elevator into the reception area of Mile High Design, he looked around quickly but didn't see Tidsdale. Without saying anything to the woman at the reception desk, he turned and hurried down the hall toward Steinman's office. Steinman's personal secretary was waiting for him when he got to Steinman's office.

"You can't see him right now," she said as she stepped in front of the door.

"Out of my way," Rinehart said as he gently, but firmly pushed her to the side.

He pushed open Steinman's office door and stepped in. He saw Steinman at his desk. He was on the phone. There was first a surprised look on Stineman's face, but it quickly turned to an angry look, but he didn't say anything to Rinehart.

"Could I call you back?" he said into the phone while still looking at Rinehart.

There was a moment of silence.

"Thank you. I'll get back to you in a few minutes," Steinman said, then hung up the phone.

"What the hell is the meaning of this," Steinman said to Rinehart.

"I'm sorry, sir," his secretary said. "He just barged in,"

"It's all right. You may go. And shut the door behind you."

Steinman's secretary looked from Steinman to Rinehart, then turned and left the office. She looked back at Rinehart just before she closed the door.

"What is the meaning of this intrusion?"

"I'm looking for Tidsdale," Rinehart said.

"Well, as you can see he isn't here. What made you think he would be here?"

"I followed him into the building. He must have gotten off on another floor."

"You couldn't think to stop long enough to ask my secretary if he was here? Don't bother to answer that. Just get the hell out of my office and don't ever come barging in here again."

Rinehart looked at Steinman through squinted eyes for a moment before he turned to leave. He was angry and wanted nothing more than to walk over to Steinman and punch him in the nose. The only thing that kept him from doing it was that Sargossa would not like it, and it was not a good idea to make Sargossa mad.

Rinehart turned and started out of the office. He started to smile to himself at the thought that one day he would get the okay from his boss to get rid of Steinman. It was something he would take a great deal of pleasure in doing, when the time came.

Rinehart left Mile High Design and took the elevator to the garage. The building was too busy with people going in and out, and from one office to another for him to confront Tidsdale now. He got in his car then drove out of the garage. He found a place to park about a half a block from the front entrance to the building. From where he parked, he could see the front door of the building as well as Tidsdale's car. He tipped back the seat and waited. He knew it could be a long wait, but it didn't matter. He would wait as long as it took. He was just biding his time until he would get his chance to get Tidsdale alone.

CHAPTER THIRTY-TWO

Using the key I had gotten from the guard at the county lockup, I unlocked the door and went inside Carlson's office. I closed and locked the door before I went to Carlson's desk and found the keys to the file cabinets and the key to the door to the file room right where he said they would be.

Since the job of searching all of the files would most likely take the rest of the afternoon and all night, or at least the better part of the night, I decided that I would search his office first. There was a possibility that Mrs. Carlson might have hidden something here while he was out of the office.

I figured that the best place to start was Carlson's desk. I did everything but turn his desk upside down, but I didn't think that was necessary since I did get down on my hands and knees and looked up under it. The result was nothing. If anyone had hidden anything in that desk, it had to be between the grains of the wood.

I next began searching the credenza. There was nothing there of any interest except for a number of CDs, about forty or so of them. I decided that I would read all the labels in the hope that something would jump out at me, but I had no luck there. Each one had the name of a person or the name of a business printed on it. I figured that they were accounting records for his clients.

The next step was to turn on Carlson's computer and begin checking each and every CD for something that didn't belong there. It was easy to get the computer turned on, but it took me a while to figure out the password that would allow me to even get into his computer. I took a stab at a couple of words that he might use and got lucky. His password to get into his computer was his name spelled backwards. It didn't strike me as much of a password since even a kid could have figured it out with a few tries.

I put the first CD in the computer only to discover that I could not look at what was on the CD without another password. Even the CDs were password protected. Not knowing too much about computers, I figured that Carlson probably had a different password for each client's CD. Since it had worked to get on his computer, I decided that it wouldn't hurt to try the name on the CD spelled backwards. It didn't work.

If that was the case, remembering each and every password would be difficult if not almost impossible, especially since there were more than forty of them. My guess was that he had probably written the password down somewhere. If he had them written down, he most likely hid them like he hid his keys to the file room. Since I had not found them under the desk like the keys, I tried looking in the drawers of the credenza. Sure enough, I found an envelope attached to the bottom of one of the drawers. Inside was a sheet of paper with the names that matched those on the CDs followed by a password. Sure enough, he had used the same method of hiding the passwords for the CDs as he had for the keys. I couldn't help but think that his idea of security was pretty lame.

I came up with the idea that maybe there was a CD in among the others that didn't have a password listed on the paper. If I found one not listed on the sheet, it was probably what I was looking for. I began checking the names on each CD against the sheet of paper. Low and behold there was a CD, only one, that wasn't listed on the sheet. Needless to say, I was feeling pretty proud of myself at that moment, but my moment of glory went away quickly when I put the CD in the computer. It almost immediately came up asking for a password. It wouldn't let me have access to the information without it.

Something told me that I had what I wanted on that CD, but there was no way for me to know for sure unless I could figure out the password. I tried a bunch of words that I thought were rather obvious without gaining access. The fact that I couldn't get access to what was on the CD seemed to assure me that I might have what I was looking for. I also noticed that the brand of CD was different from all the others. It was clear to me that the CD was not one of Mr. Carlson's.

With my limited knowledge of computers, it was beginning to look pretty bleak at the moment. Then I thought of someone who might be able to help me. I turned around in the chair and reached for the phone. I placed a call to Jackie, my girlfriend. She was much more knowledgeable about computers than I. She was a computer whiz for the state. The phone rang only twice before it was answered.

"Hello.

"Hi, honey."

"Frank? It's been a long time. Where have you been the past few days?"

"I've been working on a case."

"Are you done with it?"

"No. As a matter of fact, I need your help."

"What do you need?" Jackie asked.

"Two things. I need you to have dinner with me, tonight."

"I can do that," she said with a pleasant sound in her voice. "What's the second thing?"

"I need to break a password on a computer, actually on a CD. Do you think you could help me with that?"

"I don't know. It depends on how well the person who selected the password knows computers. How well do you know the person you think picked the password?"

"Not very well, but I don't think she's a computer expert."

"That might help.

"How about I meet you at The Rock Bottom Brewery on Sixteenth Street in about an hour? We can talk about it over dinner," I suggested.

"Great. That's only a few blocks from where I am now. I'll see you there."

"Good," I said then hung up.

All I knew for sure was if that CD proved to be nothing helpful, I would have to search the rest of the files. That chore could prove to be a long and very boring job. At the moment, I was resting my hopes on finding something on the CD that would help prove Carlson did not kill his wife. Even that depended on our ability to figure out the password. It was a long shot at best.

A quick glance at my watch told me that I had time to look around some more before I had to leave for the restaurant. I decided that I would continue to look around in the hope of finding something else that would prove Carlson didn't kill his wife, or find the password to the CD.

My continued search of Carlson's office proved fruitless. I found nothing that could even remotely help in his defense, or with getting access to the information on the CD. It was getting on toward time to meet Jackie.

I put everything back where I had found it before I left the office, except for the CD. I put that in my inside sport coat pocket. I didn't want to leave it behind in case someone got interested in Carlson's office while I was gone.

After I locked the door, I went to the elevator and took it to the ground floor. I left the building taking a right turn and began walking toward Sixteenth Street. It didn't take me long to get to the restaurant. I was shown to a booth and sat down to wait for Jackie.

Rinehart could be a patient man if he had to in order to get what he wanted. What he wanted most right now was to get his chance to teach Tidsdale that he meant what he said. He glanced at his watch and realized that he had been sitting there for a long time and nothing was happening.

It was shortly after five when he noticed several people who worked in the building were starting to leave for the day. He sat up and watched closely so that he wouldn't miss seeing Tidsdale if he should leave, all the time hoping that he wouldn't leave. If Tidsdale stayed in the building for another thirty to forty minutes, there was a good chance that he could catch him alone in Carlson's office.

"Damn" he said to himself as he saw Tidsdale come out of the office building. When Tidsdale walked right past his car, Rinehart began to wonder where he was going. Several ideas came to mind. Since Tidsdale didn't take his car, Rinehart's first thought was that he was going to get something to eat and return. His second thought was that Tidsdale might be going to meet someone close by and didn't need his car to get there. The only way Rinehart was going to find out was to follow him.

Rinehart got out of his car and began following Tidsdale on foot. In an effort not to be seen by Tidsdale, Rinehart ran across the street and dogged him from there. Tidsdale turned on Sixteenth Street and continued on down the street. When he came to The Rock Bottom Brewery, he went inside.

Rinehart stood next to a tree on the other side of the street while watching Tidsdale as he went inside the brewery. It appeared that his first thought about Tidsdale going to get something to eat was right. The only thing he couldn't be sure of was if he was going to be eating alone, or if he would be meeting someone.

Once Tidsdale was inside the restaurant, Rinehart looked both ways as if he expected to see someone following him, or possibly Tidsdale. He then looked back at the restaurant. He was trying to decide if he should risk going across the street and looking in to see if he could see if Tidsdale was there to meet someone.

Rinehart decided to take the chance and walked across the street. He looked in the window next to the door. He could see the hostess leading Tidsdale to a booth, but couldn't see if anyone was already in the booth.

"Excuse me," a woman said from behind him.

It startled Rinehart causing him to turn around sharply. Standing in front of him was a very nice looking young woman. He just stared at her.

"Excuse me," she said again. "I would like to go in, if you don't mind."

The woman's voice showed that she was not pleased that he was standing in her way and he had not made any effort to let her pass.

"Oh," he said, "I'm sorry.

Rinehart stepped aside so that the woman could enter the restaurant. He watched her as she went inside. He continued to watch as the hostess talked to her for a moment, then led her to the same booth where Tidsdale had been seated.

CHAPTER THRITY-THREE

I stood up when Jackie walked up to the booth. She slid in across the table from me and sat down.

"Am I late?" Jackie asked.

"No. I got here a little early,"

We shared a little of our day with each other then ordered dinner. While we waited, I explained a little about the case I was working on. When dinner came, we settled in to enjoy our meal. When we were done, I ordered after-dinner coffee for both of us and sat back to talk while we enjoyed the coffee.

"So you're not sure if Mr. Carlson had anything to do with his wife's death, are you?" Jackie asked.

"No. I've been trying to keep an open mind. If he did have something to do with it, I'm not sure what. So far everything I can find out has pointed to someone else having done the killing."

"He could have hired it done," she suggested.

"I'm sure he could have, but I don't think so. I think that if he is involved, he was pressured into it by someone else. But I haven't found anything to support that theory."

"I take it you're working more on the theory that he had nothing to do with it."

"At least for now I am."

"What about this CD you found?"

"I'm not sure it has anything to do with Mrs. Carlson's death. I'm not sure it has anything to do with anything involving this case at all. I won't know if it means anything to me until I find out what is on it."

"Do you know whose CD it is?"

"This is what I know about it. Unlike the rest of the CDs I found in Carlson's office, it has no password on the paper I found. Yet it does have a password. It is a different brand of CD from all the rest I found in Carlson's office which would indicate that it might have come from somewhere other than his office. And, it was in with the other CDs, but I have no idea how it got there. I do think that the CD belonged to Carlson's wife, but even that is just a guess on my part."

"That's not much help in figuring out what the password might be. So, let's assume that it was left in his office by his wife in order to make it more difficult for someone to find. There are a number of words and or numbers she might use to protect the information on the CD."

"Like what?"

"Like her birthday, her maiden name, her husband's birthday," she said.

"So I need to try everything I can think of."

"That's about it. You tell me everything you can about her and I'll make up a list of words that might work. If you think of any other words that might work while you tell me about her, we'll add them to the list. It's a long shot, but that's about the best I can do since I don't even know the woman or anything about her or what she did for a living."

"Okay," I said.

I began to tell her everything I had been able to find out about Mrs. Carlson. Jackie took a piece of paper and a pen out of her purse and began jotting down words that might work. It took us almost thirty minutes for me to tell her everything I knew about Mrs. Carlson, and possible words I thought might have some connection to her. It had taken her about thirty minutes to write down all the key words we could think off. When I had nothing more I could tell her about Mrs. Carlson, she still had one area that neither of us had thought about.

"Do the Carlson's have any pets?"

"No. I don't believe so."

"Okay. That's about the best I can do on such short notice. All I can suggest is that you try them and see if any of them work. If they don't, we'll have to try something else."

"Okay. Are you busy for the rest of the evening?"

"I have a meeting in about thirty minutes with a group of Safety Department employees to give them some instruction on a new program we just put on their computers. I should be done about nine o'clock, maybe nine-thirty."

"Could you come by Carlson's office when you're done?"

"Sure. You think you will be there that long?"

"Probably. If I get done before you show up, I'll call you and leave a message on your cell phone as to where I am."

"Okay."

After I paid the bill and left a tip on the table, I walked Jackie out to her car.

Rinehart had been waiting across the street in a dark corner of a building for close to an hour and a half. He could only see Tidsdale through the window of the Rock Bottom Brewery, and wondered what was taking them so long. Finally, they got up and he watched them as they left the table. As they came out of the brewery, Rinehart returned to his hiding place behind a tree.

Tidsdale walked the woman to her car. Rinehart didn't have to leave his hiding place as he could see where the woman had parked from there. He watched while Tidsdale gave her a kiss then stepped back while she drove off. Tidsdale then turned and headed back toward the Hammond Building making it clear that he was going back to Carlson's office.

Once again, Rinehart followed Tidsdale from across the street back to the Hammond Building. Once Tidsdale was inside the building, he walked around the corner to a small sandwich shop and got himself something to eat. He took it back to his car where he sat and ate his meal. When he was finished, he sat back to relax. Rinehart was wondering what Tidsdale was doing in the office, but if he was searching all the files he would be there for some time. He decided to wait until he was sure that the building was as empty of people as possible before he would go in to confront Tidsdale.

It was almost nine o'clock when Rinehart decided that it was time for him to pay a visit to Tidsdale. He got out of his car and went inside. He waved to the security guard who was sitting behind the desk in the lobby. The security guard waved back, but didn't say anything. He knew that Rinehart had an office on the eighteenth floor.

CHAPTER THIRTY-FOUR

I gave Jackie a kiss then watched her as she drove off. I turned and headed back to Carlson's office. When I arrived at the Hammond Building, I found the lobby to be empty except for one security guard at the front desk.

"Excuse me, but do you have an appointment in the building, sir?" the security guard asked.

"Not really. I'm Frank Tidsdale. I'm currently working for Mr. James Carlson and I'm going to his office."

"Oh, yes. My supervisor told me you were working for him. Would you mind signing in?"

"Not at all," I said as I walked over to his desk. "By the way, there may be a woman coming in a little later. I would appreciate it if you would direct her to Carlson's office."

"Certainly, Mr. Tidsdale. What's her name?"

"Jackie Harris."

"Would you like me to phone you when she arrives?"

"That won't be necessary. I'm expecting her."

As I signed in, I noticed that he wrote down her name. I set the pen down and went to the elevators. It didn't take long before an elevator arrived. I took the elevator to the eighteenth floor, got off and went directly to Carlson's office and let myself in. Once inside, I locked the door behind me. I didn't want anyone barging in while I was trying to open the CD.

As I walked toward Carlson's computer, I took the list of possible passwords out of my pocket and laid it down next to the computer. I sat down in front of the computer and turned it on. While the computer was booting up, I looked over the words that Jackie had written down. Some of them seemed almost too easy to figure, but there was no telling what had been going through Mrs. Carlson's mind when she decided on one. I also had no idea how computer literate she might have been. If she knew a lot about computers, her password could be very complicated. She might have picked something simple to make it easy to remember.

As soon as the computer was ready, I put the disk in and punched it up. It immediately asked for a password. I looked at the list Jackie had written out for a minute while I tried to decide where to start. At the beginning was the answer that came to mind, so that is what I did. I started at the top of the list and slowly began to work my way to the end.

I had no idea how long I had been working on it, but I was a little over halfway down the list of possible passwords when it accepted a password. I almost laughed out loud at the word that had been chosen as a password. It was actually two words run together, and it was a word that Jackie had written down while I was thinking about Mrs. Carlson and what her state of mind might have been at the time. The word was 'Ohshit', which seemed appropriate under the circumstances. I had to wonder how long it had taken Mrs. Carlson to come up with it. Probably not long. I also wondered what made Jackie think of it. I'm not sure, but maybe women's minds might work alike.

As soon as I got done laughing, I pressed the key to open the file on the CD using the password "Ohshit". The file immediately opened.

After the moment or two that it took to put the file on the screen, I started reading it. I quickly realized that it was a report on what Mrs. Carlson had been able to find out about certain contracts Mile High Design had entered into with regard to the construction of the new city buildings.

From what she had written in the report on the CD, it was clear that she had found a memo in among the papers she had retrieved from Steinman's office. The contents of the memo caused her to become curious as to what it all meant. She began looking into how things were being handled with regard to the construction of the new city buildings.

From what she had written in the report, she had discovered that several of the companies involved in the construction of the new city buildings were owned by a man named Donato Sargossa. A name I knew well.

It was obvious from what she wrote that she had heard of Sargossa and knew from the newspapers that he was somewhat of a mob boss in the Denver area. She also knew that he controlled several construction businesses as well as having a foothold on some of the local construction unions. With that information, she began looking into payments that were paid to Sargossa owned businesses that had contracts with Mile High Design. She had found that Sargossa's businesses were being paid for high quality materials, but were using lower cost materials and obviously keeping the difference.

It became clear that she had figured out that Mr. Steinman was in on it, too. She stated that her research of the Mile High Designs records showed that Steinman was approving the orders for the lesser quality material and signing the checks as if the higher priced materials had actually been purchased as required by the contract with the city. Mrs. Carlson's report gave no indication that she knew how Sargossa got his claws in Steinman, but I had a theory on that.

The report also showed that while she was looking into the finances, it became clear that not only Sargossa and Steinman were siphoning money off the contracts, but Steinman had been spending company money on bogus "Independent Contractors". He was claiming that they had been hired to do some of the special design work required for the city buildings when she knew that some of the "special design work" she had done herself. Mrs. Carlson was apparently unable to find any of the companies named as the

"Independent Contractors" in any phone book or in a registry of contractors within the state. She began to realize that Steinman had been stealing money from the firm by funneling it into bogus accounts at different banks, then withdrawing money from those accounts later.

Mrs. Carlson's suspicions that started her research were based on the memo that she accidentally discovered when she picked up the papers from Steinman's office. The report indicated that she had done most of her research late in the evenings at Mile High Design when there was no one around. I got the impression that she probably did some of it on her computer in her home office as well. I could only assume that she discovered the memo very shortly after she picked it up by accident in Steinman's office. She read it, then immediately put it back in the pile of reports before Mr. Steinman retrieved it from her desk.

One thing was for sure, Mrs. Carlson's report provided a pretty good motive for her murder. She was smart enough to know to follow the money, but apparently had not done a very good job of hiding her trail. The one question that came to mind was how much of this did Jim Carlson know?

Just then a heard someone try the door. A quick glance at my watch told me that it was very unlikely that it was Jackie. It was a little too early for her to be out of her meeting. I quickly pulled the CD out of the computer, deleted the information on the screen and shut off the computer. I slipped the CD under the monitor. After making sure that it was well out of sight, I pulled out one of the CDs from the pile and laid it on the credenza next to the computer. I also hid the list of passwords that Jackie and I had made up.

Rinehart took the elevator to the eighteenth floor and got off. He looked down the hall toward Carlson's office. He could see that there was a light on in the office. He had to wonder what Tidsdale was doing in Carlson's office for so long. He didn't think it was anything that should worry him or Steinman as Carlson had not been employed to handle any of the accounting work on Mile High Design's contract with the city.

The only thing that worried Rinehart was whether or not Carlson's wife had told her husband anything that could come back to haunt them. The question was had Mrs. Carlson told her husband anything, and if she had; what did she tell him?

Rinehart and Steinman were not sure that Mrs. Carlson knew anything. The only suspicion they had that she might know something was from the way she acted shortly after she had taken the memo off Steinman's desk by accident. The fact that Steinman had found the memo within minutes of its disappearance; and it was still in among the papers Mrs. Carlson had picked up, indicated that she had had little chance, if any, to actually read it. Since there were no names mentioned in the memo, there was no way that it could point to anyone in particular.

The other thing really troubling Rinehart was Tidsdale's investigation. The fact that Steinman had stonewalled Tidsdale probably made him suspicious enough to look into Mile High Design to see if they were covering up something. Rinehart figured that Steinman's treatment of Tidsdale led him to question Julie Mathews.

The fact that there were now two employees of Mile High Design that had been murdered within a short time probably caused Tidsdale to focus his investigation on Mile High Design. Rinehart was sure that if Tidsdale continued to nose around Mile High Design much longer, he might actually find something that could be a problem for Steinman and Sargossa as well as himself.

It was time for Rinehart to get Tidsdale to drop his investigation into Mile High Design and to forget everything he had learned. He left his office and went down the hall to Carlson's office. He looked around before he reached out and turned the knob. The door was locked.

He thought that he could hear Tidsdale moving around inside the office. Reaching under his coat, he drew out his gun and rested his hand at his side holding the gun slightly behind his leg. He then knocked on the door.

CHAPTER THIRTY-FIVE

I had no more than finished hiding the CD and the list of passwords when I heard a knock at the door. I got up from behind the desk and went to the door. After unlocking it, I opened it to find Rinehart standing there. He had a silly grin on his face.

"What are you doing here?" I asked.

"I thought we could have a little talk," he said as he quickly raised his hand from his side.

With the way he had been standing, I had not seen that big .45 caliber gun in his hand.

"Slowly back into the room," he ordered.

Not wanting to have a big hole in my body, I did as he said. He kicked the door closed then reached back behind him and locked the door without ever taking his eyes off me.

"If you don't mind, I'll take your gun."

"I do mind, but under the circumstances I'll let you take it."

"Very carefully, reach inside your coat and take out your gun. One wrong move and it will be your last."

Knowing what kind of man Rinehart was, I reached under my coat and took out my gun with just two fingers and handed it to him. There was no question in my mind that I would have to wait for my chance to turn the tables on him. He was a dangerous man, but he was also cautious. Sometime, somewhere he would make a mistake and I would take him.

"Turn around," he said.

Reluctantly, I turned around. I had no idea what to expect from him, but I knew it wasn't going to be good. My body was suddenly racked with a sharp pain over my left kidney. It took the wind out of me and I started to sag to the floor, but Rinehart stopped me from falling. He shoved me up against the wall and held me there with a knee pressed hard against my spine. He grabbed me by the hair and jerked my head back. Leaning over my shoulder, he whispered in my ear.

"This is the last time I'm going to tell you to drop your investigation. You continue nosing around and you will never investigate anything again. Do I make myself clear?"

I knew exactly what he meant. I also knew that I must have been making someone very nervous, which meant I was getting close to something. The only problem I had, other than having Rinehart on my back, literally, was I had no idea what I was getting close to.

"Do you understand?" Rinehart asked as he jabbed me in the kidney with his gun, again.

"Yeah. I understand," I said as I gasped for a breath.

"Make sure you do."

He had no more than said that, when I felt a sudden sharp blow to the back of my head immediately followed by the lights going out.

After Rinehart's confrontation with Tidsdale, he returned to his office. He closed the door and locked it, but didn't turn on any lights. He went to his desk, sat down and swiveled his chair around so he could sit and look out the window.

Rinehart was not interested in looking at the lights of the city at night. At the moment, he was more interested in whether or not Tidsdale would take his warning seriously. In his career as a bone breaker for Sargossa, he could not remember anyone who had not taken his warnings to heart. He had a deep feeling that he might have just met the one man who would not be bullied into backing off. In a way, he admired Tidsdale even though he knew what he was going to have to do if Tidsdale did not heed his warning.

There was only one thing that he could do now. He would have to wait and see if Tidsdale backed off. If he did, it was over and he would leave Tidsdale alone. If he didn't, he would have to kill him. Rinehart really didn't want to kill him. He didn't know why, but he had a feeling of respect for Tidsdale. It would make it harder for him to kill Tidsdale, but he would do it just the same.

Right now it was time for him to let Sargossa know that he had met with Tidsdale, and he would be spending the next few days watching to see what Tidsdale would do. He knew that Sargossa would expect him to do whatever was necessary to assure Tidsdale was out of the picture, one way or another.

Rinehart placed a call to Sargossa. He was told that Sargossa was busy at the moment, but his message would be given to him as soon as he was free. Rinehart hung up the phone then let out a long sigh as he looked at the clock on the corner of his desk.

It was almost nine-thirty. Rinehart decided that it was time for him to leave and get a good night's rest. He would have to be up early if he was going to follow Tidsdale in the morning to find out what he was going to do. Rinehart felt that with the whack on the head he had given Tidsdale, he would not be doing anything tonight. Once he woke up, he would want to go home and lie down to rest. Rinehart smiled at the thought that Tidsdale would have one hell of a headache.

Rinehart left his office, locking the door on his way out. He looked down the hall toward Carlson's office. He could see that there was still a light on. It crossed his mind that he might have hit Tidsdale a little too hard. If he had, there would be no need to worry about him.

Rinehart smiled to himself then turned and walked toward the elevators. He pressed the down button and waited for the elevator to show up. Once the elevator arrived, he got in and pressed the button for the ground floor. When the elevator arrived on the ground floor, he got out and started across the lobby.

As he waved at the security guard, he noticed a woman at the desk. He slowed his pace as he watched her signing in. It wasn't until she turned around and started for the bank of elevators that he recognized her. It was the same woman that Tidsdale had met for dinner at The Rock Bottom Brewery.

Rinehart stopped at the front door and watched the woman over his shoulder as she headed for the elevators. He wondered where she was going. There was little doubt that she would be going to meet up with Tidsdale. He turned around and walked over to the security desk.

"May I help you, Mr. Rinehart?" the security guard on duty asked.

"Who was the woman that just came in?"

"Miss Jackie Harris."

"Where is she going?"

"She's going to Jim Carlson's office to meet Mr. Tidsdale."

Rinehart stood looking toward the elevators for a minute before looking back at the security guard. He smiled. She was in for a surprise, he thought.

"Thank you," he said politely then turned and left the building.

As Rinehart walked toward his car, he began to smile to himself. He had just found the leverage that he could use if Tidsdale refused to cooperate, and her name was Jackie Harris.

Rinehart went to his car. He got in, then sat there waiting to see what was going to happen next. He was pretty sure that the police and an ambulance would be coming shortly.

* * * * * *

Jackie had not heard from Frank by the time she was done with her class. Since Frank had not contacted her, she drove over to the Hammond Building. When she arrived, she saw his car was still parked in front of the building. She parked, left her car and entered the building.

"May I help you?" the security guard asked.

"Yes. I'm here to meet Mr. Frank Tidsdale. He is in Mr. Carlson's office."

"Your name please?"

"Jackie Harris," she replied.

"Sign in here, please," he said as he laid a clipboard on the desk in front of her and handed her a pen.

Jackie signed her name on the form and gave back the pen and clipboard.

"Thank you. Mr. Tidsdale is expecting you. Go to the bank of elevators over there," he said as he pointed toward the elevators. "Go to the eighteenth floor. Get off there and turn left. You'll see Mr. Carlson's office on the right hand side of the hall."

"*Thank you,*" *Jackie said with a smile, then turned and started toward the elevators.*

The lobby was very quiet. She did notice a man walk through the lobby toward the front doors, but paid little or no attention to him. She went directly to the elevators and pressed the button for an elevator.

When she arrived on the eighteenth floor, she did as the security guard had told her. When she got to the door that had Carlson's name on it, she reached out, turned the knob and opened the door.

"*Frank,*" *she called out as she entered the room, but she got no response.*

She looked around and almost immediately found Frank lying on the floor. Jackie ran to his side and knelt down next to him. He was breathing and when she reached out and touched him, he groaned. She saw the blood in his hair on the back of his head.

Without delay, Jackie stood up and grabbed the phone. She dialed 9-1-1 and asked for the police and an ambulance. After giving the 9-1-1 operator her location, she returned to his side and held his hand while she waited.

Jackie remained beside him until the police and ambulance arrived.

CHAPTER THIRTY-SIX

I heard the sounds of people, but I couldn't figure out where they were. It was still dark and I felt as if I was lying on something that was very hard. I opened my eyes and saw a bright light directly in front of me. When I turned my head to one side, I saw Jackie. It took a minute for me to realize that I was lying on my back on the floor. I started to move, but felt a sharp pain on the back of my head.

"Don't try to move," Jackie said.

"What happened?"

"I don't know, but it looks like someone hit you on the head from behind," she replied with a concerned look on her face.

"Oh, yeah."

"Mr. Tidsdale, do you know where you are?" a man in a dark blue uniform asked.

"I'm in Jim Carlson's office, right?"

"Yes. Did you see who hit you?"

I just looked at him. I knew who had hit me, but I wasn't sure I wanted to tell them. I glanced over at Jackie and saw the worried look in her eyes.

"No. I had my back turned."

"How are you feeling?"

"Like I've been hit on the head."

"That sounds about right," the uniformed officer said with a smile.

"We're going to have you taken to a hospital to have you checked over, so just relax. We're going to put you on a stretcher. We don't want you walking until we know you're all right."

"You won't get any argument from me," I said, my head throbbing like crazy.

The ambulance personnel lifted me up and laid me down on the stretcher then wheeled me to the elevator. Jackie stayed at my side all the way down to the ground floor. I was wheeled out to the ambulance.

"I'll meet you at the hospital," Jackie said before they closed the ambulance doors.

By the time I got to the hospital, my head was throbbing so hard that it almost made me sick to my stomach. I was wheeled into the emergency room where I was seen by Doctor Muhlenberg. After asking me a million questions that didn't seem to mean anything to me, he sent me to X-ray where they took x-rays of my head. I was returned to the emergency room to wait for the results. I had a feeling that the doctor would want to admit me overnight, but I didn't want to stay there. On the other hand, I didn't really want to go anywhere else.

It wasn't long before Jackie showed up and sat down by my side while we waited for the results of the x-rays. She convinced me that it would be best if I stayed the night in the hospital if the doctor recommended it. I gave in and said I would do what the doctor wanted. She had been right. The doctor wanted to keep me overnight just for observation, and I agreed to it.

I was taken to a room where I settled in for the night. Jackie stayed with me for a little while, but when I started to doze off, she kissed me goodnight and went on home.

Once the room was dark, I laid there looking at the ceiling. It was clear that as long as I didn't do anything to make Rinehart think that I had not dropped my investigation, he would do nothing. That would give me time to figure out what was going on. I had several people who had a motive to kill Mrs. Carlson. Now all I had to do was figure out which one had her killed and who had been hired to do it. I was pretty sure that Rinehart was one of them who had killed

Mrs. Carlson, but I was also sure that there was someone else. Someone with a deep cut, probably on his hand or lower arm, caused by the knife wheeled by Mrs. Carlson.

Time went by slowly and I began to get sleepy. It wasn't much longer and I had fallen asleep.

Rinehart sat in his car waiting to see what was going to happen. It wasn't long before a police car came racing down the street and pulled to a stop in front of the Hammond Building. It was followed shortly by an ambulance. Rinehart smiled to himself. He was feeling like he might have put a stop to Tidsdale's nosing around in things that were none of his business.

After a short time, he saw a stretcher being wheeled out of the Hammond Building with Tidsdale lying on it. He watched very carefully in the hope of seeing if Tidsdale moved. He did not see him move. From where he sat, he was sure that Tidsdale had his eyes closed. It gave Rinehart the idea that Tidsdale might still be out cold. If he was, it might be some time before he would come around. He knew that he had hit him pretty hard, maybe a little too hard.

The woman he had come to know as Jackie Harris followed the ambulance attendants and stretcher to the back of the ambulance. He could not see what was going on, but when the ambulance pulled away she was still standing on the curb watching it as it disappeared around a corner with lights flashing and siren blaring. She was standing with her hand over her mouth.

Rinehart was feeling pretty satisfied with himself. He watched Jackie as she walked to her car. She got in, but didn't start it. She sat behind the steering wheel for a minute before she leaned over it as if she was crying. That was his clue that he had hit him hard enough that he would most likely be out of his hair at least for a while.

With that thought in his mind, Rinehart decided that it was time to go home and get a good night's sleep. He would check on Tidsdale in the morning to see what his status was at the hospital.

CHAPTER THIRTY-SEVEN

The night went by slowly. I woke several times during the night with a dull aching sensation in the back of my head. Jackie had gone home. She had stayed with me until well after midnight.

I woke in the early hours of the morning, somewhere around four. I pressed the button on the side of the bed that raised the head of the bed. I sat up and looked around as I listened to the sounds of a busy metropolitan hospital. It was pretty quiet on this particular floor. I could see the glow of the lights at the nurse's station just to the left of the door to my room. From my bed I could see the shadow of someone sitting in a chair outside my room next to the door. I had to wonder who had put a guard on me.

My thoughts turned to what had happened. I was mentally kicking myself for allowing Rinehart to get the drop on me. It would not happen again, I told myself.

My thoughts turned to the case. I was obviously getting close to finding out why Mrs. Carlson had been murdered, or close to who had murdered her. Someone out there was feeling the heat. I had to wonder who it was.

The names that came to mind were Sargossa and Steinman. The reason for that was the fact that Rinehart had connections to both of them, and he was the one who had found it necessary to crack my skull. But Rinehart was not the type to do anything without orders from someone else. I had to wonder who that someone else might be. I also wondered if there was someone else besides Sargossa and Steinman.

As my thoughts turned to the killing of Mrs. Carlson, I had to wonder to what degree Rinehart was involved. Since my contact with him had not given me any indication that he had any wounds, I had to wonder who else was in the Carlson home on the night Mrs. Carlson was murdered. I don't know why I thought that there were two people who where involved in killing her, but I did. It may have been the fact that she was killed with a .357 caliber pistol, when I knew that Rinehart carried a .45 caliber auto pistol. That, of course, didn't mean that Rinehart didn't have a .357 with him. It may have been the fact that I had not noticed any injuries on Rinehart. There was always the possibility that two people I didn't know had killed her, but I had no idea who it could be if Rinehart wasn't one of them.

As my head began to pound again, I lowered the head of my bed and closed my eyes. I had a feeling that I would be having headaches for at least the next few days. I would need to reduce any chances of having contact with anyone that might cause me injury for a while, meaning Rinehart. There was little doubt that he would cause me harm if I didn't back off.

Slowly, a plan started to form in my aching head. I would get the word out that I was in a coma and that it didn't look good for me. In that way, I might be able to get him to drop his guard for a little while. It would also give me time to heal and time to work out a plan to get Rinehart alone. There was no way I was going to let him get away with putting me in the hospital without paying dearly for it.

Once again I dozed off and slept until breakfast was brought around. Shortly after breakfast, Jackie showed up. I told her about my plan and had her call Wright. By mid morning we had everything arranged so that I could slip out of the hospital without actually being discharged.

The room I was supposed to be in was kept closed and a private guard was stationed outside the room to make it look like I was still being protected. In the meantime, I was recuperating at home. I spent my days going over everything that I had on the deaths of both Julie Mathews and Jennifer

Carlson. Detective Wright provided me with forensic reports on both cases.

After three days I was still convinced that Rinehart had probably killed Julie, and that he had probably killed Mrs. Carlson with the help of at least one other person. I had no idea who the other person was, but I was sure that the unknown person was the one who had left blood in the front hall and on the stairs at the Carlson house.

I was no longer having headaches and I was feeling like I was ready to continue my search for the truth. It was time to get out in the world and find Rinehart. It was time to confront him. The longer I was supposed to be in the hospital, the easier it would be for word to slip out that I was not there and hadn't been for the last few days. That information in the wrong hands would alert Rinehart that I was faking it.

Rinehart had been checking in with the hospital every day to see if Tidsdale was still hospitalized. He was pleased to see that Tidsdale had not died, but was out of commission, at least for a while.

In an attempt to visit with Jim Carlson, Rinehart was told that Carlson's attorney had restricted his visitors to only his attorney and the investigator working on the case. He was not surprised by the restrictions. He would have done the same thing if he had been Carlson's attorney. It would simply mean that he would have to find another why to search Carlson's home.

Rinehart spent a good part of each day checking on Carlson's house. After two days without anyone coming to the house, he decided that it would be fairly safe to search the house without interference and without being disturbed while doing it. The only thing he had to be careful of was getting into the house without being seen. He decided that he would get to the house by going up the alley on foot dressed as a homeless person. Since homeless people were often seen in the area, no one would think twice about it. The worst that could happen would be if he got run off by one of Carlson's neighbors. If that happened, he would just sneak around and try again later.

On the third day after Tidsdale was put in the hospital, Rinehart drove to a place on the far side of Washington Park where he parked his car. He sat in the car and watched the house for more than an hour without seeing any police cars or anyone drive by the place that might make it look like someone was keeping an eye on the Carlson home.

Satisfied that no one was keeping surveillance on the house, he drove around the park and parked his car two blocks over from Carlson's house. Making sure that he was not seen, he got out of his car and walked toward the alley *that ran behind Carlson's house. Once in the alley, he opened the paper sack he had been carrying and took out an old coat that was faded and looked dirty. He put it on along with a beat up old hat. He then started going down the alley, working his way to the gate in the privacy fence behind Carlson's house.*

After checking both ways down the alley to make sure that no one was in the alley to see him, he opened the gate and entered Carlson's backyard. He moved along the bushes that were growing along the fence. When he was as close to the house as he could get using the cover of the bushes, he dashed to the back porch. He quickly picked the lock and let himself into the house. He stood inside the backdoor and looked out to see if there was any sign that someone might have seen him. There was none.

Rinehart turned and quickly went directly upstairs to Mrs. Carlson's office. Once inside her office, he stood there and looked around. The first thing he noticed was that Mrs. Carlson's computer was missing. The printer, scanner and some of the cables used to hook up the printer and scanner to the computer were lying on the desk.

"Shit," he said.

Disappointed that her computer had been taken, he decided that since he was there, he would see if maybe there were some CDs that had been overlooked. He found none. He sat down in the chair behind Mrs. Carlson's desk to think. If she had found anything incriminating, it was too late. The police either already had it, or it would be just a matter of time before they would find what they needed and start making arrests.

It was time for him to get out of there. He had done all he could for now. The only thing he didn't know was had she found out anything incriminating; and if she had, who did it incriminate and how? He needed to get back to his office and call Sargossa. It was looking like they were going to have some damage control to do.

CHAPTER THIRTY-EIGHT

I had a pretty good idea of where to find Rinehart. He would probably be in his office. If he wasn't in his office, he would probably return to it sometime in the morning. As far as I was concerned, it was time to confront him.

It didn't take me long to get dressed and have a little something to eat. As soon as I was ready, I headed for the Hammond Building. The drive to the building was slow with the early morning commuter traffic. Once I got there I made it a point to park a couple of blocks from the building. I didn't want Rinehart to know where I was just yet. I walked into the lobby and was immediately greeted by one of the security guards.

"Mr. Tidsdale, how are you doing?" the guard asked with a smile.

"I'm fine, thank you," I replied.

"Good to see you back."

"Is Mr. Rinehart in?" I asked.

"Not right at the moment. He was in earlier but left just a short while ago."

"Do you know where he went by chance?"

"No, sir. He never tells me anything."

That didn't surprise me. The only thing I was hoping for was some sort of time line as to when he would be returning. I stood looking at the guard trying to make up my mind as to what I should do next.

"Is there something I can help you with, Mr. Tidsdale," the guard said.

Until he spoke to me, I had no idea that he was watching me so closely. I got the impression that he might be worried that I was having some sort of spell. Even though he was not on duty at the time, I was sure that he knew that I had been attacked less than a week ago and that I had been hit on the head.

"No. No, thank you. I think I'll go up to Carlson's office. I have a lot of work to do," I said as I smiled at him.

The guard watched as I turned and walked over to the elevator. I glanced back over my shoulder while I waited for the elevator. The guard was still watching me. When it arrived and the doors opened, I stepped inside and pressed the button for the eighteenth floor. I noticed that the guard was still watching me as the doors closed.

I decided that since Rinehart was not available, I would go up to Mile High Design and have another talk with Steinman. Since I didn't want the guard to know that I was going on up to Mile High Design, I would get off on the eighteenth floor and take the stairs to go up the other two floors. It would also make it a little easier to get to Steinman without someone stopping me and without anyone knowing I was there.

I had no idea how much Steinman knew, but he had to know something. I had shaken him enough on my last visit that he sicced Rinehart on me. That was enough to make me want to put a little more fear in him. If he was scared enough, he might make a mistake, and I would be ready and waiting for him.

I had no reason to think that Steinman would talk to me without the threat of death. The last thing I wanted was to give him a reason to have me arrested for harassing him. I was sure he would if I threatened him.

When the elevator reached the eighteenth floor I got off, but before I stepped off the elevator, I pressed the button that would send it back down to the fifth floor. If the guard was watching the elevator to see where it went, he would not know that I went to the twentieth floor. He would think that I had gone where I said I was going. If the guard told Rinehart when he came in that I was looking for him and I had gone to Carlson's office, he would not suspect that I was actually in Steinman's office.

Once the elevator was on its way down, I walked to the end of the hall to the stairwell that would take me to the twentieth floor. If my directions were correct, the stairwell should put me at the end of the hall that Steinman's office was on. It should also put me behind his private secretary. I had no doubt that it would be locked to prevent entrance to the hall from the stairwell, but I was not often stopped by a locked door. The stairs could also be used by Steinman as an escape route in case of trouble, and as a fire escape if necessary.

When I got to the top floor, I was not surprised to find the door locked. There was a small window with wire running through it, but I could see all the way down the hall to the reception desk. I couldn't see anyone at the desk because all I could see was the very front of the desk.

I could also see Mr. Steinman's secretary's desk, but she was not sitting at it. There was no one in the hall at the moment. It was as good a time as any to pick the lock.

It took me a couple of minutes to pick the lock. It turned out to be harder than I thought it would be. When I started to open the door, I hesitated when I saw Steinman's secretary come out of his office. She had several files in her arms. She stopped just outside Steinman's office door and turned to look back. I could hear her say "Yes, sir," before she started down the hall toward the receptionist desk. That little comment told me that Steinman was in his office even if it gave me no indication if he was alone.

I quickly opened the door, stepped into the hall, than closed the door behind me. Keeping an eye on the hall, I moved up close to the door to Steinman's office and listened. I didn't hear anyone talking so I assumed that he was alone.

I stepped into his office, closed and locked the door behind me. Steinman looked up from the papers on his desk at me. The expression on his face made it clear that he was surprised to see me. He had probably heard that Rinehart had cracked my skull. He started to reach for the intercom.

"You touch that and I will break every bone in your hand, and that's just for starters," I threatened as I stepped closer to him.

He hesitated for only a second before he pulled his hand back away from the phone.

"How did you get in here?" he demanded, but the tone of his voice gave away his fear that I was there to do him harm.

"I walked in," I replied as I walked toward him.

"What do you want?"

I could see by the look on his face that he was scared as well he should be. I didn't have anything on him I could prove, but I was sure he knew that I could make his life miserable.

"You know, I found out something that I would be willing to bet you wouldn't like your people in LA to know."

"You can't prove anything."

"Now that's a strange response to what I said, especially since you don't know what I know. I would say you have a guilty mind."

"I have nothing of the sort," he blurted out, but with little conviction behind it.

"I think you do. And I think you have every right to be scared to death, but not from me."

"If not you, then from whom?" he asked.

He was suddenly getting a little more confident. I got the impression that he was beginning to want to know just what it was that I knew and how much I knew.

"If I were you I would be scared to death of Rinehart."

"Rinehart? Why should I be scared of Rinehart? He works for me."

"Does he?" I asked with a grin.

I could see the look on his face change.

"What do you mean by that? He has worked for me for three years. He came highly recommended for his skills as a security expert."

"I'll bet. Do you know what he is really skilled at?"

"I don't get what you're asking. He's a security expert."

"Actually, he's a bone breaker. Since you might not understand that term, I'll explain. He works for the mob and enforces the wishes of his boss by breaking the bones of those who make his boss unhappy. You know, like broken arms, legs, hands, that sort of thing. By the way, do you know who his real boss is?

"I don't know what you're talking about," he said, every inch of his body showing how nervous he was getting.

"His real boss is Donato Sargossa."

"I don't believe you."

"You better if you want to live very long."

"Why would a man like Sargossa want to kill me?"

"Because you know too much."

I could see that Steinman was really beginning to worry now. He had no idea how much I knew, but the fact that I knew about Sargossa was already more than he wanted me to know. I had put the fear of Sargossa in him. In his case that was far worse than the fear of God as far as he was concerned.

"I want to know what you know about the death of Julie Mathews and Jennifer Carlson."

"I don't know anything about it."

"I don't think that's the right answer, but it really doesn't matter. Once I find out why they were killed, I'll have all I need to go to the police."

I wanted him to be scared, but I didn't want him to think that I knew enough to have the police knocking on his door just yet. From the look on his face, I had accomplished what I had come here to do.

"You think about what I said."

Steinman didn't say anything as I turned and walked over to the door. I unlocked it and opened the door. Steinman's secretary had a surprised look on her face when I stepped out into the hall.

"Don't worry. Your boss is fine," I said as I turned and walked down the hall toward the reception desk.

When I got to the elevator, I pushed the button then waited for it to arrive. As soon as it arrived, I got on and pressed the button that would take it to the eighteenth floor. I got off and went directly to Carlson's office.

I knew it was only a matter of time before Rinehart would know that I had talked to Steinman. Once he found that out, he would come looking for me, only this time I would be ready for him.

Rinehart left the Carlson home and drove back to his office. As he drove into the underground garage, he nodded to the guard on duty at the garage gate. He parked, then went to the elevator and took it to the eighteenth floor where he got off and went directly to his office. After locking the door behind him, he sat down at his desk and placed a call to Donato Sargossa. The phone was answered on the third ring.

"Yeah," the voice on the other end of the line said.

"Rinehart. I need to talk to the boss."

"Just a minute," the voice said.

It was almost fifteen minutes before Sargossa picked up the phone. It was his habit to make anyone who called him, or stopped in unannounced to wait. It was his way of showing them that he was in control of everything.

"Jacob, my boy. I hope you have some good news this time."

"I don't think so, Mr. Sargossa."

"Do we need to meet?"

"I think what I have to say might best be said in private," Rinehart said, not sure if Sargossa's phones were tapped.

"Okay. Meet me at the usual place in about two hours. I have something to clear up here, first."

"I'll be waiting for you."

There was no confirmation. The phone simply went dead.

Rinehart sat there for several minutes before he made a move. There were a lot of things running through his mind. Since he had no idea if there was anything to worry about, he couldn't help but think that there was.

Rinehart kicked back in his chair and began to think about Tidsdale. He wondered if the beating he had given

Tidsdale was going to be enough to get him off the case. He had his doubts.

Just then the phone began to ring. Rinehart sat up then reached over and picked up the receiver.

"Yes."

"You should have taken care of that Tidsdale like I told you," the voice screamed into the phone.

"What are you talking about, Mr. Steinman? He's in the hospital with a cracked skull."

"Like hell he is. He left my office not fifteen minutes ago, just fifteen minutes ago," he screamed."

"Take it easy. Why didn't you call me?"

"I tried the minute he left, but you either didn't answer or the line was busy."

"I must have just missed you. What did he want?"

"I think he knows about my arrangement with Sargossa."

"What makes you so sure?"

"He said that you work for Sargossa. Is that true?"

"Yes. It is. And I would suggest that you settle down."

"How long has this been going on?"

"Since the day you hired me. I've always worked for Sargossa. I take my orders from him."

"Well, see where it got us. That Tidsdale knows everything."

"I doubt that."

"He knows there's a connection between the deaths of Carlson and Mathews."

"He's only guessing. He can't prove anything."

"I wouldn't put money on that. You've got to get rid of him before he can prove it. Do you hear me?"

"I hear you, but I'm not going to do anything until I talk to Sargossa. I've got a meeting with him in a little while."

"You better kill Tidsdale. If I get arrested, I'm not going down alone, and you can tell Sargossa that," Steinman said, then slammed down the receiver.

It was obvious that Tidsdale was not going to back off. In addition to Tidsdale, Rinehart knew there was going to be a problem with Steinman. If Steinman panicked and spilled his guts, there would be hell to pay. With the way Steinman was acting, there was little doubt that Rinehart should probably take him out before he got so scared that he talked. He would talk to Sargossa and see what he wanted him to do about both of them.

As Rinehart leaned back in his chair, he wondered if Tidsdale might still be in the building. If he was, he would most likely be in Carlson's office. Since there was little chance that anyone would be visiting Carlson's office, he thought about going down the hall to find out. It would be easy to take him out using a pistol with a silencer on it.

He sat up and opened his desk drawer. He took out a pistol and attached a silencer to it. If he was going to kill Tidsdale, he wanted it to be done with a minimum amount of noise.

Rinehart started to tuck the gun with the silencer under his coat but suddenly thought better of it. He knew that he needed Sargossa's okay if he was going to kill him. Besides, Tidsdale would be easy to find.

Since Rinehart had over an hour before Sargossa would be meeting him in front of the Marriott Hotel, Rinehart decided that he would go get himself something to eat, then drive over to the downtown Marriott and wait for Sargossa. There was no need to spend a lot of time waiting around the office.

Rinehart left his office and headed for the elevator. He took the elevator to the main floor. He walked up to the counter where the security guard was on duty.

"May I help you, Mr. Rinehart?"

"Did you see Mr. Tidsdale this morning?"

"Yes sir. He came in this morning and went up to Mr. Carlson's office."

"Did you see him leave?"

"No, sir. As far as I know he is still in Mr. Carlson's office."

Rinehart knew that he had been to see Steinman. A quick look at his watch told him that he didn't have time to confront Tidsdale now. He would go get a cup of coffee and a roll at the Marriott, talk to Sargossa about what he should do about Tidsdale and Steinman then do what he was instructed to do.

"Is there anything else I can help you with?" the guard asked wondering what Rinehart was thinking.

Rinehart looked up at the guard, then said, "No."

Rinehart turned and went back to the elevators. He took the elevator to the garage and got into his car. He drove to the downtown Marriott.

CHAPTER THIRTY-NINE

I sat behind Carlson's desk waiting for Rinehart and thinking, mostly thinking. There was little doubt in my mind that once he got wind that I had talked to Steinman, he would be in a hurry to find me. It was only a matter of time before he would come to Carlson's office looking for me. I also knew that it could be a rather long wait.

I wondered if Rinehart had returned to his office. It was probably not a good idea for me to go to his office and confront him there. That would make it hard for me to say that I beat the hell out of him in self-defense. On the other hand, I wanted my pound of flesh. But it would be so much better if I could prove he murdered either Mathews or Carlson, or both. I would settle for a conviction for either one of them.

Along with thinking about Rinehart, I began to think about Steinman and Mile High Design. The more I thought about it, the more I began to believe that I had enough evidence to get an investigation started into Mile High Design's accounting practices of city money spent on the new city buildings. I was sure that the CD I had would go a long way in getting the city to look into it. I looked under the computer monitor and found the CD right where I had left it. I picked it up and put it in my coat pocket.

To get an investigation started, I would need to get hold of Wright and let him know what I had. I reached over, picked up the phone and placed a call to Wright.

"Denver Police Department, Precinct One, is this an emergency?"

"No. I'm Frank Tidsdale. I would like to speak to Detective Donald Wright."

"One moment, please."

It wasn't long and Don came on the line.

"What's up, Frank?"

"I need to have a little talk with you."

"About what?"

"About a CD I found in Carlson's office. I think you would be very interested in what it has to do with the murder of Mrs. Carlson and possibly the death of Julie Mathews. I think you will find that it provides a clear motive for the death of Mrs. Carlson."

"Where would you like to meet?"

"I think that since Rinehart will probably be looking for me, it might be a good idea if we were to meet in your office."

"When?"

"As soon as I can get there?"

"Okay. I'll be waiting for you."

"I'll be there in about ten minutes," I said.

As I hung up the phone, it suddenly occurred to me that I had the only CD that would be of any help in convincing the police that there were some rather questionable accounting practices going on. It caused me to wonder what would happen if I ran into Rinehart? With the way things were going for me lately, I wasn't too sure what he would do. The last thing I wanted him to do was to get his hands on the only CD, at least the only one I knew about. I decided it would be a good idea to make a copy of it and hide it so if he got the CD I was carrying, it wouldn't matter if he destroyed it.

I looked around until I found a clean CD. After putting the information on the computer, I copied it back off onto the clean CD, then on to a second CD. I made sure that all the CDs had the same information on them before I deleted the information from the computer. I hid the CD that Mrs. Carlson made under the computer monitor where I had hidden it before. I put one of the copies in a file cabinet in the file room and the other one in my sport coat pocket before I left for the elevator.

I kept an eye out for Rinehart. The last thing I wanted to do was to run into him in the elevator. I took the elevator to the main floor and started walking toward the door. I was only about half way to the door when the guard called to me.

"Mr. Tidsdale."

"Yeah," I said as I turned and walked toward him.

"Did Mr. Rinehart find you?"

"No."

"He was looking for you. I guess you just missed him."

"I guess so," I replied. "Thanks."

Turning toward the door, I quickened my pace. Once outside the building, I hurried to my car. I kept a close watch to make sure that I was not being followed as I drove to the police station.

Rinehart was waiting outside the Marriott Hotel when Sargossa's Cadillac pulled up to the curb. The backdoor opened and he got in. He quickly discovered that Mr. Sargossa was not in the car. Instead there were two of Sargossa's bodyguards. Rinehart looked at the two men. The fact that Sargossa was not in the car caused Rinehart to become a little worried.

"Where's the boss," Rinehart asked.

"Back to the barn," one of the bodyguards said to the driver without answering Rinehart's question.

Rinehart was sure that he had done something that had upset Sargossa. When Sargossa sent his bodyguards out to get someone, it was not a good sign. It was especially not a good sign when the two bodyguards didn't talk. They rode to Sargossa's house in silence. It was the longest trip that Rinehart could remember, although it only took about fifteen minutes.

After going up the long circular drive to the front of the house, the driver stopped the car. The two bodyguards got out and escorted Rinehart into the house, one on each side of him. They led Rinehart into the den off to the right of the foyer. Sargossa was waiting for him.

"Have a seat, my boy. I'm sure you are wondering why I had you brought here."

"As a matter of fact, I am," Rinehart replied.

"I thought it might be best if we have our little discussion here. Now what is it that is so important that you needed this meeting?"

"Well, sir, first of all, Mr. Frank Tidsdale has not backed off."

"I didn't think that would require you to call me. I thought we had discussed that before. You had your instructions with regard to him. Isn't that so?" Sargossa asked.

"Yes, sir."

Well, then I expect you to follow my instructions. Do you need help getting it done?"

"No, sir," Rinehart replied.

"You said 'first of all'. I take it there is something else you wish to discuss with me?"

"Yes, sir. It has to do with Steinman. It seems that Tidsdale had a talk with him this morning. Steinman called me shortly after his visit from Tidsdale. He was very agitated. He said Tidsdale knows about his arrangement with you."

"That could prove to be a problem, but I wouldn't get too excited about it. Was there anything else?"

Yes, sir. Tidsdale told him that I work for you. I told Steinman that I took my orders from you, not him.

"How did that set with him?" Sargossa asked, with a slight grin on his face.

"Not very well. Steinman said that Tidsdale knew there was a connection between the deaths of the Carlson woman and the Mathews woman."

"What did you tell Steinman?"

"I told him that he was only guessing and that Tidsdale couldn't prove anything. - - - ,"

"Can he prove it?" Sargossa asked, interrupting Rinehart.

"No, sir. I don't believe he can."

"But you're not sure."

"No, sir. Not a hundred percent sure."

"Then you need to do something about him."

"Yes, sir. There is one other thing."

"What's that."

"Steinman was demanding that I get rid of Tidsdale before he could prove anything."

"That doesn't sound like too bad an idea."

"No, sir. It doesn't. But the thing that has me worried about Steinman was his comment about if he gets arrested. He said that if he gets arrested, he was not going down alone. He also said that I could tell you that before he slammed down the phone."

"Well, I see your concern," Sargossa said thoughtfully.

Rinehart sat quietly while Sargossa stood up and walked over by the window. It was clear that he was thinking of the best way to make the problem go away. He suddenly turned back around and looked at Rinehart.

"I want you to make sure that Tidsdale is disposed of in the manner that we discussed earlier, and I want it done today. Do you understand?"

"Yes, sir. But what about Steinman. If he gets any pressure put on him by the police, he might talk."

"You let me worry about Steinman. You just take care of Tidsdale."

"Yes, sir," Rinehart replied.

Rinehart stood up as Sargossa looked over at one of the bodyguards and said, "Have the driver take Mr. Rinehart back to the Marriott, then return here immediately."

Rinehart followed the bodyguard out to the car and got in. The bodyguard gave the driver instructions to take Rinehart back to the Marriott and return, then stood back and watched as the driver drove down the circular driveway to the street.

CHAPTER FORTY

When I arrived at the police station where Wright was waiting for me, I looked around. I didn't see anyone that might cause me to be suspicious. I went into the police station and immediately talked to the desk sergeant. I didn't have to tell him who I was there to see, he simply pointed down the hall toward Wright's office.

"He said to expect you."

"Thanks."

When I got to his office, I knocked on the door. He immediately told me to enter. I opened the door and stepped into his office. I noticed that Latimer was sitting in a chair up against the wall. He had that same stupid grin on his face. I had to wonder what it was that he found so funny.

"You have something for me?" Wright asked, getting right to the point.

I glanced over at Latimer. I wasn't sure that I wanted him to see what I had.

"Well?" Wright said.

"If he isn't willing to show us what he has regarding this case, then maybe we should arrest him for withholding evidence and take it away from him," Latimer said with a grin.

Latimer would like nothing better than to slap me in cuffs. With his show of arrogance I was almost willing to let him try, but that would just prolong the case and make it easier for those involved to fold up shop and disappear into the night, so to speak. The case was far more important than Latimer, but then almost anything was more important than Latimer.

"You'd like that wouldn't you. Let me explain a small but very important fact of life to you. What I have is a copy of the original CD. Since it is not the original, I would have to verify it in order for you to use it in a court of law. How fast do you think I would do that if you tried to arrest me? And how fast do you think it would be before you are out pounding a beat?"

"That's enough," Wright said angrily. "No one is arresting you. And Latimer, if you can't be in the same room with Tidsdale and keep your damn mouth shut, you are more than welcome to leave. If you stay, you will keep your damn mouth shut. Is that clear?"

I didn't wait for Latimer to respond to Wright. Reaching in my pocket, I took out the copy of the CD and handed it to Wright.

"You will find everything you need to start an investigation into Mile High Designs accounting practices. It will also provide you with a motive for Mrs. Carlson's murder. The only thing it doesn't provide is the name of who killed her, or who ordered her killed."

"Where is the original," Latimer asked.

The tone of his voice showed that he might be a little more willing to work with me. I found it a little hard to accept this sudden turn around in his attitude. I guess it was my suspicious nature, but I wasn't ready to give him the information he seemed to want.

Wright looked at Latimer, then at me. I got the impression that he was wondering why the change of heart by Latimer, too. He might have also been wondering if I would tell him where the CD was. I guess he figured that I wasn't going to tell him.

"By the way, Tidsdale, are you ready to tell me who it was that almost killed you? I know you were hit from behind, but I think you know who did it."

"You're right. I do know who did it, but I'm not ready to tell you."

Again, Wright looked from me to Latimer, then back to me. If I had to guess, he was trying to decide if I wouldn't tell him because Latimer was in the room. He would have been partly right. The fact was I wanted my chance at Rinehart first.

"You take a look at the CD. Let me know what you think," I said as I stood up.

"You're not staying around while I look at it?"

"I've already seen it. I don't know what good it will do for me to see it again."

"Okay. I'll talk to you later."

I turned and left Wright's office. I was no longer concerned about being followed. The police had a copy of the CD. Even if the original was found, I had another copy and I could verify the copy in court if necessary.

It was now time to find out who had murdered the young woman who had stuck her neck out to help me. I had a pretty good idea who was involved, I just couldn't prove it. My next stop would be the morgue. I was hoping that the M.E. would be able to help me figure out who had killed her.

Rinehart got out of Sargossa's limo in front of the downtown Marriott and watched it as it disappeared around the corner. All the way back to the Marriott, Rinehart had been thinking about how he was going to kill Tidsdale and have it look like an accident. One of his first thoughts was to frame him for the death of someone. He smiled at the thought of having him framed for the murder of Steinman, but there was a problem with that. Sargossa wanted him out of the way immediately. With all the friends Tidsdale had on the police force, it would take too long to have him put away. Plus, it would not satisfy Sargossa as it would not get rid of him for good and quickly. Rinehart started off toward where he had left his car.

As he was walking toward his car, he thought about an auto accident. That would be a good way to get rid of him, but it was hard to plan one so it looked spontaneous in such a short time.

It was at that moment he remembered that there had been a rash of muggings in the area of the building where Tidsdale had his office located. There had been three within a four or five block area of the building in the last couple of months, and most of them had taken place either near the entrance to the underground garages of nearby buildings or actually in the underground garage. However, there had not been one at the building where Tidsdale's office was located. Maybe it was time for one in his building's garage, Rinehart thought.

Before Rinehart could kill Tidsdale in the underground garage, he would have to study the MO of the previous muggings; otherwise it would not look like his death was from a mugging by the same person or persons that had been committing them.

Rinehart suddenly remembered what Tidsdale had told him a while back. He had said that he could learn a lot in a library. He smiled to himself as he turned the corner and headed for the Denver Library.

Once Rinehart got to the library, he went to the counter and asked for help. A young woman directed him to the archives. The young woman's name was Lisa. She helped him find all the articles about the muggings in the area he was interested in.

Rinehart began by reading everything he could find on the muggings in the area around Tidsdale's building. He made a list of all the evidence that had been reported to have been found at the scene of the muggings. He didn't want to miss a thing if he was going to make Tidsdale's death look like the result of a mugging gone badly. Rinehart also knew that not all the evidence found at the scene of the muggings would be released to the press. He would just have to do his best to make it look like the other muggings.

Once he had as complete a list as he could, Rinehart left the library and returned to his office. He put together a plan to kill Tidsdale in such a way that the police would think he was the victim of a mugging by the same people that had been committing them in that area over the past couple of months.

Once his plan was complete, he gathered all the things he would need to carry it out. Then it was time to go to the garage and wait for Tidsdale to show up.

CHAPTER FORTY-ONE

The morgue was one place that was the least enjoyable place to visit, but I had little choice. If I was going to find out what the cause of death of Julie Mathews was, I had to start there. The M.E. and I were on a first name basis. We had worked together on a number of occasions during my time as a police officer.

When I arrived at the morgue, I found Martin Dodd at one of his examining tables. On the cold stainless steel table laid a man that I would guess was in his mid-thirties, although it was hard to tell. It looked like he had been dead for at least a week, probably longer.

"What's going on?" I asked to get his attention.

Martin looked up and smiled.

"Say, guy. What brings you down here to the dungeon of death?"

"I'd like a bit of information."

"How can I help you?"

"I was wondering what you could tell me about the death of Julie Mathews. I understand that she came across your table not too long ago."

"Yes, she did. To bad. She was so young, and pretty, too."

"What can you tell me about her death? What did you find?"

"Can you wait a few minutes? I just got this guy a few minutes ago."

"Sure. What's his cause of death?"

"A bullet hole in the head. He took the shot up close and personal. It was done with a small caliber gun pressed against his head just back of the left ear. Professional job would be my guess."

"Really."

"Yeah. He was shot some time ago, at least a week, maybe more, would be my guess at this point. He has a deep cut to his right hand that looks like it might have happened about the same time."

I just stood there looking at the body. Was it possible that the man whose blood we found on the floor in Carlson's house was lying on Martin's table at this very minute?

"Tell me. Does the cut on his hand look like it was a defensive wound?"

"Yeah. I'm sure it is, but it doesn't add up. He was killed by a shot to the head up close, not by a knife. And the knife that cut his hand was razor sharp. If it wasn't for the depth of the wound and the cut, it could have been made by a razor. But I think it was a very sharp kitchen knife, probably one of those ceramic knives that the chefs like to use."

"Martin, you may have found the missing link to a murder that I have been working on."

"No kidding," he said as he looked up at me.

"Yeah. I want you to compare his blood with samples taken in the Jennifer Carlson murder case. We found some blood on the floor of the house that didn't match the victim or the husband. I got the impression that it came from a third party."

"I can do that. I'll let you know how it comes out."

"Great. If I got you one of the knives from the set, could you tell if the knife that cut him was the same kind?"

"I might, but it's a long shoot. If you can get one, I'll see what I can find out."

"You know who this guy is?" I asked.

"Not yet, but I haven't run his prints, yet."

"I'll leave you one of my cards. Give me a call when you find out something."

"Sure."

As I turned to leave the morgue, I thought about calling Wright and telling him what I found. But I decided that it was a little too early.

"Say, you still want to know about Julie Mathews?"

"Yeah. I guess I got a little distracted."

"Come over to my office."

I followed Martin out of the morgue to his office. He picked up a file from the basket on his desk and sat down. I sat down in a chair in front of his desk. I noticed that Martin was not the most organized person that I had ever met. In fact, his office looked like an oversized waste basket.

"Well, let's see," he said as he looked through the file. "Okay. Here. Miss Mathews suffocated. She was not strangled. She was smothered in the comforter on her bed. From the looks of the marks on her body and what the comforter told us, she had been pushed down on her bed. Someone had laid down over her while pushing her face into the comforter until she suffocated. I can tell you this, she didn't die quickly.

"We also found that she had been undressed after she was dead, then redressed in a nightgown. She was then placed very carefully in her bed to make it look like she had died in her sleep. Whoever killed her didn't know anything about forensics. It clearly showed that she was murdered," Martin said.

"What kind of evidence did you find that might lead to her killer?"

"We did find a couple of dark brown hairs. They are from a male, but we don't know who."

"If I could get a hair, could you tell me if it was from the same person?"

"Sure. It would be best if you got a hair with the root still intact. That way I could do DNA testing and prove it beyond a doubt. You have someone in mind?"

"Yes. I'll see what I can come up with."

"You want me to run it against the guy on the table?"

"It wouldn't hurt. But if he's been dead for a week or more it wouldn't be him."

"I'll run it just in case."

"You might run any hairs you find on the guy on your table against the one found on Miss Mathews. There may be a connection between the two."

"That sounds like a bit of a reach, but I'll do it."

"Let me know what you find out," I said as I stood up.

"Will do."

"Oh. You might want to keep it quiet for awhile."

"Okay."

I left Martin's office and returned to my car. I got in, but didn't start the car right away. I had to wonder if I was reaching for answers that weren't there. I wasn't sure if there was a connection between the body Martin had on his table and Julie Mathews. Only time would tell.

I reached down and started my car. I drove back to my office to think.

Rinehart drove into the garage under the building where Tidsdale's office was located. He had no idea if Tidsdale was in his office or not, but it didn't really matter. He had been given orders to kill Tidsdale and make it look like an accident. He was also told to make it quick, and he knew Sargossa would accept nothing less.

Rinehart had only been in the garage for about twenty or thirty minutes when he saw Tidsdale drive in. He watched as Tidsdale parked his car only a short distance from the elevator.

As Rinehart reached for the handle to open his car door, he caught sight of another car coming into the garage. Rinehart turned his attention to the second car and cursed. When he looked back toward Tidsdale's car, he saw him disappear into the elevator. He hit the steering wheel of his car in frustration. He had hoped to get it over with quickly and then leave. Letting out a sigh, he leaned back in the seat of his car to wait for Tidsdale to come back to the garage. He would try again then.

Rinehart began to think that he might need a plan B if he was going to get the job done. Since he had nothing else to do, he began to mentally work on a new plan, just in case the one he had planned didn't work. His first thought was to mess with the brakes on Tidsdale's car, but he knew that was not a very dependable way to get rid of someone. Besides it was too easy to detect if someone decided that it might not have been an accident.

Having Tidsdale be attacked by a mugger was still the best idea that he had come up with. If it didn't work, he might just have to plan to shoot Tidsdale and dispose of his body in a way that it wouldn't be found for a very long time, if at all.

Just then, the elevator door opened. Rinehart looked toward the elevator in the hope that Tidsdale was returning to his car. He once again started to get out of his car, but quickly closed the door when he saw it was not Tidsdale. He was now thinking that his idea wasn't going to work.

As impatience started to cause Rinehart more frustration, he began to think about just going to Tidsdale's office and killing him there. It wasn't what Sargossa wanted, but it would get him out of the way. Rinehart was confident that he could do it without leaving any evidence that would point to him or Sargossa as being the killer. After all, he had gotten rid of Jack Vernon after he messed up the job of getting information from Jennifer Carlson. Rinehart smiled to himself as he thought about how good he was at taking care of loose ends. Especially the kind of loose ends that could put him in jail for a very long time.

He decided that he would wait a little longer. If Tidsdale didn't come down to the garage in the next hour, he would go to Tidsdale's office and take care of matters there.

CHAPTER FORTY-TWO

By the time I got back to my office, I had had a chance to think about what I found out at the morgue. The fact was that I had learned almost nothing. I had my theories, but that was all they were, theories. Until I had some kind of proof nothing would change. If Martin could tie the body on his table to the blood in Carlson's house, it would show beyond a reasonable doubt that there was someone other than Jim Carlson in the house when his wife was murdered.

The police now had a motive for Mrs. Carlson's murder. It was pretty cut and dried with the evidence provided by Mrs. Carlson's CD of what she had discovered at Mile High Design.

I still didn't have a solid motive for the murder of Julie Mathews. The only thing I could think of as a motive was that someone was worried about what she might know. That would mean that the motive for her death was to shut up a witness. However, having talked with her, I doubted she knew anything.

Just as my thoughts turned to the guy on the slab at the morgue, my phone began to ring. I reached over and picked it up.

"Tidsdale Investigative Agency"

"Franky, you got a minute."

"Always for you. What's up?"

"You asked me to keep nosing around. Well, Steinman is in deep debt to Sargossa. He's been gambling at a large house in the foothills. The house just happens to belong to Sargossa. On paper it is rented to a dummy company that just happens to be used to launder money into Sargossa's organization."

"Well, that's what we suspected. Is there any way to prove that?"

"All you have to do is follow the money, but being the nice guy I am, I've done that for you. Give me your fax number. As soon as you get the information, be sure to wipe out my number from your fax machine."

"No problem. Is the information reliable?"

"Rock Solid. You can take it to the bank, so to speak," he said with a slight chuckle in his voice.

"Great. Thanks for your help."

"No problem. Say, there's one more thing."

"What's that?"

"The word is that Rinehart is out to kill you. It seems you didn't take his warning seriously."

"Oh, I took it seriously. I just wasn't about to back down. I think he killed that young girl who worked for Mile High Design just because she talked to me."

"Well, he's out to get you now."

"He's not the only one out to get someone. He's about to find out that I'm out to get him."

"You be careful out there. Rinehart is as mean as they come."

"I will. Thanks for the info."

"You're welcome," he said, then the phone went dead.

I looked at the phone as I hung it up. That was the second time I had been warned to watch out for Rinehart. I must not have paid as much attention to the first warning as I should have since I ended up getting my head cracked. I was not about to let it happen again.

My thoughts were interrupted by the sound of my fax machine coming on. I got up and walked over to see what my friend was sending me. It took a few minutes, but it was well worth it. The fax machine spit out six sheets of paper showing addresses of buildings and houses that were owned by Sargossa, several bank accounts both in and out of the city that belonged to Sargossa and a list of companies that had some connection to Sargossa. I quickly noticed that Mile High Design was not listed as one of the companies. The last sheet of paper listed the owner and board of directors of Mile High Design. My friend had been right. Mile High Design was actually owned by a San Francisco company that had offices in several western cities. Steinman was listed as the President of Mile High Design, but it was only a title. The paper for the business was owned by the San Francisco company.

I quickly deleted the address and phone number on the fax from the machine. Once that was done, I decided to share this new information with Wright. It might help him in his case. I made a copy of the faxes and safely put the original fax in a secure place. I put the copies in my coat pocket.

I was about to leave when my phone began to ring again. I reached over and picked up the phone.

"Tidsdale Investigative Agency"

"Tidsdale, this is Wright."

"Yeah. I was about to come and see you."

"Oh. Why?"

"I got some interesting information on Mile High Design."

"Well, I have some interesting information for you. We went to Mile High Design to have a little talk with Steinman about the death of Jennifer Carlson. When we got to his office, we found him slumped over his desk. It looked like he killed himself. There was a .38 caliber pistol next to his hand. It probably has his fingerprints on it."

I didn't say anything for a moment or so. I had to think.

"Let me ask you this. Do you think he killed himself?" I asked.

"Not for a minute. We're looking for Rinehart."

"That makes two of us. But I don't think Rinehart killed Steinman."

"What makes you think that?"

"He's a little too close to Steinman. I think one of Sargossa's muscles probably did it."

"You may be right. What's the information you have for me?"

"It's a list of banks, companies, and houses owned by Sargossa. It will show you where all the money goes. Along with the other information you have on Mile High Design, it should help you close him down. Where are you now?"

"At Mile High Design."

"I'll see you in a little while."

"Okay," he said then hung up.

I had just stood up and was getting ready to leave my office when the phone began to ring, again. I couldn't help but wonder who it was this time. I reached over and picked up the phone.

"Tidsdale's Investigative Agency."

"Frank, Martin here."

"Do you have something for me?"

"Yeah. I have the name of the guy on my table. It's Jack Vernon, a small time hood. Does his name mean anything to you?"

"No. Have you checked out the other things I asked about?"

"No. Not yet. The DNA tests might take a little while. I thought you might like to know his name. You could check it out and find out who he was working for."

"Thanks. Would you get back to me when you have the rest of the information I need?"

"Sure. Talk to you later."

"Okay," I said, then hung up.

I couldn't remember ever hearing of Jack Vernon. The fact that he was a small time hood, and he had a deep cut on his hand led me to believe he might very well have been the other person in the Carlson house. I'd have to wait for the DNA results to be sure.

I left my office locking the door behind me. As I started for the elevator, I got to thinking about the warning I had received from my friend. I stood back away from the elevator with my hand under my coat and on my gun as I watched the doors open. There was no one there so I stepped on the elevator and pushed the button for the main floor.

Again, I was prepared for anything that should happen. When the door opened, I found the lobby was empty. I walked over to the stairwell and walked down to the garage instead of taking the elevator the rest of the way down. I didn't want any surprises in the garage where I would be an easier target.

Time had gone by very slowly for Rinehart. It seemed to him as if he had been sitting there for hours just waiting for Tidsdale to come back down. He wondered what Tidsdale could be doing in his office that would take him so long.

Rinehart's mind began to wonder what Sargossa had in mind for Steinman. There was little doubt that he would have to kill Steinman to keep him from talking. It was clear that things were beginning to fall apart.

Rinehart knew that if Steinman was to talk, he would be arrested. He began to wonder if Sargossa would have him killed just to make sure that there were no loose ends. Although Rinehart had never given Sargossa reason not to trust him, he knew that Sargossa would cover his own ass at any cost. Rinehart knew that as far as Sargossa was concerned, he was expendable.

That thought got Rinehart to thinking. Maybe it would be a good idea for him to go ahead and kill Tidsdale, but when that was done he should simply disappear. He had a bit of money in a wall safe in his office in the Hammond Building. He had set it aside for an emergency. To his way of thinking, that was an emergency. He also had a private bank account under a different name in Santa Fe, New Mexico, that no one knew about. It would provide him with enough money to leave the country and live comfortably for some time in some country that would not extradite him back to the U.S.

Rinehart smiled to himself as his thoughts turned to leaving Denver and letting Sargossa fend for himself. He had been treated well by Sargossa over the years, but he knew that Sargossa would give him up in a heartbeat to save his own neck. He was not going to jail to save Sargossa from going to jail.

With that firmly set in his mind, he had one thing to do before the put his plan to disappear into action. And that was to get rid of Tidsdale.

CHAPTER FORTY-THREE

At the garage level there was a small window in the door to the stairwell. I took a minute to look out. There were not many cars in the garage at this hour, but there was one that interested me. I could see someone sitting in the car. He was looking toward the elevator. I watched him for a few minutes before he turned enough for me to see his face and for me to recognize him. It was Rinehart. It didn't take a rocket scientist to figure out what he was doing there at this hour. I looked around to see if there was anyone else in the garage. I couldn't see anyone.

Staying hidden behind the door, I began to form a plan in my head. It was time to get even with Mr. Rinehart for the beating he gave me. The plan that formed in my mind was rather simple, and I was ready.

I took my gun out of my shoulder holster and held it in my hand down at my side. In my other hand, I carried the envelope that had the copies of the fax I had received earlier. I slowly opened the door and stepped out of the stairwell. I moved quickly behind one of the large square concrete posts. It was clear that he had not seen me.

After taking a minute to plan my next move, I began working my way from one post to the next as I moved closer to Rinehart while he sat in his car. I was very careful to keep his blind spot in the car between him and me. I didn't want him to see me until I was very close to his car. When I got close enough to his car, I stepped out and pointed my gun at him through the open window.

"Good evening, Mr. Rinehart," I said.

He jerked around and was reaching for his gun at the same time.

"I wouldn't do anything stupid," I said sharply.

He stopped and looked at the business end of my gun which was only about a foot from his head. I could see that he was trying to think of something to do, but he knew his options were very few at the moment.

"How's it feel to be on the other end of a gun?" I asked.

"I'll let you know when you no longer have the upper hand."

"I have been thinking about this moment for some time. I have even been thinking about what I would do when it came."

"Have you decided?"

"As a matter of fact, I have. But first, I would like you to know that we found your partner."

"What partner?"

"The one who helped you kill Jennifer Carlson."

Rinehart didn't make a move, but I noticed a slight tightening of his jaw. I knew I was right.

"Mr. Jack Vernon. Does that ring any bells for you?"

"No," he replied, but not with a great deal of enthusiasm."

"That's okay. It really doesn't matter because he's in the morgue. The M.E. is going over him very carefully. He found some hair on his clothes that we think will match up to you."

"So. I knew him."

"Yes, you knew him. I also think you killed him so that he wouldn't be able to get his hand treated for the nasty cut that Jennifer Carlson inflicted on him. You probably knew that if he went to a hospital or doctor's office to get the cut taken care of the police would be notified. If that happened, they would be able to match his blood to the blood found on the floor at the Carlson house. You couldn't take the chance that if he was caught he wouldn't talk. Am I right so far?"

Rinehart didn't answer me. He just looked at me with hate in his eyes.

"Well, that's okay. It's time for you to get out of your car. I suggest you do it with a great deal of care as I have a hair trigger on this gun. I'd really hate to accidentally shoot you."

I knew that if I gave him even a little bit of a chance, he would take it. He wanted me so badly that he would very likely take even the slightest chance to get at me.

I watched him very carefully as he got out of the car. I noticed that as he straightened up, he shifted his feet. That was my clue that he was about to try something. Rather than give him a chance at me, I let go of the envelope as I shot out a quick hard punch to his jaw that sent his head twisting to one side. It threw him off balance.

I pressed my attack by swinging him on around, pushing him hard up against the car and hitting him in the kidney at the same time. Between hitting the car and my hitting him in the kidney, I had taken some of the wind out of him, along with most of the fight. While he was trying to recover, I relieved him of his gun.

"I think it's time I got even. Then we'll see what the police have to say to you."

With that said, I laid his heavy .45 caliber gun across the back of his head, just like he had done to me. And like me, his lights immediately went out and he slid unceremoniously down the side of the car to the floor of the garage. I can't say that I enjoyed doing that to him, but it was not something that would keep me awake at night, either.

It was time to call the police to come and pick Rinehart up. I placed the call, then leaned up against the front fender of the car to wait until the police arrived.

As soon as the police arrived, I had them contact Wright. I would have done it myself except that I wasn't sure where he was. The last time I talked to him, he was at Mile High Design investigating the death of Steinman. It didn't take long before he showed up in the garage where

Rinehart was lying on the floor waiting for an ambulance to take him to the hospital.

"Well, it looks like you got even with him. I take it he's the guy who put the knot on your head," Wright said as he looked at Rinehart.

I was about to answer him when I saw Latimer walking toward us. The last thing I wanted was to get into another pissing match with him.

"I'll talk to you later," I said nodding my head toward Latimer, then turning away.

Wright turned and looked over his shoulder. He then looked back at me and shook his head.

"You do this to him?" Latimer asked as he looked at Rinehart.

"Shut up," Wright and I said at the same time.

Latimer stopped in his tracks. He had a surprised look on his face.

"Latimer, why don't you go back to the Mile High Design office and see how the forensic team is coming along with their investigation," Wright said calmly.

"I'd rather stay here and see how Tidsdale explains how this guy got the back of his head bashed in," Latimer said with that stupid grin of his.

"That was not a suggestion. That was an order," Wright said.

The stupid grin on Latimer's face disappeared rather quickly. It was obvious that he would rather hang around and give me a hard time, than to do his job. But it was also clear that Wright was not going to let him.

Reluctantly Latimer turned and left. I wasn't sure if he went back to Mile High Design or not, but he was gone and that was all I cared about.

I invited Wright to my office after the ambulance had picked up Rinehart, and after Wright had given instructions to put a guard on Rinehart around the clock. His instructions included that there were to be no visitors at all, and he was to be shackled to the bed.

Once in my office, I made coffee for Wright and myself. While I was making it, I explained everything I had that could be used against Rinehart. I had just finished telling him what happened between Rinehart and me when the phone rang. It was my friend in the morgue.

I listened to everything Martin told me. I even made a few notes so I wouldn't forget any of it, then hung up.

"That was Martin Dodd in the morgue. The body that was found earlier today was that of Jack Vernon, an enforcer for Sargossa. It was his blood on the floor and on the hand railing in Carlson's house. The hair on his clothes wasn't his own. Martin is going to be checking it against hair from Rinehart. My guess is that it will be a match. It's also going to be checked against the hair found on Julie Mathews's comforter.

"I think it will prove two things. That Rinehart and Vernon were in Carlson's house and killed Jennifer Carlson. I think it will also prove that Rinehart killed Julie Mathews in order to keep her from becoming a witness to what was going on at Mile High Design," I explained.

"It looks like Carlson didn't kill his wife after all."

"No, he didn't. In fact, he didn't do anything. Everything he said appears to have been the truth."

"I guess I can let him go. I'll get hold of the ADA and tell her. She won't like it. I think she was planning on making a name for herself on this one," Don said with a grin.

"You're probably right. I have to make a call to Moore and tell him what's been going on."

"Okay. Will I see you in the morning? I'd like you to come in and file charges against Rinehart for attacking you in the garage and for assaulting you in Carlson's office."

"Yeah. I'll see you in the morning."

I watched as Wright stood up and left my office. I leaned back in my chair to take a deep breath and a sip of coffee. This case had turned into more than I had thought it would in the beginning. It felt good to be able to close it, and to be able to clear Mr. Carlson of all charges.

I sat up and called Mr. Moore. I explained everything that had happened and that I was able to clear Mr. Carlson. Mr. Moore told me that he would run by the county jail to get Carlson out before the evening was over.

"I want to thank you for all your hard work," Mr. Moore said.

"It will be thanks enough if you pay my bill."

"Gladly. And there might be a little something extra in there for you."

"Thank you," I said.

"Can I call on you again?" Moore asked.

Sure. Anytime I can be of service," I replied then hung up.

As soon as I was done talking to Mr. Moore, I placed a call to Jackie. It didn't take her long to answer the phone.

"Hello."

"Can you have dinner with me tonight?"

"Frank?"

"Were you expecting someone else?"

"No. I just wasn't expecting to here from you. And yes, I'd be delighted to have dinner with you."

"I'll pick you up in about twenty minutes?"

"Sure. Will we be spending the night together?"

"I was hoping we would."

"Your place or mine?" she asked with a slight giggle.

"How about your place?"

"Okay. I'll be waiting for you."

"Love you," I said, before I hung up.

I smiled to myself as I thought of how this day was going to end. I could think of no better way for it to end than to be spending the night with Jackie.

Carlson was sitting on the edge of his bunk when the guard came down the hall. He looked up when the guard stopped in front of his cell, but he didn't stand up.

"You've got a visitor."

"Who is it," he asked as he stood up.

"It's your attorney. He says he has good news for you."

Carlson watched as the guard had the cell door opened. He then followed the guard to the visiting room. When he entered the room he could see a big smile on Mr. Moore's face.

"I've got good news. I'm getting you out of here right now. You owe a great deal to Mr. Tidsdale. He has found proof that you had nothing to do with your Jennifer's death. The ADA has dropped all charges and signed your release, with a big apology. I think she is hoping that you don't sue her for false arrest since she didn't have any solid proof that you had done anything."

"You mean I can leave here right now?" he asked, almost afraid to be too excited.

"That's what I mean. Get your stuff. I'm putting you up at a hotel for tonight where you can get cleaned up and get back into your own clothes."

"What about my house?"

"I'm sure it will be difficult for you to return there, so I will go with you in the morning. It will require some cleaning. You might want to have that all done before you move back in."

"Yeah. I hadn't thought about that," Carlson said sadly. "I guess I didn't think I would be seeing it again."

"Right now, get your things. I'll wait while you change your clothes and get checked out. We'll talk about everything tomorrow."

Mr. Moore watched as the guard led Mr. Carlson to a place where he could get his personal belongings and change into his own clothes. It was only a matter of minutes before Carlson returned and left the county jail as a free man.

"You owe Mr. Tidsdale a great deal of thanks for getting to the truth," Mr. Moore said as they walked to his car.

"I know," was all that Carlson said as he stopped next to Mr. Moore's car.

Carlson looked up at the night sky and took a deep breath. He knew what it meant to be a free man. It was finally over and he could once again walk the streets. He looked over at Mr. Moore, smiled, then got in the car.

www.ingramcontent.com/pod-product-compliance
Lightning Source LLC
Chambersburg PA
CBHW070854180626
46817CB00003B/770